Readers love
Sue Brown

The Fireman's Pole

"As always, a Sue Brown novel is a complete package that lures you into the story completely and wraps you up in the magic."

—Joyfully Jay

"This is definitely a character-driven story, with some surprises, and a well-crafted plot to keep everyone aligned and in their places. All the stars for this book. Read and enjoy!"

—Happy Ever After, *USA Today*

Island Counselor

"…the best kind of love story. It's just so easy to accept them as a couple…"

—MM Good Book Reviews

Island Doctor

"Going back to the island was like visiting old friends while looking forward to meeting new ones."

—Rainbow Book Reviews

"*Island Doctor* is a good strong romance, the men are as sexy as all get out, it is low in angst, high in love… overall a really great read."

—*Divine Magazine*

By Sue Brown

Chance to Be King
Falling for Ramos
Final Admission
Grand Adventures
The Layered Mask
The Next Call
The Night Porter • Light of Day
Nothing Ever Happens
The Sky Is Dead
Stitch
Stolen Dreams
Waiting

COWBOYS AND ANGELS
Speed Dating the Boss

DREAMSPUN DESIRES
#44 – The Fireman's Pole

FRANKIE'S SERIES
Frankie & Al
Ed & Marchant
Anthony & Leo
Jordan & Rhys
Frankie & Friends Anthology

THE ISLE SERIES
The Isle of… Where?
Isle of Wishes
Isle of Waves

ISLAND MEDICS
Island Doctor
Island Counselor

MORNING REPORT
Morning Report
Complete Faith
Papa's Boy
Luke's Present
Letters From a Cowboy
Letters From a Cowboy Anthology

SUE BROWN

SPEED DATING the BOSS

Published by
DREAMSPINNER PRESS

5032 Capital Circle SW, Suite 2, PMB# 279, Tallahassee, FL 32305-7886 USA
www.dreamspinnerpress.com

This is a work of fiction. Names, characters, places, and incidents either are the product of author imagination or are used fictitiously, and any resemblance to actual persons, living or dead, business establishments, events, or locales is entirely coincidental.

Trade Paperback ISBN: 978-1-64080-650-4
Digital ISBN: 978-1-64080-649-8
Library of Congress Control Number: 2018931585
Trade Paperback published May 2018
v. 1.0

Printed in the United States of America

This paper meets the requirements of
ANSI/NISO Z39.48-1992 (Permanence of Paper).

To Clare London, who's been my "officemate" for many years.
To many more visits to the Office.

CHAPTER 1

"INCOMING!"

At the shout Daniel Collins dropped to the floor. A projectile skimmed the top of his buzz cut and narrowly missed the bottles behind him.

"Quit throwing glasses at me," he yelled, knowing he was wasting his breath and likely to get smacked in the mouth. It was futile. Everyone was too liquored up to pay any attention to the barmen cowering behind the thick mahogany bar.

That was their usual Friday-night entertainment at their favorite bar. Cowboys and Angels was a long established blue-collar bar, not a place for Wall Street suits or hipsters. Late afternoon, students came in search of jugs of cocktails and cheap beer. They vanished by early evening in search of music and dancing and left behind the construction workers and builders who came for the extensive list of draft beers and a chance to relax. On a Friday night, they'd get paid, arrive at Cowboys and Angels in time for happy hour, and drink with their buddies until closing. A fight was added entertainment. They'd throw punches with random glee, not caring where they connected. Then they'd go home, arms slung around the guy they'd been beating up ten minutes beforehand singing at the top of their voices.

So, Friday night as usual.

"They started early tonight." Dan's coworker Bradley ducked as a barstool went flying over their heads to crash into the fridge.

Dan cursed as the stool rebounded and caught him on the cheek. He was convinced he was going to end the evening in the ER, with stitches and a concussion. "Ariel's in the bar."

"Where the hell is Gideon? He's supposed to keep her under control." Bradley lobbed the stool back over the bar, not caring where it landed. From the pained grunt, he could tell it made contact with someone.

"Get him down here," Dan ordered.

Arms over his head, Bradley crawled along the bar to the phone and dialed the boss's number. "Boss, get her out of here now, or you won't have a bar left." He nodded at Dan. "He's on his way."

That was one of the things Dan appreciated about his boss—no questions, no discussion, just action. His daughter, Ariel, was like that too, except she was normally the center of all the trouble.

Time to shut the fight down before it got out of hand—*more* out of hand. Dan grabbed the baseball bat tucked behind the bar, sent up a quick prayer that he wasn't about to get glassed, and got to his feet.

"Stop!" he yelled it at the top of his lungs, honed by years of practice. For a moment the action continued. A bottle crashed by his ear. "Cut it the fuck out," he yelled again, feeling the sting in his other cheek. "The next person who twitches a muscle gets banned for life." The occupants of the bar froze as though Dan had hit Pause on the remote control.

"Sorry, Dan."

He didn't know who made the muttered apology, and he didn't care. Nobody moved a muscle. Their attention was fixed on the baseball bat Dan was smacking into one hand. So far Dan had never had to use the bat, and he intended to keep it that way. Dan saw a movement out of the corner of his eye and swung around, bat ready for action. Then he relaxed at the sight of the tall figure. "Boss."

"Good job," Gideon drawled.

Dressed in a tight black T-shirt with the blue Cowboy and Angels logo and jeans that molded his ass, he stood like a giant in the middle of the destruction. Originally from Texas, at six foot five, Gideon was two hundred and fifty pounds of solid muscle. Despite being ten years older, he could bench-press Dan—and had—without breaking a sweat. There were men there who made Gideon look small, but they all listened to him. Not for the first time, Dan wished he had Gideon's physical presence.

Gideon picked his way over the broken glass and tipped-over furniture to arrive at his daughter's side. He held out his free hand and hauled her off the floor in one smooth move. "Ariel, darlin', what happened this time?"

Ariel tossed her head and grinned at him. She had no shame. "No idea, Daddy. I was just here for a quiet drink with my friends." She pointed to the two young men either side of her who stared at Gideon. Both of them wore terrified expressions.

"Darlin', that's the biggest pile of horse puckey you told me since the last time you destroyed my bar." Gideon sounded more resigned than annoyed.

An NYU senior, Ariel was twenty-one with blonde hair the color of ripe wheat, baby-blue eyes, and a cute smile for everyone. She was the sunny day to Gideon's night, since he had dark curls and deep gray-green eyes. Ariel was the belle of the ball, and a pain in Dan's ass. He preferred the nights when she didn't come into the bar and expect everyone's attention. It wasn't that he didn't like Ariel, but Dan was fond of the quiet life, and Ariel was too high-maintenance for him. His tastes ran to denim-clad asses, broad shoulders, long legs… and maybe looking like his boss.

There was nothing anyone could say to the boss about his precious daughter. He adored Ariel, and she got away with absolute murder. Dan liked her. They all liked her, but she was an incredibly beautiful spoiled brat. Gideon had lost his wife and young son to a carjacking. Dan got his job at Cowboys and Angels about a year after they died. It was obvious Gideon and Ariel were still distraught from the loss of Sarah and Simon. There were photos of the family everywhere in Gideon's apartment—happy, smiling faces, unaware of the tragedy in their future. After their deaths Gideon focused all his attention on Ariel. It wasn't as though Gideon didn't know he indulged her, but he would do anything to make her happy. Her saving grace, in Dan's eyes, was that she knew just how spoiled she was, and she tempered it with a kind heart and a wicked sense of humor.

Gideon held her hand and looked around at the men prostrate at their feet. "Get out now, all of you."

There was a hush and a pause, as though they were waiting for more instructions. Then Gideon raised an eyebrow, and everybody moved. There was a rush for the door as the men fought to get out, and finally the place was empty.

"You can come out now, boys," Ariel trilled.

Bradley and the other barman got to their feet. Dan sighed at the chaos around the wood-paneled bar. It was going to be another night of clearing up, another night when he would get fewer tips and plenty of cuts and bruises. He ought to get combat pay for working at Cowboys and Angels. Who was he kidding? He'd been saying that for five years, and yet he was still there.

As if he'd read Dan's mind, Gideon rumbled, "You boys injured?" He'd been in New York for a quarter of a century—yet the Texas drawl remained, his voice like a rumble of thunder in the far distance—compared to Dan, who'd lived in Brooklyn all his life.

Dan gingerly touched the graze on his cheek. It had already stopped bleeding. "No more than usual."

Gideon strode over to him. "Show me," he demanded as he tilted Dan's chin to inspect his injuries.

Dan stood, self-conscious as always under Gideon's steely gaze. They were so close Dan could smell the coffee on Gideon's breath. He could have made one slight move and brushed Gideon's mouth with his own. It wasn't as though he hadn't dreamed about doing that a million times.

Thankfully oblivious to Dan's thoughts, Gideon gently touched first one and then the other cheek, and try as he might, Dan couldn't help but flinch away from the gentle touch.

Gideon frowned at him. "Where does it hurt?"

"It's fine." If Gideon didn't step out of Dan's personal space, Dan was liable to do something stupid.

"There's no glass in this one, and it's stopped bleeding. I'll clean it out." Gideon righted a bar stool and pushed Dan onto it.

"I can do it," Dan began, but he subsided under Gideon's hard stare.

Dammit, Gideon knew just how to make Dan sit and stay like a pet dog.

"Give me the first aid kit." Gideon held his hand out to Bradley, who handed it over and vanished in the direction of the janitor's closet.

Once Gideon had cleaned Dan's wound to his satisfaction, Dan put on gloves that were left under the bar just for that purpose and collected the larger pieces of glass to put in the trash can. Gideon and Ariel righted the furniture, and Bradley swept up.

"No broken tables or stools this time," Gideon said. "That's a record for you, darlin'."

She winked at him. "I'll have to do better next time."

Gideon looked over as Dan snorted. "Got something to say?"

"No, boss."

Dan continued to clear up and left Gideon to talk to his errant daughter in private. When they had vanished, Bradley rolled his eyes, and Dan snorted again. He might have a huge crush on the man, but Dan wasn't stupid. No staff member said anything negative about Ariel to Gideon's face, not if they wanted to keep their job. And Dan did want to keep his job. Of all the bars he'd worked in, Cowboys and Angels was his favorite.

Not that Dan wanted to be a barman there forever. He had plans for his future, and they were almost within his grasp. Another year, possibly two, and he would be ready for the next stage of his life. Then he'd leave Cowboys and Angels—and Gideon—behind. Dan stared at the piece of glass in his hand. He would miss Gideon, but he couldn't spend the rest of his life crushing on a man who didn't know he existed. He just wished the thought of a future apart from Gideon didn't hurt so much.

"Dan?"

He looked up to see Gideon studying him with a worried expression. "Yeah?"

"Are you okay?"

Aside from wanting you? "I'm fine. Just tired."

"Finish up here, and you can go."

"And leave you to clean up my bar?" Dan teased.

Gideon raised an eyebrow. "*Your* bar?"

"My bar," Dan said, and they grinned at each other.

It was an old joke. It was Gideon's bar, but he had other businesses and didn't spend much time downstairs. Dan was the closest thing to a manager that Cowboys and Angels had. Of course, if Gideon actually made him manager, Dan's plans for the future would change. But Gideon was reluctant to let go of the reins. It was his baby and the one business he'd operated with his late wife.

"Dan, you're standing on a piece of glass," Bradley said, interrupting their staring contest.

He looked down to see a sharp piece of glass and moved hastily to pick it up. Gideon turned away to talk to Ariel.

Bradley and the other barman approached him. "We can't go on like this," Bradley said softly enough not to attract Gideon's attention.

"You mean Ariel?" Dan asked.

They both nodded.

"I'll speak to Gideon." He looked over to where Gideon was talking to his daughter. They were both laughing, and despite the difference in their coloring, Dan could see the family resemblance.

"When?" Bradley demanded.

"Tomorrow," Dan promised. "You're right. Gideon and Ariel need to face up to reality or there won't be a Cowboys and Angels left."

CHAPTER 2

THEY ONLY lost about an hour of business, but the cleanup took twice as long. It was nearly five in the morning when Dan left the club with Gideon's cheery goodbye rattling in his ears as he locked the door behind him. Dan shoved his hands into his pockets and covered his head with a watch cap in a futile attempt to keep warm in the early hours of the winter day. The temperature had dropped considerably, and he was freezing after an evening in the overheated bar.

Fortunately the Uber was warm, and Dan struggled not to doze off as he flicked through the messages he'd received during the evening. His mom, his best friend, a date that had gone disastrously wrong trying to set up another evening—no chance there—and his dentist. Why did his dentist call him in the evening? Dan didn't care enough to listen. It would have to wait until Dan's brain worked again. Finally he arrived home, fed his large gray cat and told her she was a worthless beast, and flung himself onto his bed. Still wearing his jacket and shoes, he fell asleep with SmokeyJo's rumbling purr in his ears.

Dan woke up to his phone jangling obnoxiously in his ear and the realization that he'd slept on top of his comforter again. His apartment was freezing, and his breath a white cloud in the cold air. *Apartment* was a generous term. It was more of a largish room with a bed stuck in a nook, a small bathroom and an even smaller galley kitchen, but it was rent controlled, and it suited Dan. He turned on the space heater and replaced his jacket with the warmest hoodie he could find. The jeans became thick sweats, and he rolled on even thicker socks. The coffee was dripping into the pot before he picked up his phone and checked who'd called him.

It was Disastrous Date again. The man did not take a hint. Dan wasn't interested in another evening of listening to tales of the man's sexual encounters. Dan liked sex. Hell, he loved sex with the right person, but he preferred doing to listening, and he had no intention of becoming another conversation piece for.... Dan struggled to remember the man's name. Peter, Paul? He shook his head. That wasn't right, but he didn't care enough to find out. He poured the steaming dark brew into the largest clean mug he could find. He would have to do the dishes soon or he'd be drinking from the coffeepot itself.

At least the man was interested in him, more than anyone else had been for a long time—*more than Gideon was.* Dan shut down his traitorous thoughts. His love life had been as barren as a desert recently, and he struggled to think of the last time he was in a relationship. His job didn't help, because he didn't work office hours and he had to take every shift he could just to pay the bills. It wasn't like the customers of Cowboys and Angels were interested in him.

His friends asked him on a regular basis why he didn't work in a gay bar. They didn't get that Dan preferred not to be hit on by the customers. Gideon employed him for that reason and the fact that Dan wasn't going to hit on his daughter. And Gideon, the other reason Dan stayed at Cowboys and Angels, wasn't interested in Dan either, but Dan's heart was just stupid enough to hope that one day the situation might change.

He looked at the message from Disastrous Date and almost called him back. Then he snorted and shoved his phone into his pocket. He wasn't that desperate, not yet, but he was getting close.

SmokeyJo slunk over to him and wrapped her gray silky body around his legs, reminding him that her stomach had been empty for a very long while and it was about time he paid her the attention she deserved.

"You were fed when I got in, you lying whore," Dan reminded her. "You can't be that hungry again."

She meowed at him piteously, which Dan took to mean that she needed food at least every hour on the hour. Dan filled a bowl with kibble. SmokeyJo sniffed and gave him a look that said he'd failed again.

"That's all you're getting." He scratched her behind the ears, and she scowled and purred, an adorable combination that Dan fell for every time. Then she settled down to nibble at the despised dry food.

He looked at the clock and was pleased to discover he didn't have to be into work for another six hours as he was only doing the evening shift. Dan's stomach growled, which reminded him that, unlike SmokeyJo, he hadn't sat down to eat since lunch yesterday. If he didn't eat soon, he would pass out, and his precious cat would eat his face in some evil, twisted revenge. He looked in the fridge and grimaced at the eggs and not-quite-rotting vegetables. It was about time he visited the local store. Though he wasn't at home much, Dan enjoyed cooking, and he made omelets on a regular basis, so he'd had a lot of practice at using up eggs and old veggies.

As he fried the peppers and onions, Dan listened to his mother's querulous voice chastise him for not calling the night before. It was another voicemail message. Dan had a love/hate relationship with his mother and found it best to keep his distance. She didn't understand why he needed to keep half a state's distance between them, but his sister understood. She'd picked a college on the other coast to get away, and she never moved back, no matter how much their mother complained. Dan would call her over the weekend, when he was fortified by more sleep and more caffeine. Liquor would probably help, but he didn't drink much. He preferred to keep his head clear.

He added a touch of seasoning to the beaten eggs and poured them into the vegetables. It became more of a scramble than an omelet, but Dan didn't mind. It tasted just fine. He was still shoveling eggs down his throat when his phone rang again. This time it was his best friend, and he didn't mind answering the call. "What do you want?"

"Nice greeting," Marty said, "and it's great to hear from you too, dickwad."

"Yeah, yeah. What do you want?"

Marty Kennedy had been Dan's friend since grade school. They went through their school years dealing with bullies, broken hearts, and the occasional broken bone. The broken bones had been Dan's, because he tried to save Marty from numerous falls. Marty was the clumsiest man in existence.

"I'm calling to invite you to my wedding," Marty announced.

Dan choked on the last mouthful of his breakfast. He spent the next few minutes recovering from a coughing fit and then drinking water so he could speak again. Marty, of course, spent the time cracking bad jokes about Dan's ability to eat, breathe, and live at the same time.

"What the hell did you just say?" Dan finally managed to wheeze out.

Marty chuckled in his ear. "I said I'm in love."

"No. That's not what you said. You said, 'I'm calling to invite you to my wedding.'"

"If you knew that, why did you ask?"

Dan was going to need a lot more coffee for this conversation, and he topped off his mug. "You met someone?"

"That's usually how it works… unless you want to marry your coffeepot or your car. Did you know people marry their cars? I'd marry a Mustang or maybe a Pontiac Firebird. You'd probably marry your coffee maker."

Dan ignored the segue into Strangeville. "You're in love, and I didn't know about her?"

"When was the last time I saw you?" Marty pointed out. "You're always busy. You work every evening, and I can't remember the last time we got together or even had a proper conversation."

Marty wasn't bitching, or if he was, he was just being honest. They had let their friendship slide recently. Dan had been so involved with the bar and his studies that he barely had time to scratch his ass.

"Yeah, yeah. I know. I've been meaning to call. I've just been so busy."

"I know, dude, and it's not like I've made the effort either. I've been tied up with Lena. You know what love is like."

Dan let that go without comment. He'd never been in love, and his relationships had been short and sweet—or not so sweet and sometimes downright dirty. "So how long have you known your fiancée? What's her name?"

"Lena. Lena Dawson. Six months, more or less."

"How much more or how much less?" Dan asked warily. He *knew* Marty.

There was a huff, and then Marty said, "Okay. I've known her for four months, but before you say anything, it's nothing I haven't heard from the parents already."

Dan could think of a lot of things to say to that, and most of them involved cuss words and the suggestion that he get an MRI. He looked at his schoolbag with his assignment and textbooks which was how he'd intended to spend his day and said, "What are you doing at the moment?"

"My laundry, like I do every Saturday morning. Nearly finished, as it happens."

"Your usual place? Do you want to meet for a coffee?"

Laundry and coffee had long been Dan and Marty's way of catching up, but even that had gone by the wayside recently. Dan realized, with a touch of shame, he hadn't even noticed Marty's absence from his life.

"Sure," Marty said. "But I haven't got long. I said I'd meet Lena this afternoon. She wants to sort out the registry at the department store."

It was becoming far too real for Dan. He'd never thought about getting married, let alone doing the whole white-wedding affair. "I'll be with you in thirty. Usual place? Get me a latte."

"A latte? You're becoming middle-aged, bro."

Dan didn't need to hear that, even if he was feeling his age. "I'm not the one getting married. Again," Dan pointed out. "And I expect that latte to be hot."

"You'd better get your ass outta bed, then," Marty shot back. "And say hello to your lovely SmokeyJo. Tell her she needs a better owner."

"You can't have my cat." This was an old, old argument.

"Why not? She loves me. She loves me better than you do. And I'd remember to feed her."

"I do remember to feed her." The damn cat would never let him forget it if he missed a meal.

Marty made a scoffing noise, told him to hurry up, and then disconnected the call. Dan flipped him off even though Marty couldn't see it.

He'd perfected the art of the quick shower, though he never understood why people needed to spend an hour just to wash their body. He took three minutes, tops, and that was if he was going to wash his hair. Admittedly, he didn't have a lot of hair to wash. He kept his hair in a buzz cut. That way no fucker could grab hold of it in a fight. When he arrived at Cowboys and Angels, his hair had been longer than Ariel's. That lasted two fights and losing a strip of scalp to a liquored-up construction worker. The guy was apologetic, but the next day, Dan headed to the barbers.

Three minutes and forty-five seconds later, Dan jammed on his navy watch cap—because his head got cold easily without hair—picked up his wallet and walked out of his apartment. As he was on the third floor, he ignored the bone-creaking elevator that only worked on a day ending in *Z*, took the stairs two at a time, and waved at his elderly neighbor from the floor above as they passed.

"Morning, Mrs. G."

"Morning, Dan. Wrap up warm, son. It's cold out there." Mrs. Gryniewicz managed a tired smile and carried on climbing stairs without breaking her stride. She'd told him more than once that taking the stairs was the secret to her longevity.

As he reached the sidewalk, Dan's phone beeped, and Gideon's number flashed up.

Need you at 5.

No *please* or *thank you*, no asking if he could come in early. For a moment Dan was tempted to tell Gideon to find someone else. He tapped out his answer.

Sure.

Because Dan had *Mug* tattooed across his forehead… and the hots for his very straight, alpha boss.

CHAPTER 3

DAN PUSHED through the heavy crowd in the coffee shop, knowing Marty would have found a seat as far back as he could. It was something to do with fear of cars flying through the window. Marty watched way too many cop shows. Dan gingerly skirted around a stroller that held a tiny baby asleep with a thumb in its mouth and headed for the man waving in the far corner. Marty stood as Dan reached the table, and they hugged and thumped each other on the back. Then Dan sat down and reached for the large mug Marty pushed toward him. He buried his nose in the fragrant steam and inhaled.

"You're going to snorkel it if you're not careful." Marty picked up his own mug of something topped with cream and chocolate. He was slim to the point of being skinny and, unlike Dan, didn't need to watch what he ate. He never put on a pound.

"I don't care. I got to bed at nearly six this morning. There isn't enough caffeine to make up for that." Dan chugged down a quarter of the mug and sighed in satisfaction.

"How's the college course going?" Marty asked.

"I'm almost done."

Marty gave him a broad smile. "That's great, Dan."

Dan had never gone to college. He barely graduated high school. But three years of working for other people had convinced him that he wanted his own bar someday. So Marty encouraged him to attend community college to take some business courses. Walking into class the first day was the hardest thing Dan had ever done, but constant work paid off, and a couple of business courses and studying every spare hour had turned into an almost completed degree in business and economics. Every hour studying and assignments that left him sleeping over his textbooks took him closer to his goal, although juggling a full-time job and school left him feeling like a zombie most of the time.

"It's all thanks to you," Dan admitted.

Marty waved a hand and nearly sent his cup flying into Dan's lap. "You took care of me. I'm glad I could do that for you, but remember to invite me to your graduation."

"You're the first on the list." Dan slurped again and then looked at his sandy-haired friend. "So, you're getting married?"

Marty bit his lip. "She's the one, Dan. I swear it. The minute I met her I knew she was the one for me."

"Have you introduced her to your parents?"

"Yeah. They took it about as well as you might expect."

Dan wasn't surprised that Mr. and Mrs. Kennedy weren't thrilled at their son's announcement. Marty had been married twice before, the first time just out of high school, and then again at twenty-three. Both marriages had lasted less than a year. Dan wasn't thrilled either, but Marty was his friend, and he would do his best to support him.

"Tell me about Lena."

It was the right thing to say. Marty's face lit up, and he pulled out his phone. He scrolled for a moment and showed Dan a picture of a pretty black girl with huge eyes and a beautiful smile. "She's the most amazing woman I've ever met. Kindhearted and intelligent. I mean really intelligent. She makes me look like a third grader."

Dan whistled. Marty was a structural engineer and no slouch in the smarts department. "What does Lena do?"

"She's an attorney and set to make partner early."

That was one up on his previous wives. They were great girls, but they'd seen Marty as a meal ticket for life. "Where did you meet her?"

"I met her in here," Marty said. "We collided, and I threw a cup of coffee all over her. She was furious because she was wearing a new suit."

Dan chuckled at him. "She's lucky she only ended up with a coffee shower and not broken bones."

"I'm not that bad," Marty protested, and then at Dan's raised eyebrow, he said, "I'm not."

"I know you, remember?"

Marty made a noise in the back of his throat as though Dan were talking off the top of his head. "Anyway, she didn't stay angry… much. And after I offered to dry-clean her suit, she forgave me. We haven't spent a night apart since that day. She's an amazing girl, Dan, and I want you to meet her."

"She sounds wonderful, especially if she can put up with your shit," Dan said. "But, and I say this as the man who's had your back through two divorces, I'm with your parents on this one. Why are you getting married so quickly? If she's as amazing as you think, why can't you take your time to get to know each other?"

Marty pressed his lips together as though he were holding back angry words, but then he said, "Lena is from a very religious family."

"So are you," Dan pointed out. "What's that got to do with—oh… she's pregnant?"

People looked over, and Marty made shushing noises and nearly knocked over his mug again in the process. "The whole shop doesn't need to know."

"So, she *is* pregnant?" Dan moved the mug away from Marty. He didn't know much about straight couples and marriage, but he knew Marty's parents, and they were going to be livid when they found out their precious son had knocked up another girl. Yes, there was another one back in high school, but that had been "handled" with an adoption. Marty had escaped one shotgun wedding, only to get married for real six months later. That was the first one. But now Marty was an adult, and he'd obviously decided to do the right thing by Lena.

Marty took on a mutinous expression, as though he were sure of Dan's disapproval. "It wasn't planned, but it's the best news ever. I love Lena, and I can't wait to spend the rest of my life with her and our baby."

Dan eyed him thoughtfully. He was honestly surprised by Marty's pronouncement. "What do you need from me?"

Marty's expression changed to a pleased smile. "I want you to be my best man."

"Your best man? Isn't that like third in command at the wedding? What do I have to do? You're going to want a bachelor party, aren't you?"

"Hell, no. I've done that twice already. I'd rather have a night in with my gorgeous fiancée than go out drinking with the boys."

Dan leaned forward and rapped Marty on the forehead with his knuckles. "Who are you and where's my friend Marty?"

"Marty grew up."

Dan wasn't sure how he felt about that remark. Was Marty implying that Dan *hadn't* grown up? Dan was adult enough for his own liking. He had a job, an apartment, nearly a degree. He even had a cat, dammit.

What more did he need to be classified as a grown-up? "I'll be your best man if you want me to, but don't you want to ask your brother?"

Marty gave a wry smile. "If Todd is my best man again, then I won't get away without a bachelor party. He'll have me naked and tied to a lamppost before midnight."

"That was the last bachelor party." Dan frowned and tapped the table with one finger. "Or was that the party before?"

"I don't know. I'm not even going to think about it." Marty shuddered. "All you have to do is get me to the church on time and don't forget the rings like Todd did last time. I'm not putting a plastic flower on Lena's finger."

"You're having a church wedding?"

"They'll give us a blessing." Marty bit his lip. "Dan, if I tell you this, you can't tell anybody else. I mean it. It has to be a secret."

"Sure, dude, whatever you want. You know I have your back."

"We're already married. Lena and me, I mean. We got married last week, as soon as we found out about the baby. We're just doing the formal bit for the parents."

Dan shook his head. "You are the most impulsive man I've ever met. I don't know what to say. But whatever you need me to do, I'll be there. That's a promise. Just don't get me between the parents. I don't do religion. You know that."

Marty looked at him speculatively. "Are you planning on bringing a date?"

"I doubt it. I can't think of anyone to ask. I certainly haven't got any boyfriends waiting in the wings."

"What about that date you had a couple of weeks ago?"

"He was a disaster. Thanks for reminding me. He's the last person I would bring to a wedding. Besides, the last thing you need is for me to bring an ole gay to the happy event. Not with two sets of holy rollers there."

"So you're going to play straight for the day?" Marty asked.

"It wouldn't be the first time," Dan pointed out. "I've done that at your last two weddings."

"My parents know you're gay, dude. As for Lena's family, they'll get over it."

"I know your parents know about me." And hadn't that been an uncomfortable explanation for a sixteen-year-old boy to handle. To give

Mr. and Mrs. Kennedy credit, they didn't throw him out of the house, but he remembered the strained meetings afterward. "But it's one thing to know and another to have it rubbed in your face. I'll go stag, and everyone will be happy."

"Except you."

Dan shrugged at Marty's perceptive comment. "It doesn't matter. This is your day, and nothing is going to get in the way of a good wedding." Marty blinked rapidly, and Dan could see the sheen in his eyes. "Dude, you're not going to blub, are you?"

"Fuck off," Marty muttered as Dan laughed at him.

"Daniel!"

The light soprano cut through the background noise of the coffee shop.

"Oh hell no. What are they doing here?" Dan's stomach turned as he looked up to see Ariel making her way around the tables, a mischievous smile on her face. He groaned again as he saw Gideon behind her. He looked like hotness on two legs, even dressed in a thick winter coat and boots. It was so unfair when Dan looked like the walking dead.

Marty looked over and shot him a wicked grin. "Who're you bitching about? Ariel or her hot daddy?"

"You shouldn't know anything about daddies," Dan muttered.

Marty rolled his eyes. "Oh, Dan, you are so naïve."

Dan stared at him, unsure if they were on the same page. Because there were dads and then there were *daddies*.

"Don't worry, I'll keep your secret," Marty assured him.

And Dan breathed a little easier, because there was no way he was going to discuss his penchant for daddies—and one in particular—with his straight best friend.

Chapter 4

ARIEL BOUNCED over to them before Dan could reply, and Marty got to his feet to kiss her cheek. He'd gotten to know her over the five years Dan had worked at Cowboys and Angels. From the start Dan warned Marty about having any ideas about Ariel, but he knew Ariel wasn't Marty's type. Marty had preferred mature women… up to now.

"You get more beautiful every time I see you," Marty said, and Ariel beamed at him.

Gideon growled for form's sake, and Ariel snorted at him. She plopped down onto a chair, and the men had no choice but to follow her. Gideon sat next to Dan, and because the place was busy, they had to sit close together. Dan tried not to shift as the long, warm length of Gideon's thigh pressed up against his.

Once they settled, Ariel asked, "What are you doing here?"

"Discussing Marty's wedding," Dan informed her.

Ariel's eyes went comically wide. "You're getting married?"

Marty pressed his hand against his ear to counter the piercing squeal. "Do you want to let the whole block know? Yes, I'm getting married."

"Again?" Gideon asked. He never forgot anything. Dan had learned that to his cost and was very careful what information he disclosed.

Marty scowled, but he nodded and pulled out his phone again to show them the photo of his fiancée. "I'm marrying Lena in four weeks, and I've asked Dan to be my best man."

Ariel's squeal was loud enough to burst the eardrums of every customer in the store. "That's so exciting. She's so beautiful."

"You're a lucky man," Gideon said.

Dan caught the hint of sadness in his voice and knew Gideon must be thinking about his late wife. He wondered how Gideon felt every time he saw a happy couple, but practicalities interrupted his thoughts. He turned to Gideon. "I'm gonna need that Saturday off. It's the beginning of March?" He looked at Marty for confirmation, and Marty nodded.

"The first weekend."

Dan didn't anticipate it being a problem as he would willingly swap a shift with someone and he couldn't remember the last time he'd taken any vacation time.

"We'll look at the rosters tonight," Gideon rumbled.

"Who are you gonna take as your date to the wedding?" Ariel asked.

"No one. I'm going stag."

She didn't look impressed. "You can't do that. You have to take a plus-one."

"Got no one to take, baby girl. And I don't want to upset the parents of the happy couple." Dan had been to many weddings—gay and straight—by himself. In fact he struggled to think of a single wedding that he'd been to with a plus-one. At least if he went stag, he could escape when he wanted to.

"I told you, my parents know you're gay, and they wouldn't have a problem with you bringing a man," Marty said. "And as for Lena's parents, they just have to put up with it. Lena doesn't care. She knows you're gay."

"You told your bride-to-be that your best friend is gay?"

Marty looked puzzled. "Yeah. Of course I did. You're my best friend. Why wouldn't I tell her?"

Dan couldn't think of a good answer.

"Times are changing," Gideon said. "In my day no one would have taken a man as their partner or at least they wouldn't have been open about it. They would have been cousins or roommates or something. But now it's different, and it's a good thing. You need to catch up, Dan. Find a date and take him to the wedding."

Dan shook his head, annoyed at the pile-on. "I'm happy going by myself. Besides, I'm gonna have to look after the groom and make sure he gets to the church on time. I won't have time to take care of anyone else."

"You could invite them to the wedding reception," Ariel said.

Dan looked at them sourly. "Enough with the date I haven't got."

"What about that date you had… when was it?" Gideon said.

"He spent the whole time telling me about all the men he'd fu—got into his bed. I don't need to be another notch on his bedpost or a discussion point over dinner with his next date. And before you ask, I can't remember the last time I went out with someone else before him."

Ariel shook her head, and Dan caught her mischievous expression. He didn't want to think what was coming next. "That's really sad. You need more time off, Dan. You should ask your boss for a proper vacation."

Gideon fidgeted beside Dan. "He's old enough to arrange his own vacation times. You keep your nose out of it, missy."

Ariel pouted. "I'm only trying to help."

"I know you are," Dan soothed, "and your dad is just grumpy at the thought of giving me any time off."

Gideon smirked at him. "Well, yeah, you're the best employee I have."

It was all banter and joking, but Gideon's words left a flutter in Dan's heart.

"When are we going to meet Lena?" Ariel said.

"Right now," Marty pointed to the door. "She just walked in."

Dan looked over to the door to see a slim black woman in a red coat standing hesitantly in the doorway. Marty got up and waved to attract her attention. She saw him and smiled, and any reservations Dan had about their relationship went out the window when he saw the love and joy on her face. He had never been a believer in love at first sight. Lust, yes. He thought about his first sight of Gideon at their initial interview. Love was overrated, but maybe it did exist for other people. Then Gideon sighed and pushed closer to him. Sometimes lust turned to love, even if nothing else happened.

Lena pushed her way through the crowd and joined them at the table.

Marty kissed her on the cheek and put his arms around her. "This is my wonderful fiancée, Lena. Lena, this is my best friend, Dan. This is his boss, Gideon and Gideon's daughter, Ariel."

"I thought I was going to meet your best friend, but we have a crowd?"

Ariel smiled at her. "Dad and I just crashed Dan's morning coffee. I'm really nosy, and it's been a long time since I've seen Marty."

"That might be my fault," Lena said. "I've been hogging Marty's time recently."

Still waiting to formally greet Lena, Dan had the chance to watch her interact with Ariel. Marty hadn't stopped grinning like a loon since Lena walked in the door. It was obvious that Lena hung the moon and stars in Marty's world. She leaned against Marty, her fingers entwined with his as she carried on an animated conversation with Ariel.

Gideon nudged Dan's leg again, disturbing his thoughts. "I'm sorry if your work time interferes with your love life."

Dan snorted. "Don't give me that. You have a bar to run, and you know I'm gonna be there most days. If I wanted a love life, I'd get a different job."

"Ariel has a point, though. It ain't good for a man to be alone. You need company sometimes."

"I could say the same for you," Dan said pointedly. "I don't think I've ever seen you with a date."

There was that sad look Gideon always got when he was thinking about his wife and son. "I wasn't ready before, and now I don't seem to find the time to go dating. Between business and my daughter, I'm always busy."

Dan looked at Marty. "Do I get a proper introduction now?"

Marty stuck his tongue out at Dan's teasing. "If you can stop gabbing about how sad your love lives are. Lena, this is my best friend and my best man and possibly the saddest dude in the universe when it comes to music. Dan, meet the love of my life."

Dan stood and held out his hand to Lena, but she bypassed it and hugged him.

"I've heard so much about you," she said as she stepped back. "Marty talks about you all the time."

"I'm really sorry about that."

She laughed. "Oh no, I want to hear more. I'm sure you've got plenty of stories from when you were kids."

Dan grinned at her. "You bet I have."

"Not until after the wedding," Marty protested. "I don't want to put her off."

Gideon also got to his feet and held out his hand to Lena. "I think I'm the only one who hasn't said hello. Pleased to meet you, Lena, I'm Gideon Tyler."

As Lena shook his hand, she frowned and held on to his hand for a minute. "I know you."

"I doubt it," Gideon said. "I don't think we move in the same circles."

Lena was still frowning, and then she snapped her fingers. "I know! You helped at the children's hospital's Christmas party the year before last. You were Santa Claus. I was there too. My niece was in the hospital at the time."

Dan blinked at the thought of Gideon playing Santa, and from the stunned expression on Ariel's face, it was news to her too.

A smile spread across Gideon's face. "You're right, and you're very perceptive if you realized that was me under the padding. How is your niece now?"

Lena smiled at him. "It's your drawl. I don't get to hear many Texans in New York. Rosie is doing fine now. She has cerebral palsy and has to spend time in the hospital occasionally."

"Daddy? Is there something you need to tell us?" Ariel had a wicked grin on her face. "I've never heard anything about this."

Gideon groaned and said, "There's a good reason you haven't heard anything. Because I know you'd never let me forget it. It was a one-time thing because a friend couldn't play Santa. You remember Bill Thomas? He had a heart attack just before the party, and I was asked to step in. He was well enough to be Santa at the last party." He caught Dan's amused expression and stabbed a finger at him. "If you tell anybody else in the bar, you're fired."

"You run a bar?" Lena asked.

"I own a bar," Gideon corrected.

"*I* run the bar." Dan thought he'd get a rise out of Gideon, but his boss ignored the comment and continued talking to Lena.

"I doubt you'll have heard of it. It's called Cowboys and Angels."

"I've not only heard of it, I've been there." Lena caught the skeptical expressions on Gideon's and Dan's faces. It certainly wasn't a bar frequented by attorneys and the social circle Lena must have moved in. "It was a long time ago. A friend from Harvard was in town and took me there, and I don't think he knew what type of bar it was. Marc was more interested in the beer. He owns a microbrewery now. We left after a fight broke out."

"Good move," Marty said. "That's usually when I leave too."

Gideon smiled at her, and Dan realized she'd impressed his boss. "You're both welcome anytime. I'll make sure Ariel is somewhere else—less likely for fights to break out."

Dan was sure that fights broke out if someone breathed funny, but he wasn't going to contradict Gideon. Ariel felt no such compunction and started bickering with her father. When Marty ignored them both and offered to buy everyone a drink, Dan looked at his watch. He needed to eat before he started work.

"I'm going to take Dan away for a late lunch," Gideon said suddenly. "I've made him start work early today, and he needs to eat."

Gideon just read his mind.

Ariel nodded. "I'm going to meet friends. I'll see you later, Daddy." She kissed him on the cheek.

"Make sure you call me if you're coming home," Gideon ordered. Officially Ariel lived close to NYU, but she came back to the bar so often that Gideon still waited up for her.

"Yeah, yeah," Ariel muttered, but she didn't protest again, and Dan was pleased. She was a good girl at heart. Then he rolled his eyes at himself for thinking like a proud parent.

Marty looked at Lena. "It's just you and me, then, sweetheart."

She smiled at him sweetly. "A quick coffee and then the department store."

They all laughed at Marty's loud groan. "Do I have to?"

Dan patted his back. "Never mind, man. Just get it over with."

"It's not like we need anything new," Marty protested. "We've got two apartments full of stuff."

Lena kissed Marty on the cheek. "But this is a time to get new things. Times are changing."

They walked away to the counter, and Gideon raised an eyebrow at Dan. "Is that what I think it means?"

Dan nodded, but Ariel looked confused. "Is anyone going to clue me in?"

"I'll tell you later," Dan said. "Much later. When you're over thirty."

He ducked as Ariel threw a sugar packet at him, but she got him square on the nose. Then she punched the air in triumph, and Gideon shook his head.

"You should know better than to take on my daughter."

Dan shrugged. "It's fun to try."

"And you'll always fail," Ariel assured him.

He looked over to Gideon for support and found him studying him with an expression Dan couldn't place. "Are you okay, boss?"

Gideon started, as though he'd been lost in thought. He opened his mouth to speak, but a well-aimed sugar packet to the nose stopped him in his tracks. Ariel crowed, Gideon growled, and Dan picked up his hat and waited for father and daughter to finish.

CHAPTER 5

AS SOON as they hit the sidewalk, the icy wind made Dan shiver, and he wished he'd worn a thicker jacket. He pulled his hat out and shoved it on his head.

"I've got gloves if you can deal with the colors. Ariel knitted them at school." Gideon pulled a bright yellow and purple stripy woolen pair out of his pocket, but Dan shook his head.

"I've got gloves." He pulled out his own sedate navy pair and put them on. "I think Ariel gave me the scarf to match your gloves."

"She knitted presents for everyone that year." Gideon didn't seem to feel cold, and he stuffed his gloves back in his pocket.

As he walked along the sidewalk next to Gideon, Dan was acutely conscious of the height difference between them. Gideon was at least seven inches taller than him and much broader, and he seemed to take up the space around him as they walked. Dan's previous hookups—he never bothered with the term boyfriend—had all been around his height or smaller, and Gideon was huge in both body and personality. Dan had worked with him for five years and still felt overwhelmed.

"Dan?"

Gideon had been talking to him, but Dan didn't have a clue what Gideon had said. He flushed and said, "Sorry, what was that?"

Gideon gave him an odd look. "I asked where you wanted to eat?"

"Let's go to the diner on Washington Avenue," Dan said. "They do the best burgers, and I'm really in the mood for some meat." When he realized what he'd said, he sighed. Out of the corner of his eye, he could see Gideon's lips twitch, and he wished he'd kept his mouth shut.

"That's fine," Gideon said. "I like it there."

By the time they reached the diner, Dan was hunting for something to say, but Gideon didn't seem to mind the lack of conversation. He led the way into the warm room and greeted the waitress by name. She pointed to a booth, and the two men settled themselves. Their legs brushed for a moment, and then Gideon found his own space.

"I guess you come here a lot," Dan said.

"More than I should," Gideon admitted. "I used to bring Ariel and Simon here when their mom wanted a break from cooking."

"You didn't offer to take over?"

"Sarah would never let me near the kitchen. Her parents were chefs, and Sarah learned from them."

"I like cooking. I just don't get the time," Dan admitted. "My mom taught me too, and she's a very good cook. Is that why you've never offered food at the bar?"

Gideon shook his head. "Ariel would like me to offer food, but it would change the style of the bar, and I like it as it is. Too many places have become restaurants rather than places to drink and socialize. Cowboys and Angels is for guys to come in after work and relax. If they want to eat, they can go home or to a burger bar. I want somewhere they can drink and let off some steam."

"They let off steam a bit too often," Dan said dryly. "Don't you get fed up with replacing the furniture?"

It was a conversation they'd had too many times, and as usual, Gideon shrugged it off. "It's cheap, and I've got the money. They do a lot less damage than they used to."

Dan touched the bruise on his face and huffed. Gideon only came in after the worst was done, but Dan still came home damaged every time there was a fight. Gideon followed Dan's fingers and narrowed his eyes.

"You're still hurt?"

"No more than usual."

"Did Ariel start the fight again?"

"She doesn't help the situation." Dan said it as diplomatically as he could. It wasn't as though they hadn't had this discussion before either.

Gideon grinned. "This is why you've lasted so long at my bar."

"Oh yeah? Go on, then. Tell me why I've lasted so long,"

"You tell me I waste my money and my little girl causes trouble, but you're not obnoxious about it."

Dan gave a wry smile. "I like my job, Gideon. Cowboys and Angels is your place. If it were my bar, I'd do things differently."

Gideon leaned back in his seat and picked up his coffee. "Okay. You tell me what you'd do if Cowboys and Angels were yours."

"Is this a trick question?" Dan could usually read Gideon's expression, but not now.

Gideon shook his head. "I really want to know."

Dan had had a lot of time to think about what he'd do with the bar. He licked his lips. Okay. Gideon had dangled the bait. Maybe it was time to hook the fish. "First I'd put a muzzle on Ariel." Gideon let out a bark of laughter, obviously not angry at Dan's forthright comment. "You're spending money night after night cleaning up her mess. You could spend that money elsewhere. She's not a little girl anymore. I know she's *your* little girl, but she's an adult. She's almost finished college, and she needs to grow up." He saw the laughter changing to a frown and held up his hand. "That's all I'm gonna say. I want to see the bar change, but I don't want to change the patrons. I like that we've got a place for working men to go to. I don't want to be a fancy wine bar, and I don't want to be a sports bar. I like it as it is. But I'm tired of the customers smashing the furniture over each other's heads, and the décor needs updating. We're not in Texas. We're in New York, and if it were my bar, we'd reflect that.

"I'd also put in a small amount of food. Burgers, fries, chicken wings. Give the guys something to soak up all that beer. It doesn't have to be a large menu, but something basic. You should look at what other bars do. They're offering food, and they don't get the trouble. We're gonna lose customers. Just because you *can* pay for the damage doesn't mean you should. And last, I'd make sure I was visible as the owner or manager. You hide upstairs too much. People only see you when there's a fight." Dan ran out of breath and decided to end it there. He hadn't intended to say so much, but once he started, he couldn't stop.

Gideon stared at him, and Dan had visions of being handed a pink slip, even though Gideon had told him to be honest. "You've thought about this long and hard, huh? Is this from the course?"

"I've worked for you for a long time." Between the bar and his business courses, he'd had ideas over the years.

"But you never said any of this to me before. Why not?" Gideon's tone was more curious than annoyed.

"Would you tell your boss that you think he's doing it wrong?" Dan pointed out. "I just have different ideas, that's all."

"It's okay. I'm a big boy. I can take a little criticism. Let me get this straight," Gideon counted off his fingers, "One, you think I need to rein in Ariel. Two, I need to change the décor to reflect New York and change the furniture so the customers can't hurt each other with it. Three, I need to provide a food menu. Four, I'm being a lousy boss by hiding away."

"I didn't say you're a lousy boss. You're a good man to work for, and I wouldn't have stayed as long as I have if I thought you were bad at your job. I just think you could make changes."

A long silence followed, and Dan started to worry. Just because Gideon had said to be honest, didn't mean he accepted the criticism.

Gideon smiled. "How would you like to become my manager?"

Dan stared at him. "What did you just say?"

"How would you like to become the manager of Cowboys and Angels?"

"That's what I thought you said." Dan took a deep breath and exhaled. "Yes."

Gideon's smile widened. "Just yes?"

"Well, subject to terms and conditions. You're gonna give me a pay raise? When do you want me to start?"

"Yeah, yeah. You get a pay raise and benefits. Once we've discussed benefits, the job is yours."

Dan took a deep breath and tried to hide his excitement. The experience of running Cowboys and Angels would look great on his business plans for the future, and the pay raise would help with his rent. "Okay tell me the terms."

"I can't tell Ariel what to do. She's got me wrapped around her little finger." Gideon's smile turned wry, and Dan nodded. "But my manager? He'd be a different matter. He could tell Ariel to behave."

Dan held back an eye-roll. Trust Gideon to make Ariel top of the list. "You want me to be the bad guy?"

"Yeah. Do you think you can do that?"

"If you don't interfere, yeah."

Gideon snorted. "Don't hold back, Dan."

"I'm not gonna take the job if you want a yes man," Dan said bluntly. "There are plenty of other guys who can do that."

Gideon leaned forward and caught his gaze. "I offered you the job precisely because you're not a yes man. You get carte blanche to run Cowboys and Angels how you want. I need to step back from the bar. Other interests need my time."

Dan's eyes opened wide. "Are you serious?"

Gideon held up his hand, and Dan noticed the small hairs curling around his watch. "Carte blanche within reason. My bar is for drinking, not a restaurant. But if you can find a small menu we can agree on, then we'll talk. I'm open for change. You get a pay raise, and you'll need to find someone else to take your place."

Dan shook his head. "This is the last thing I expected you to want to talk about."

"I have a couple of conditions," Gideon said.

"What are they?" Dan asked suspiciously.

"I want you to take some evenings off. Time away from studying and working."

"But you just said—"

Gideon held up his hand.

"This is a condition. I know what I just said, but your comments about dating struck home. You're not even thirty yet, and I can't remember the last time I saw you date someone you were excited about."

Dan felt a bit defensive. Why was everyone on his case about his love life? "I don't date at the bar. It's not a place to pick up guys."

"I know it isn't, but God knows I know what it's like to be alone. I also know what it's like to be in a loving relationship, and I think you should have the chance."

"I'm not on the shelf yet. I just haven't found anyone I like." *Except you.*

Oblivious to Dan's inner conversation, Gideon continued. "Find a date for Marty's wedding."

"I don't want to date," Dan said tightly. "I'm fine going stag."

"Humor me."

"How am I supposed to find a date?"

Gideon let out a booming laugh. "Well, son, if you need me to tell you that, you've been doing it wrong all these years."

Dan refrained from pointing out that he was not Gideon's son. He'd had many fantasies about Gideon over the years, but the daddy-and-son relationship wasn't one of them. "Why do I feel like there's a conspiracy here?"

"Because you read too many of them conspiracy sites?"

"How do you know.... Oh, of course, Ariel told you?" At Gideon's nod, Dan sighed. "I *do* read conspiracy-theory websites. But I don't actually believe them." He kept the tinfoil strictly for cooking.

"Thank heaven for that. I don't want to discover my manager is a closet flat-earther."

"I'm not a closet anything," Dan pointed out. "And definitely not a flat-earther. You know way more about me than I know about you."

"That's the way it's meant to be," Gideon said. "A good boss should always know about his staff."

Dan had a momentary panic thinking Gideon might know about his unrequited crush. But he was fairly sure he'd managed to keep that one from Ariel. She would never have kept that juicy piece of gossip quiet.

At that point their food arrived, and Gideon dove in with obvious enthusiasm. Dan's stomach rumbled as he picked up his knife and fork, and he moaned as the taste of bacon flitted over his tongue. Gideon looked up with a grin, and Dan flushed.

"Good?"

"Very good," Dan mumbled through a mouthful of bacon, egg, and hash browns.

Eating was more important than talking, and both men agreed on pancakes to follow. Dan relaxed in Gideon's company, at least until coffee, when Gideon mentioned the wedding again.

"I don't need a date."

With a wicked grin on his face, Gideon sat back against the vinyl seat. "A bet, then."

"What kind of bet?"

"I've been thinking about that. How about $500?"

Dan frowned. "You want to bet $500 on what?"

"If you find a date, I'll keep Ariel out of the bar for the next three months and pay you a $500 bonus."

"That's ridiculous." Dan didn't have $500, and Gideon knew that.

"You're turning down a quiet bar?"

"And if I don't find a date, I have to pay you $500 and keep Ariel quiet?"

Gideon shook his head, but mischief was written all over him. "Not quite."

"What, then?" Dan asked warily.

"If we, and by *we* I mean Ariel, find you a date, you donate to a charity of my choice and Ariel is all yours to deal with."

"You've got to be joking. There's no way I'm going to let Ariel pick me a date." That idea was just horrific. Dan turned it over in his mind as the waitress topped off their coffees. The whole thing was a joke to Gideon, but Dan could use $500. Was he a man or a mouse? He could find a date for himself.

Gideon picked up his cup. "Five hundred dollars and no fights."

"You're on." Dan was going to win that bet. He raised the cup to Gideon in mock salute. One date. He could manage that.

Dear Reader,
By now, you must be HORNY & HOT.
How big is your Cock?
7" 8" ---- 10"
I have a 9" Cock. Cut.
I like you to play with my Cock, and I will suck your Cock. I want you to CUM in my mouth. Then, I want you to FUCK me.
I have lots of CONDOMS and rubs.
I am a doctor.
Would you like to be Fucked with my 9" Cock?

CHAPTER 6

IT WAS supposed to be his day off. Gideon had promised him that after an eleven-day stretch he could have the whole day off and not return until the following evening. Dan fully intended to stay in bed, cuddle his cat, and not move for twenty-four hours. He was asleep, buried in pillows and comforters, his dreams full of a guy with dark curls who looked suspiciously like Gideon pushing him facedown into his bed and thrusting into him until Dan's toes curled and he forgot his own name.

The sound of his phone was an unwelcome intrusion. Dan fumbled around for the phone and dislodged his purring cat. He knocked the phone onto the floor, and after more cursing and fumbling through his discarded clothing, he eventually managed to pick it up, only to have missed the call.

Dan cursed again He would have to open his eyes to see who called. He wasn't any happier when he cracked open one eye and realized it was Cowboys and Angels' number. He was tempted to ignore the call, but then he heard the beep of a message. He rolled over onto his back and called the bar. Gideon answered immediately.

"Dan?"

He could deny all knowledge of knowing anyone called Dan, but the petty satisfaction wasn't worth the aggravation. "Yeah. Is there a problem?" *Please don't ask me to cover a shift.*

"I know you're tired, but I really need you in the bar this evening."

Dan groaned. "Gideon, I'm dead on my feet. Isn't there anyone else?"

"Bradley and Luis are sick, and Juan is away. I've got Eddie and Liam here till four, but then I'm on my own. If you come in, we can work together."

"Bradley and Luis are both sick?"

Dan's suspicious tone must have communicated itself to Gideon. "I know. It did seem unlikely, but they both said they'd been puking."

"What about Ariel or her friend, what's her name, Rachel? She wanted more shifts."

"They've got lectures tonight. I know I promised you the time off, and I'll make it up to you."

It was the sense of desperation in Gideon's voice that made Dan say, "Okay, okay. I'll be there at five."

"Thanks, dar—Dan. See you later."

Dan rolled out of bed and was unsurprised when SmokeyJo conveyed her displeasure by hocking up a hairball.

He'd had almost ten hours sleep. That was enough, surely. Dan rolled out of bed and padded into the bathroom. A hot shower might wake him up, so he stood under the pounding stream of water and closed his eyes. His apartment was blessed with a powerful shower, and he leaned against the tiles and relished the feel of the water running over his tired body.

"If you're not careful, you're going to fall asleep standing up," he muttered.

He squeezed shower gel into his hand and ran it over his body. Dan had little hair on his head, but he was furry on his chest and belly, the brown hair a shade darker than his head. Idly he wondered whether Gideon liked body hair, but then he cut that thought off. Gideon was straight and, since women didn't usually sport chest hair, off-limits. After five years Dan was very good at cutting off any unwanted thoughts, if not dreams. He rinsed himself and got out of the shower to towel dry.

SmokeyJo poked her head around the bathroom door and mewed at him. He scrubbed his head dry and then answered her meow. "Yes, I'll feed you before I go. But you don't deserve it. Just saying."

She sniffed and walked away, tail held high and with a contemptuous swagger. Dan sighed. He should have gotten a dog.

COWBOYS AND Angels was virtually empty when he walked in. Gideon was behind the bar, and he looked relieved when he saw Dan, although his opening greeting was a harsh "About time."

Dan glared at him because it was exactly five o'clock. He'd spent what little free time he'd had finishing his assignment, then apologized to SmokeyJo before leaving her again. In the back he removed his coat, hat, and gloves, aware he was still out of sorts and not ready to make nice.

Gideon appeared in the doorway. "I'm sorry about that. I didn't mean to be an asshole."

Dan grunted. "We need more staff, boss."

"Agreed. I want you to look at it as part of your new duties."

"I didn't know I'd accepted the job." Dan frowned. Or had he? Yes, he had agreed to take the post. God, he was so tired.

Gideon raised an eyebrow. "You're going to turn me down? I'm giving you everything you wanted in the place."

"Except sleep," Dan bitched. "I'm really lacking in sleep."

"I know that, and I'll make up it up to you. I can't believe Bradley and Luis were both sick."

Dan had a sneaking suspicion he knew exactly what was wrong with the two barmen. There was a new bar opening across town, and separately, both men had asked Dan if he would cover their shifts. If he hadn't worked so many days, he would have said yes. But he wasn't about to snitch to Gideon. He would make his feelings clear to them on his own time. Dan grinned viciously. They would be covering his shifts for some time to come. They just didn't know it yet.

"Do I want to know what you're thinking about?" Gideon asked.

Dan shook his head. "I don't think you do."

"If you're my manager, you're supposed to be on my side."

"I'm not your manager yet. When I am, I will always be on your side. Unless you're being an asshole, in which case I'll tell you, and that will be me being on your side too."

Gideon shook his head. "I'm beginning to regret this decision."

"No, you're not."

"No, I'm not," Gideon said softly as he walked back into the bar.

Dan was worried he'd fall asleep—he was that tired—but the bar got so busy he didn't have time to stop and think, let alone sleep. Partway through the evening, he realized how much he enjoyed working with Gideon. He hadn't worked a shift with his boss since his early days, and they just fit. Unlike some of the other barmen, he didn't have to prod Gideon to work. Gideon knew what needed to be done, and he just got on with it. They deferred to each other when necessary, and when a customer got rowdy, Gideon had Dan's back.

Still, he wasn't unhappy that Gideon made a decision to close the bar a couple of hours early, and because there weren't any fights to clear up, the bar was closed and cleaned by 2:00 a.m. Dan sat down wearily and rubbed his eyes.

"I'll give you a ride home," Gideon said.

"It's okay. I can get a car." But Dan couldn't bring himself to move. He could barely raise his head.

"I'm driving you home."

Dan was too tired to argue. He yawned and got to his feet. "Could you just transport me home now?"

"You can stay here if you want. I have a spare room."

"The offer is very tempting, but I have to get home to feed SmokeyJo. If she doesn't get food every couple of hours, she'll die. At least that's what she tells me."

Gideon looked amused. "You do know she's just playing you, don't you?"

Dan yawned again. "Of course I do. But I let her think she's in control."

"Come on, then. I'll have you in bed in ten minutes," Gideon said as he walked toward the back to get his coat.

Dan was glad Gideon couldn't see his face at that moment, because all his feelings would be on display. Goddammit. Crushes on unattainable guys were the pits. He put his coat on and smiled when Gideon returned. "I'm ready."

"HEY, YOU'RE home."

Dan mumbled and snuggled down, annoyed at being disturbed.

"What am I going to do to wake you up?" The voice sounded amused, but Dan could really do with it shutting up. He needed sleep. "Am I going to have to carry you upstairs?"

"I'm awake. Awake." Dan sat up abruptly, arms flailing, and then realized he was still in Gideon's car. "Did I fall asleep?"

Gideon rolled his eyes. "You were snoring before I put the belt on you."

"I'm sorry." Dan knuckled his eyes in a futile attempt to wake up.

"No worries. Let's get you to bed before you fall asleep again." Gideon got out of the car and came around to open Dan's door.

Dan scowled as he got out of the car. "I can open my own door."

Gideon pushed the door shut. “I know you can. I also know you’re asleep on your feet. If I leave you here, you’re probably going to fall asleep in the doorway and die of hypothermia.”

“I’m not that helpless,” Dan protested.

“That would be more believable if your eyes weren’t already shut. I wouldn’t be a good employer if I didn’t make sure my staff were safely tucked up in bed.”

“You never worried about me before.” Dan slapped a mental hand over his mouth. Obviously being tired had lowered some of his defenses.

Gideon put an arm round him and guided Dan to the door before he answered. “That was remiss of me. I won’t make that mistake again.”

“It’s okay,” Dan mumbled. “You’re a good boss. The best.”

“I really ought to be recording this for future reference so I can remind you when you tell me all the things I do wrong.”

“No blackmail.”

“No blackmail,” Gideon agreed. “What floor are you on?”

“Third floor. No, don’t use the elevator. We could be stuck in there forever.” Dan pointed to the stairs.

Gideon half carried him up the stairs. “Thank God it’s only the third floor,” he puffed as he manhandled Dan into the hallway. “Which is your door?”

By that time Dan was resting his head on Gideon’s chest and was more than ready to go back to sleep, but he waved to his front door.

Gideon propped him against the wall. “Give me your keys.”

Dan fumbled for the keys and handed them to Gideon, who tried a couple before he found the right one. SmokeyJo greeted them as they entered the apartment. Her meows changed to something more questioning when she spotted Gideon, but they turned to purrs as Gideon bent down to pet her. Dan stood in the middle of his room, not sure what he was meant to do next.

“You go to bed,” Gideon said.

“Gotta feed the cat.” Dan wandered in the direction of the kitchen cabinets.

Hands landed on his shoulders and steered him toward the bedroom. “I’ll feed the damned cat. Get into bed before you fall down.”

Dan landed on the bed without even taking off his boots and jacket. It wasn't like he hadn't done it a hundred times before. He was asleep before he properly settled, and he stirred only slightly when he felt gentle hands undress him and guide him under the covers. But it wasn't enough to fully wake him as he slipped into a dreamless sleep.

Chapter 7

DAN GRUMBLED in annoyance as sunlight filtered through his eyelids and interrupted his dreams. He must have forgotten to close the blinds before he went to bed. Too lazy to get up and close them, Dan slung an arm over his eyes. But despite being warm and comfy and listening to the purring in his ear, it was obvious that sleep was a distant memory. Dan sat up and scratched his belly. SmokeyJo rumbled her displeasure at being disturbed, and he rubbed behind her ears in apology.

"I must have been tired last night," he told her. "I don't remember getting undressed. How did I get here, Smokey?"

He frowned as he tried to work through his memories. He didn't remember much after closing up the bar for the night. He hadn't drunk anything, so he could only put it down to exhaustion. But he was at home, undressed down to his briefs, and in his own bed, so he must have gotten a car. Dan shuffled to the edge of the bed and heaved himself up. He took one step, tripped over his boots, and landed heavily on the floor. The downstairs apartment thumped their ceiling in annoyance. Dan yelled out an apology and received another thump in response.

His knees and palms stung as he got to his feet and threw the boots toward the front door. He narrowly missed SmokeyJo and once more had to apologize to her. He also received another *thump thump* from downstairs.

Why were his boots by the bed? He always put them by the front door unless he fell asleep on the bed still dressed in his outerwear, which happened more than Dan liked to admit.

He dressed in sweats and a hoodie and headed to the kitchen cabinets. SmokeyJo weaved around his legs in an open display of pleading. "Did I feed you last night?" The empty tin of kitty crap on the counter suggested he had, and Dan congratulated himself. He might have forgotten everything else, but he never forgot to feed his cat.

Dan frowned as he noticed a piece of paper stuck to the fridge, held on by a fridge magnet. That wasn't there yesterday. He pulled it off. It was an empty envelope with a note on the back in a scrawling cursive he recognized.

> *Don't come in today.*
> *Gideon*

WHY WOULD Gideon leave a note on his fridge? More to the point, when had Gideon been in his apartment?

Small snippets of memory plopped into the tired void of Dan's mind. Gideon insisting he drive Dan home. Gideon's arm around him as he stumbled up the stairs. Gideon saying something about feeding the cat. Dan looked at his boots and then at himself.

"Oh fuck. Please tell me he didn't undress me."

Who else would have stripped him of his clothing?

SmokeyJo meowed imperiously. She wasn't interested in his mortification, so he fed her, made himself coffee, and returned to bed. If he was going to nurse humiliation, he could at least do it in comfort. On impulse he picked up his phone, intent on dialing Gideon's number, but he had a message.

Hey, what are you doing tonight? I'm free. If you want to get together for dinner and a fuck you know where I am.

Dan nearly threw his phone across the room, but Disastrous Date wasn't worth a broken phone. "What's it gonna take for you to get the message?" SmokeyJo meowed her displeasure at the shouting, and he apologized profusely. He deleted the message and called Gideon instead.

"I'm surprised you're awake," Gideon said by way of greeting.

"Did you take me home last night, or did I just imagine that?"

"I brought you home."

"And put me to bed." Dan flushed bright red at the thought. At least Gideon couldn't see that.

"I wasn't going to leave you sleeping in your jacket and boots."

"It wouldn't be the first time," Dan admitted.

"I had a feeling that was the case. You didn't even stir as I undressed you. I've never met anyone who sleeps as soundly as you."

"I've always slept like the dead."

"You looked so warm and cozy lying there, I was tempted to get in and join you."

Dan's mind went to a completely different place, he was sure, from Gideon's. He'd had visions of Gideon in his bed, but they never involved sleeping. "You would've had to fight for space with the cat."

"I'm sure SmokeyJo and I could have come to some arrangement." Gideon sounded very sure of himself.

"She could out-stubborn you any day."

"Maybe I'll try that out someday."

Before Dan could think of anything to say to that, Gideon continued. "Ariel wants to talk to you about your date."

Dan buried his face in the pillows and groaned. "I hoped she'd forgotten."

"Have you met my daughter?"

"I'll come in later."

"You stay in bed. I'll get her to call you this evening."

"I'll be awake."

Maybe. Dan didn't think he'd ever be able to move out of his bed again.

"It can wait 'til tomorrow if you're asleep, dar—Dan."

That was the second time Gideon had stumbled over his name.

"Are you shorthanded?"

"Bradley is covering your shift tonight. Luis is in too. They're suddenly well again."

Dan smirked at Gideon's unimpressed tone. "Thanks for covering my shifts."

"Going back to the dating question, have you found your plus-one yet?" Gideon asked suddenly.

Dan covered his face. He'd been so busy with work and an assignment that he hadn't even thought about it since their initial discussion. "I've still got time."

"Three weeks left. Let Ariel do it for you."

"Five hundred dollars, Gideon. Five hundred dollars. I'll find my date, and I'll be the one laughing."

"I didn't think you'd accept the bet."

"Just shows you don't know me as well as you think."

Gideon snickered. "I know you a lot better after last night. Tweety Pie briefs? I expected something far more sedate."

"Ariel bought them for me for Christmas. I hadn't had time to do my laundry," Dan protested.

"Hey, I won't judge a man for wearing cartoon underwear." Gideon paused. "She bought me Simba boxers."

Gideon got the king and Dan got the small yellow bird.

"Why does that not surprise me?" Dan muttered.

"*The Lion King* is my favorite movie."

Dan blinked. "That does surprise me."

"I like animation."

"Especially if they're kids' movies?"

"I used to watch them with Ariel and Simon."

Dan was so tuned to Gideon that it was easy to catch the hurt in his voice. "They remind you of happier times?"

"They do. I guess that sounds silly."

"I used to watch Tweety Pie with my grandfather. Paw-paw used to look after me when my mom went on a date," Dan admitted. "He didn't like new cartoons, so we watched all the old ones together."

"I used to do the same with my father."

Dan was caught by a sudden yawn. "Oh, sorry. Last night is catching up with me again." He stretched and yawned.

"You need to sleep," Gideon said briskly.

"Yessir."

"Smartass."

Dan laughed. "That's you."

"Go and dream of the man of your dreams."

"I wonder about you, Gideon. I've never met a straight man who would say that."

"What makes you think I'm straight? What the hell are you doing, Liam? Oh hell. I've got to go."

Dan was left staring at the phone. Gideon? Not straight? What the hell?

BY THE following Monday, Dan had gotten himself into a knot about finding anyone to take to the wedding. Ariel had said nothing about finding him a date, but he didn't think for a moment that Gideon or she would have forgotten. The Tylers didn't forget. But Dan was doing his best to forget Gideon's startling announcement.

At a quiet moment during the day, Dan took the opportunity to call Marty at work and explain the whole bet debacle to him. He had to wait for Marty to stop howling with laughter.

"Thanks for your support," Dan snapped when Marty finally shut up.

"You're welcome." Marty laughed again.

Dan chewed on a hangnail. "How am I going to find a date at this short notice?"

"Don't you people use an app or something? Antonia, it's supposed to go over there." Marty's attention was definitely elsewhere.

"'You people?' Nice. I've done Grindr before." It was fun in his early twenties, but he was approaching thirty and was a down-to-earth, maybe too-old-fashioned kind of guy. He preferred to meet his dates face-to-face.

"Where do you normally meet your dates?"

"At a bar or a club."

"Why can't you do that, then? Oh, for fu—!"

Dan heard a huge crash, and then Marty said, "I've got to go. Go speed dating if you have to. Just find a date."

"Speed dating?" Dan stared at the disconnected phone. "What the heck is speed dating?"

CHAPTER 8

DAN JUMPED as Ariel squealed loudly. The last time he checked, she was writing an essay at the far end of the bar. Now she was an inch away from his ear.

"Speed dating? That's perfect." She beamed at him. "Leave it to me."

Dan stared at her with a sinking feeling. "What are you going to do?"

"Find you a date, silly. We'll set up a speed-dating night at the bar."

"Ariel, baby, Cowboys and Angels doesn't do events. We're not that type of bar. You know that."

She tossed her hair. "Only because you guys never make an effort to organize anything. I've been telling Daddy he needs to hold events here. I have a ton of contacts who can help. All we need is another nineteen men as potential dates."

Dan shook his head. "I only need one date."

"You need to find the right one. Look, you can call that guy who keeps bothering you, or you can let me help. Come on, Dan, you don't want to be taking a man you hate to Marty's wedding."

"I can find my own date, thank you. Wait, does the speed dating count as me finding myself a date or you finding me a date?"

Maybe he *should* call Disastrous Date. It would shut them up and get the dude to stop texting him.

Ariel tossed her head again, and her ponytail bounced wildly. "You find a man at this event, and Daddy has to pay up."

Gideon had been watching them talk from the other side of the bar, but he hadn't gotten involved until then. "That wasn't the bet, darlin'."

"It's only fair, Daddy," Ariel pointed out. "And an event like this will bring in more customers. It's perfect."

"How do we get it organized?" Gideon asked.

"You aren't serious, boss?" Dan protested.

"Deadly serious. We'll have to do it on a Monday night, and we need to warn the regulars."

"They're not going to be happy."

"It's one night, for a couple of hours," Ariel said. "Come on. It'll be fun."

Dan could think of a million things more fun than speed dating, but from the determined looks on Gideon's and Ariel's faces, he wasn't going to win the battle or the bet. It was kind of spooky how fiercely determined and identical their expressions were.

It was annoying, but Ariel was right. Dan had also suggested to Gideon that they hold special events and private functions. He just never thought he would be the focus of the event.

Gideon shook his head. "Ariel, darling, you get the men here. And Dan, you make sure there are drinks and food for them." He twinkled at Dan. "And make sure you look your prettiest. I'll forget the $500."

Ariel burst into peals of laughter, and Dan stalked away to the basement, where he could bitch to the kegs about his absurd situation. Ariel and Gideon could laugh themselves senseless at his expense, and then he'd remind them who really ran the bar, and life would return to normal. Or not.

FOR THE rest of the week, life did return to normal as Dan dealt with a series of issues at the bar. He didn't have time to think about the dating event. Three of the barmen caught the flu, the dishwasher broke down and flooded the kitchen, and there was an issue with the lines of one of the beers. The barrel had been changed, but one of the barmen told him it wasn't working, so he was in the basement again, trying to sort out the problem.

"Dan?"

He looked up as Gideon clattered down the wooden stairs to join him. "Hey."

"Problems?" Gideon came up behind Dan, so close Dan could feel Gideon's breath on his neck.

"Damn thing's still not working right. Liam changed the barrel yesterday, and it hasn't worked since. There are no kinks in the line."

"Did he clean it through?"

Gideon stepped forward to take a closer look at the line, and his long body pressed against Dan's. For one moment Dan forgot how to breathe, but then he focused on what Gideon had said.

"Juan told him to, but it's Liam." Gideon insisted the lines be cleaned and replaced regularly, and usually Dan or whoever the senior barman was took care of the barrels and lines, but Dan hadn't been on the shift, and Liam wasn't the most conscientious of the staff. The customers liked him well enough, but he frustrated the hell out of Dan. "I'll clean the line now. Hopefully that'll fix the problem."

"Okay. I'm gonna talk to Liam." Gideon sounded resigned.

Dan pressed his lips together. He wasn't the manager yet, but when he was, Liam was going to pull his weight or he'd be out on his ear.

Gideon looked over his shoulder and obviously caught Dan's expression. "You wanna talk to him?"

"Why do you keep him on? He's lazy and inefficient."

He'd had that argument with Gideon before, but Gideon always insisted that Liam just needed more training. Dan had pointed out Liam got the same training as all the other staff, and they didn't fuck up, but Gideon insisted that Liam stay.

"He's Sarah's nephew."

Dan frowned. "Sarah? Your wife?"

"Yeah. He couldn't find a job after high school, and his mom, Sarah's sister, asked me to help. I didn't realize how lazy he was."

"You never told me." Dan felt strangely hurt, which was stupid, because he'd never really talked with Gideon about personal stuff.

"Liam asked me to keep it quiet, and I agreed. He said he didn't want people using him to get at me. I didn't think he was gonna take advantage of our relationship."

"He's been here two years," Dan pointed out. He should have noticed. Gideon had no issues firing staff who didn't match his standards, but Liam had always been off the table.

Gideon sighed. "It's the one thing I can't do. I can deal with anyone but family."

"If you're making me manager, Liam either pulls his weight or he's fired," Dan warned. "And you back me up, family or not. Are there any other family members you want to spring on me?"

"None. Just Ariel and Liam." The relief in Gideon's voice suggested Dan could ask for the world if Gideon didn't have to deal with his errant family.

"Do you need to talk to his mom first?" The last thing Dan wanted was to get caught between Gideon and his late wife's family.

Gideon shook his head. "He's not a kid. There's no reason why he can't stand on his own two feet now."

Footsteps sounded on the steps from the bar.

"Dan? Is the line fixed?" Bradley appeared. "Oh hey, Gideon. I didn't realize you were down here. Is it fixed?"

Dan shook his head. "I'm gonna clean the line. See if that solves the problem."

"'Kay."

Bradley clattered back up the stairs and left Dan and Gideon behind. Dan shivered, bone-cold after the time he'd spent down in the basement.

"Send Liam down here," Gideon said. "We'll clean the line. You go back up, Dan."

Dan shivered again, and his teeth chattered. "Are you sure?"

"You stay down here any longer and you'll turn into an icicle." Gideon gently pushed Dan to the stairs.

"Thanks." He took the stairs two at a time and headed for Liam, who looked at him warily.

"Am I in trouble?" Liam asked.

"Don't know yet," Dan said. "Did you clean the line when you changed the barrel?"

Liam flushed and looked away. "No. I meant to—"

"Just get downstairs. Gideon's down there." He couldn't fail to notice Liam brightened at Gideon's name. Dan pressed his lips together. Any reprimand this time was up to Gideon. He would talk to Liam separately, but it was time Liam found out who was in charge. "I'll talk to you later."

"Liam, get your butt down here," Gideon roared.

Dan worked his way through the waiting customers, soothed his regulars who were annoyed at the temporary loss of their favorite beer, and made lists of what was needed for the speed-dating evening. He and Ariel would meet later to finalize plans. He also dealt with a blocked toilet in the men's bathroom and averted a potential fight with two guys over a card game.

After a while a subdued and cold-looking Liam emerged, followed by Gideon. Dan didn't have time to talk to either of them because it was happy hour and a gaggle of students entered in search of cheap drinks and good music. To Dan's amusement, Liam went as far away as he could to man one end of the bar.

Gideon joined Dan to help at his end. "It's working again, and if Liam screws up again he's out the door."

"Great. Buck will be happy."

"I'll take him a pint."

Dan poured the beer and handed it to Gideon, who went over to Buck, a customer who'd been coming to the bar for as long as it had been open. The old man gave a toothless grin and a salute as Gideon handed him the glass and exchanged a few words with him.

"He's a happy man," Dan said on Gideon's return.

Gideon flashed him a bright smile. "Buck likes the idea of us serving burgers and fries."

"You asked him?"

"I don't want our older customers to feel pushed out."

"What did he say?"

"That it was about time the old girl got a makeover and I stopped playing at running a bar." Gideon gave a wry smile. "Buck thinks I need to hand the bar over to someone who knows what they're doing."

Dan tried and failed not to snort with laughter. Buck was renowned for telling it like it is. "Did he have any suggestions?"

"He said I could do worse than ask you to take over. He said you wouldn't fuck it up as much as I do."

"What did you say?"

"I said I'd consider his idea."

"You didn't tell him you'd already asked me?"

Gideon grinned. "Not yet. Let it be a surprise."

"At least someone 'round here appreciates me."

"Gideon thinks the sun shines out of your ass, Dan," Bradley said as he walked past with a tray of empty glasses.

"'Course I do," Gideon said cheerfully.

Dan rolled his eyes, flipped them off, and served the next customer.

CHAPTER 9

ONCE ARIEL got the bit between her teeth, Dan was shocked at how quickly she managed to organize the event. She rushed around like a whirlwind and spent hours on the phone.

Dan watched her with bemusement. When he mentioned it to Gideon, his boss just laughed.

"Ariel was born to organize things like this."

"Then why have you never had any events before?"

Gideon shrugged. "No one suggested something I wanted to hold at Cowboys and Angels."

"So you decided to start with a gay speeding-dating event?" Dan asked dryly.

"Gotta start somewhere." Gideon's eyes twinkled over the set of accounts he was looking at.

"I feel like I ought to help more." Dan had offered to help repeatedly, but Ariel had turned down all his offers.

"All you have to do is agree on the food and turn up looking pretty on the night," Gideon said.

Dan growled. "I'm gay, not a girl. I'm not pretty for anyone."

"I'm sorry," Gideon said unexpectedly. "I didn't mean to imply anything."

The anger drained out of Dan. "I know, I'm sorry for snapping. I'm just nervous."

Bone-fucking petrified.

Gideon slid off his stool and came to stand in front of Dan. "Just relax about the speed dating. It's supposed to be fun. You might get a date, and if not, you get a chance to meet other men."

"This is so wrong."

"The point is, you don't get a choice. You said she could find you a date, and now you're stuck with it."

"You could put a stop to this. She is your daughter."

Gideon laughed and squeezed his shoulder. "Hell no. And miss watching you squirm for a couple of hours? I'm not gonna miss this for the world."

"I thought you liked me."

"I do like you. But I'm more than happy to watch you go through a couple of hours of hell. Besides, it's good business for the bar, and it keeps her from getting into trouble."

"About that. When it gets around that you're hosting gay men, you might not find it's such good business."

"I'll take that hit." Could anything shake that confidence?

"Is there anything I can do to make you change your mind?" Dan begged.

Gideon chuckled again, and Dan knew that any hope of a reprieve was out of the window. "Not a chance in hell. But if it's any help, Ariel already has plans to help you."

"What kind of plans?" Dan asked suspiciously.

"You'll have to wait and see," Gideon said. "I need to get back to these accounts." And he was gone upstairs to his apartment, leaving Dan alone in the bar.

"I'm doomed," he muttered.

Just then Bradley walked in with a crate of bottles. He laughed derisively at him. "You've taken this long to work it out?"

Dan stalked off, shaking his head. How could he get out of this?

THE DAY of Dan's Day of Doom, as he'd termed it, he was banned from the bar during the day, but that didn't mean he could sleep in. On the contrary, he was in the clutches of the Tylers for the entire day. Ariel told him to expect a visitor at ten in the morning, which made Dan real grumpy because he'd been working the night before and only got to bed at four. But he was showered and dressed, and at ten o'clock precisely, the doorbell rang.

Dan deleted yet another text from Disastrous Date and stomped over to open the door. His jaw dropped as he surveyed the man on his doorstep. "What the hell are you doing here?"

Gideon leaned against the doorframe, dressed in a dark navy peacoat, tight jeans, and a smug smile that Dan wanted to wipe off his face. "Morning to you too. Are you ready?"

"Ready for what?" Dan asked warily as he stepped back to allow Gideon into his apartment. Gideon seemed to swallow up the oxygen.

"I thought Ariel was gonna tell you." Gideon looked far too innocent to believe that.

"No, she hasn't said a word," Dan managed through gritted teeth.

"She wants you to have a makeover before tonight's event."

Dan stared at him in horror. "Oh hell no. We had that conversation about me being a girl. I'll be clean, and I'll even iron my shirt. But she's not going to primp and preen me like some doll."

"Calm down. I canceled most of the appointments. But you have to make an effort, Dan. It's a new world out there, and this is New York. A clean shirt won't cut it."

"I'll stick with the old world, thanks very much."

Gideon fixed Dan with a hard stare. "You're going to do this, because Ariel wants it. She's made a huge effort for you. Now suck it up and get your coat on."

Dan swallowed back the angry retort brewing on his lips. Gideon was his boss, and no matter what he thought, Gideon was right. Ariel had worked tirelessly, and it was one night. He'd get through whatever torture Ariel had devised for him. "Okay."

Gideon ignored Dan's rather ungracious response and said, "Let's go. Your first appointment is at ten thirty."

Dan picked up his jacket, wallet, and keys. "Where are we going first?"

Gideon consulted a list. "The barbers. Ariel wants your stubble tidied up."

Dan grunted. He planned to do that before the wedding, but he'd been too busy. At least he could be grateful that was one less job to do. "If you give me the list, I could do it myself. You don't have to babysit me for the day."

"She's given me a list of orders." Gideon looked at Dan as though he were mad. "And if she tells me to do something, I do it. Besides, count yourself lucky one of her professors changed a lecture time. She was going to escort you herself, and you'd have to suffer through a spray tan because she wants one."

Dan nearly choked at the thought of standing naked while somebody covered him in orange crap. "I'm not having a spray tan."

"Relax. It's one of the appointments I canceled, along with a facial, an appointment with a personal shopper, and an eyebrow-threading session."

Dear God, what was left? "What did you keep?"

"Hair, a mani-pedi, a massage, and waxing back, sac, and crack." Gideon burst out laughing as Dan scowled. "No massage?"

"You lay one waxing strip on me, and I'll rip your arm off."

Gideon nudged him. "You're so easy to wind up. I canceled that too."

"Yeah, yeah. Get out of here."

Dan manhandled Gideon through his front door and locked up as Gideon headed for the stairs without Dan needing to remind him. He said hello to Mrs. Gryniewicz from the floor above.

She waved at him and then studied Gideon. "He's better than your last one."

"He's my boss, not my boyfriend," Dan said hastily, almost feeling the amusement radiating off Gideon.

"That's a pity." Mrs. Gryniewicz looked at Gideon. "You treat him well, boss man. Dan's a good boy."

"I know he is," Gideon assured her.

She carried on up the stairs and left Dan furiously blushing.

Gideon's smirk was huge as they carried on down the stairs. "You're the color of my sweater."

"Shut up."

They reached the sidewalk, and Dan went to head off in the direction of his barber, but Gideon caught his arm.

"Where're you going?"

Dan was confused. "I thought I was getting my hair done? My barber's this way."

"You are, but Ariel made the appointment. The hair salon is in the other direction."

"Hair salon?" At Gideon's nod, Dan felt a sinking feeling in the pit of his stomach. "I don't need a hair salon. I can get a buzz cut for $20 around the corner."

"Dan, this is Ariel's day, and you'll do what she wants. You're not paying for this."

Dan shoved his hands into his pockets. He wasn't moving a step until Gideon got one thing straight. "I don't need charity."

"It's not charity."

"If I'm not paying for it, it's charity."

"Call it a bonus from me for putting up with us. Whatever will soothe your conscience. But it's going to happen."

Dan had heard that voice before—usually as Gideon stopped a fight with a single shout. "Do I have a choice?"

"No. Get moving or we'll be late."

Sullenly Dan followed Gideon to a hair salon a few blocks from his apartment. To his relief it looked like a small establishment his mom would've gone to, not a snooty place like the one Ariel frequented. Dan had picked her up there once or twice when Gideon couldn't make it. After the first time, Dan met her outside. The women in there could have slain him with one red-painted talon.

Gideon pushed the door open and ushered Dan into a small, brightly lit salon full of women, their heads covered in foils and things that Dan had only seen in science-fiction movies. Their conversations faltered as they all looked over, and Dan felt conspicuously on display. Only Gideon's hand resting in the small of his back stopped him bolting. Then a short young Hispanic man rushed toward them.

"Gideon, where have you been? Dear God, what have you done to your hair? Don't tell me you went to Antoine's?"

Gideon bent down for a kiss on either cheek. "Baz, it's good to see you. It's been too long."

Baz fluttered around Gideon and led him to a chair. "I have to do something with this mess."

"The appointment's not for me. It's for my friend." Gideon indicated Dan, who hovered uncertainly by the door.

Baz turned to Dan and then back to Gideon. "You know I'm a hair stylist, right?"

Dan turned, ready to walk out of the salon and away from the arrogant little man, but Gideon pinned him to the spot with a "Stay there."

"Baz, we need your help. Dan needs a special date, and Ariel, you remember her, has organized a makeover day for him. She came to you because you're the best. You can see he needs a tidy up and a shave. You're the best I've ever met with a hot shave."

Baz huffed, but then he smiled. "I see what you're doing, trying to flatter me. Anyone else I would say no, but because it's you, just wait here."

He rushed away, and Gideon walked over to Dan. "I'm sorry, I should have warned you. Baz can be a bit temperamental when he first meets someone."

"Temperamental? Is that what you call it?" Dan was unimpressed. "I call it being an asshole."

"Yeah, that too. He did it to me too the first time. But he'll have his moment, and then he'll take care of you."

"I could get a shave and less attitude for half the price."

"But it wouldn't be half as much fun or as good a shave," Baz said. As Gideon was effectively obscuring his vision, Dan hadn't seen Baz approach. "Come with me. I have time to do both of you today."

"I don't need—" Gideon started but gave in under the weight of Baz's glare.

"I am not allowing you to walk out of my salon looking like—that." Dan smirked, but he quickly erased it when Baz turned on him. "Do you have something to say?"

Dan shook his head. "No."

"Good." Baz pointed to two vacant seats.

Dan sat where he was told and let himself be gowned by a teenage boy with a startling mohawk and piercings all over his face. He wished he could feel as relaxed as Gideon seemed. He settled right in next to him with a ready smile for the young man.

Being shaved by Baz was an experience. At the end of his session, Dan had to admit the man had skills with a razor. Dan couldn't shave for shit without ripping up his skin, but the fuzz over his scalp was neat, and he had the smoothest chin he'd had since he hit puberty. Baz rubbed some scented oil into his skin and stood back to examine his work.

"Much better. Now I'm going to leave you here and harass your boss."

Dan frowned. "How do you know he's my boss?"

"Gideon talks about you all the time."

"He does? I guess I work for him, so it makes sense."

Baz got a look Dan couldn't interpret. "He doesn't talk about anyone else. Just you."

"Don't give away all my secrets," Gideon said from the other chair. He was gowned, and his hair had been washed by another pretty young man who fluttered around Baz as though he were the second coming. Baz took it as his due and barely noticed the boy.

Baz snorted. "You have too many secrets, Gideon. You ought to loosen up."

Dan felt a pang of jealousy at the obvious closeness of their relationship. He wasn't used to seeing Gideon being friendly with anyone. Of course he didn't know Gideon outside the bar. Dan didn't have a friendship with Gideon as such. They'd only ever been boss and employee.

He made an effort to thank the pretty young man for offering a magazine. Then he glanced over to see Gideon watching him with a slight frown. When Gideon caught his gaze, the frown was erased, and Gideon focused his attention on Baz. Dan flicked through the magazine. He had zero interest in photography, but it helped him to avoid watching Gideon as Baz scolded him for not coming sooner. Dan did *not* need the mental images *that* produced.

If Baz was a demon with the razor, he was equally a demon with scissors. At the end of an hour, Gideon gave a sigh of relief as Baz pronounced himself satisfied.

"Next time, don't leave it so long," Baz scolded. "Those curls needed serious work."

"Yes, Baz." Gideon stood, handed the gown to the pretty man, and rolled his shoulders. He glanced over to Dan, who was pretending to read a magazine about men's health.

"Anything interesting?" Gideon asked.

Dan looked up, confused. "Huh?"

"The magazine?"

Dan couldn't recall a word he'd read. The only advantage of the magazine was good eye candy, even if nothing came close to Gideon. "Yeah. I guess so. If you're into fitness." Dan did all the weightlifting he needed sorting out the deliveries.

Gideon nodded as if in agreement. "You don't need to go to the gym. You've got a great body."

"Uh… thanks."

"You're welcome. Let's get out of here before Baz threatens me with a razor." Gideon stroked his chin.

Gideon didn't need another shave. He had the smoothest chin of any man Dan had ever known. Even on his days off, Gideon always shaved. He settled the bill, and Dan hung awkwardly by the door again, embarrassed at someone else paying for him. Then they were on the sidewalk, and Dan could breathe again.

"Hey." Gideon squeezed his shoulder. "It's okay."

Dan met his gaze. "That obvious, huh?"

"You've got that deer-in-the-headlights look."

"I feel like that," Dan admitted.

"Is it the speed-dating event?"

Dan could hardly tell Gideon that he was more rattled by Gideon's hands on him than the damn event. "It's what you've got planned for me today. A mani-pedi? No. No. No."

"Every man has them now. It's not just women. Look." Gideon splayed out his nails. They were neatly trimmed and well cared for, a sharp contrast to Dan's raggedy nails.

"They're not going to make me wear polish, are they?"

Gideon sighed and rolled his eyes. "Dan, I don't want to turn you into a girl. You're a handsome man. All I'm doing is smoothing out the edges for a potential date and for the wedding. Ariel will be happy, and all will be right with the world."

Dan was still reeling from the idea that Gideon thought he was handsome, but he managed to say, "You know you're meant to be in charge."

"You really don't know much about women, do you?"

There wasn't much Dan could say to that.

Gideon looked at his watch. "We're late. Vera will kill me." He grabbed Dan's hand, and they set off down the street for half a block, at the most. Gideon halted outside a lavender-fronted shop with a large purple sign that read Vera. "Whatever she says, don't show your fear, or she'll eat you alive. I mean it. The woman is a nightmare."

He opened the door to a jangle of bells, and Dan was overwhelmed with the scent of lavender and the sheer purpleness of the place. Everything was a shade of purple, from the walls to the accessories. And that included the lady with the mauve hair who was tapping her foot impatiently.

CHAPTER 10

"YOU'RE LATE." She touched her watch.

"I'm sorry, Aunty," Gideon said in a meek tone Dan had never heard before. He would have laughed if he hadn't been so terrified.

"Where is he?"

Gideon stood to one side and tugged Dan into the store. "Dan, this is the proprietor of Vera. Aunty Vera, this is Dan, the new manager of Cowboys and Angels. He needs a mani-pedi."

"I know what he's booked in for, Gideon. I'm old, not stupid."

"Sorry, Aunty."

Dan stepped forward and offered his hand. "Afternoon, ma'am."

She took his hand, but instead of shaking it, she turned it over and studied his nails. From the pinched expression on her face, she obviously didn't like what she saw. "I'm not a miracle worker, Gideon."

Dan was getting mighty tired of dealing with the sneers and the attitude from everyone. He tried to extract his hand from hers, but she hung on, stronger than an old lady had a right to be.

"You come with me, Dan. I'll manicure your fingers while your feet are soaking. Gideon, this is my grocery list. You can come back in an hour."

He took the list and scanned it. "Okay. If there's anything I can't get, Ariel can bring it around tomorrow. See you later, dude."

Dan panicked and mouthed, "Don't leave me here."

"You'll be fine." Gideon chuckled. "You're in good hands with Aunty Vera."

Sure I am. That's what everyone thinks before they realize they're in the hands of a serial killer.

He sat where Vera told him to and watched as she bustled around for a few minutes. He expected to be taken to a modern salon with rows of people having their nails done, not a room straight out of the 1950s.

Vera looked over at him. "Take your boots and socks off, son."

"Yes, ma'am. Sorry." He hastily undid the laces of his boots and prayed he didn't have any holes in his socks.

"You haven't done this before, have you?" It was more of a brisk statement than a question, but he answered out of politeness.

"I've never had a manicure or pedicure before, ma'am."

Vera put a bowl in front of him, squirted something foamy and minty-scented into the water, and told him to put his feet in there. Then she pulled up a stool beside him and sat down. Dan winced at the creak of her bones, but she paid it no mind.

"You're a very polite boy, but call me Aunty Vera. Everyone does."

"Yes, ma'am… Aunty Vera. Are you Gideon's real aunty?"

"No. I wasn't blessed with a family or even nieces or nephews. Gideon and Sarah adopted me not long after they were married. Or I adopted them. Anyway, he's family to me."

"He's very lucky to have you," Dan said, and he meant it sincerely.

She patted his cheek. "You're a nice boy, even if you have got terrible nails."

Dan looked at his fingers. His nails looked fine to him, but he was a barman. Who was he to argue?

An hour later Gideon backed cautiously into the salon, laden with bags from a store Dan recognized as a grocery near Cowboys and Angels.

"Shut the door, Gideon," Aunty Vera ordered. "You're letting the cold in."

"Yes, Aunty Vera."

"Put them in the back. I'll empty them out when you're gone."

Dan would've gotten up to help him, but he had one foot on Vera's lap, and she had a pointed stick that looked as though it could do real damage.

Having deposited the groceries, Gideon returned to where they were sitting. "How are you doing?"

Dan waggled his fingers at Gideon. "I have beautiful nails."

Gideon caught Dan's hand and studied his fingers. "Yes, you do."

Dan had to work hard not to blush.

"We're almost done," Aunty Vera said. "Five minutes, at the most."

"Good. We've got one more stop today."

"You're gonna have to feed me, man." Dan's stomach growled loudly, and Gideon chuckled.

"Okay, next stop is the deli. I can't have you going feral and eating the masseurs."

Another rumble from Dan's stomach signified its agreement. Gideon pulled up a seat and started a conversation with Aunty Vera, so Dan tuned out and focused his attention on the up-coming DDD. He'd tried hard to avoid thinking about it for a week. It wasn't that he cared about the outcome. At best he'd get a date for the wedding. At worst, he'd meet nineteen guys he could cross off his dating list. *Heh, what dating list?*

"Dan?" Gideon interrupted his thoughts.

He blinked and realized Gideon and Aunty Vera were staring at him. "Hi… umm… I'm sorry. I was thinking."

"We could see that," Aunty Vera said. "You're finished for now. I expect to see you back here at the start of next month.

Dan sent a panicked look to Gideon. This was a one-time thing, wasn't it?

"He'll be here," Gideon said cheerfully. "Okay, Cinders, time for lunch."

There was no obvious exchange of money with Aunty Vera, so Dan pulled his wallet out to give her a tip, but she told him to put it away.

"But—"

"Just do what she asks," Gideon said.

"But—"

Dan wasn't allowed to do anything except kiss Aunty Vera on the cheek and be ushered out into the crisp winter day.

Back on the sidewalk, Gideon smiled at him. "Food next, then the massage."

Dan bit his bottom lip. "Could we make this the last stop? I don't want to offend you or Ariel, but I'm not real keen on the idea of being massaged."

He wasn't really keen on being touched by strangers, and after his hair and nails, Dan had reached his people limit. To his relief Gideon didn't argue—much.

"Ariel thought it might relax you before tonight." At Dan's skeptical look, he laughed. "I told her a bottle of bourbon would have a better effect. She said she wanted you relaxed, not trashed."

"I don't need relaxing. I just need it to be over."

"You know I'll be there, and Ariel and Bradley. We have your back."

"I know you do." Dan's stomach interrupted them with a loud rumble. "I've gotta eat or I'll be passed out before the first dude walks through the door."

His phone beeped, and he looked at it.

Free 2nite. Wanna meet?

No. No. No. What did it take to get through to the man?

"What's wrong?" Gideon asked.

"What?" Dan looked up.

"You're scowling at the phone."

For a moment Dan was tempted to tell Gideon about Disastrous Date and how he wouldn't leave Dan alone, but that would make it seem as though Dan weren't capable of getting rid of an asshole who couldn't understand no.

"I'm fine." He slipped the phone in his pocket. "Where're we gonna eat?"

"We could go to the deli. Or pizza?"

Dan thought about it for ten seconds. "Let's get pizza."

"You read my mind."

"Ariel won't kill me about the massage?"

"I'll tell her to take the appointment. She'll be fine."

They walked toward the pizzeria with a comfortable silence between them. The air was getting chillier by the day, and Dan wished he'd brought a hat.

Gideon caught Dan running a hand over his head. "Problem?"

"I'm cold," Dan confessed. "I left my hat at home."

Gideon fumbled in his pockets and pulled out his gray wool cap. "Here you go."

"Don't you need it?"

"I'm fine. You take it."

He handed it to Dan, who jammed it on his head and sighed with relief at the instant warmth. "That's good. Thanks."

"You're welcome. I don't wear hats that much. I don't know why I even carry it around."

"So you can loan it to employees who forget their own," Dan suggested.

"That must be it," Gideon said with a soft smile, and Dan's heart did a flip.

CHAPTER 11

DAN ARRIVED at Cowboys and Angels at 8:00 p.m., bathed and wearing black pants and a black shirt with short sleeves that displayed his muscles way too much. Gideon handed him a bag at the end of the day and told him to wear that or else. Dan would pay for the clothes. He wasn't a damn doll to be dressed up.

He shed his coat, but he didn't have time to feel self-conscious because he was immediately captured by Bradley with a query about a delivery earlier that day. Dan didn't know if it was a calming tactic or not, but it worked, and by the time they finished, he was able to contemplate the evening without wanting to run… much.

Cowboys and Angels had been transformed. From somewhere Ariel had found square tables and chairs not usually in the bar, and they now lined the available floor space in neat rows of five. And there were flowers on them, for heaven's sake. If they were really interested in guys dating, Dan thought they should've had condoms and lube. A few other men gathered at one end of the bar and eyed each other with open curiosity.

Ariel bounced up to him, dressed in a tight-fitting, low-cut, flame-red dress. His first thought was the dress was going to be wasted on tonight's customers. Then again, maybe that was the reason she was wearing it. No one was going to hit on her. "What do you think?"

"It's a nice dress," Dan said cautiously.

"It's a fabulous dress, but I meant the bar."

Dan looked around. "It's like being back at school."

"But just for one night and no math on Monday morning."

"That's a bonus." Dan would have preferred the math, and he was looking forward to Monday—The speed dating would be over, and life would return to normal.

"Are you ready?" she asked.

"I'm ready as I'll ever be."

Ariel waved at Bradley, who handed Dan a double of something.

Dan sniffed cautiously at the glass. "What is it?"

"Jack."

"Knock it back, and let's get this evening underway," Ariel said. "It's about time we got the best man a handsome date."

Dan did as he was told as he felt the liquor burn through him. He handed Bradley the glass and gave Ariel the bravest smile he could manage. "I'm ready."

Ariel smirked at him as though she knew exactly how brave he was and picked up the microphone. "Guys, we're ready to start. You all have a number and your table order. You'll have five minutes with each table. You each have a piece of paper to make notes. When the whistle blows you move. Let's get started."

"What number am I?" Dan asked, still confused about the whole proceeding.

Ariel rolled her eyes as though he'd just asked a really stupid question. "You're number one, of course. This is all for you."

"Oh yeah." As though he could forget.

She waited till everyone was settled and then blew a loud whistle right by Dan's ear. He winced. His palms were sweaty as he waited for the first man to sit down at his table. It only took a minute, and the seat opposite him was occupied by a handsome thirtysomething Asian man, with large eyes and a very nervous smile. Dan smiled back just as nervously. "Hi."

"Hi. I'm Mr. Two."

They stared at each other for a moment, and then the ridiculous mess of the situation made Dan's lips twitch, and he started to chuckle. Fortunately the man opposite him wasn't offended, and he joined in.

"I'm sorry, I'm really bad at this," Dan confessed when he sobered again.

"Is it your first time?"

"Does it show?" Dan said dryly.

"It's nice to meet someone as inexperienced as me. This is the first time I've been to anything like this too." The man looked around and then leaned over and lowered his voice as though he didn't want to be heard. "I must say, this is the last place I expected to host a gay evening."

"Oh?" Dan made his voice as neutral as possible.

The man nodded. "I don't know how much you know about this place, but it isn't somewhere a gay man should set foot in. Except perhaps tonight."

"I'm the manager," Dan said flatly.

He would have laughed at the look of horror on the man's face, but somehow it wasn't funny.

"My God, I'm so sorry… I didn't mean…."

Dan relented and gave the man a wry smile. "It's okay. You're quite right. I can't believe this is going on either."

"Why are you hosting a gay-themed evening? Obviously you're gay, but your customers? Not so much."

"Because…." Dan sought around for an explanation that didn't make him look completely stupid. "My boss is trying to get me a date for a wedding. And although I told him I could get my own date, he thinks putting me through this ordeal will be quicker."

The man stared at him. "I'm trying to imagine my boss doing the same thing. No, isn't happening."

"You don't think he would?"

"It would be a cold day in hell before my father tried to get me a date with a man."

It took Dan a minute to realize what the man meant. "You work for your father?"

"Yes, for my sins. He's a wonderful man, but he's not comfortable with having a gay son." He grimaced. "This would be ideal if it were setting me up with a nice Japanese girl."

"I'm sorry." Dan struggled to think of something to say. "Well, have fun tonight. My boss keeps reminding me this is supposed to be fun. Why don't we both relax, enjoy ourselves, and meet the other guys."

The man gave him a smile that made Dan's awkwardness worthwhile. "Thanks, man. I'll do that." He looked a little awkward himself. "You won't be offended if I say you're not my type?"

Dan grinned at him. "No worries. You're not my type either, but I don't think you'll have any problems finding someone tonight."

He could see the boost that gave the man's ego. "You shouldn't be here either," the man said. "I'm surprised you don't have the men lining up at your door."

"Two problems," Dan counted them off on his fingers. "One, I work in this bar, and two, I work in this bar. That's why the boss has to find me a date."

"Well, good luck, man."

The whistle blew, and Mr. Two smiled as a new man took his place.

"Hi, I'm Mr. Four."

"Mr.... er... One." Dan realized he hadn't bothered to ask the previous guy's name. Mr. Four didn't seem anxious to give his out, so Dan just waited.

There was that awkward look again, and then Mr. Four started to talk and didn't stop for the whole five minutes. Dan listened with the attentiveness he would give any customer of Cowboys and Angels and surreptitiously studied the guy as he talked. Mr. Four was probably pushing fifty rather than forty. Not bad-looking but starting to show signs of wear and tear. He'd probably been a jock, and from the muscles in his arms, Dan would guess he worked out every day. He still hadn't stopped talking, but at least he wasn't like Disastrous Date. His monologue wasn't about the sex he'd had and what position he favored. No, he was mainly about work, his family, and his children. Mr. Four was in the middle of a messy divorce. When the guy finally paused for a breath, Dan leaned over and said very quietly, "This isn't the right place for you, you know. You need time to get over your marriage and make time to be with your kids."

From his frown Mr. Four didn't like that answer. "But I'm lonely."

"There's no reason you can't go out and have fun. But you're looking for a relationship here, and it's really obvious you're not ready for it."

The man flushed an angry red, and for a moment, Dan thought he was going to storm out of the bar. Then he slumped back, his expression one of utter defeat, and he nodded. "I know you're right, but I just thought.... I haven't done this before."

"Speed dating or being gay?"

"Either... both."

"Try spending a little time being gay before you worry about the dating," Dan suggested.

"I don't know what to do."

"Try the Pink Palms. It's a gay bar, and the men won't eat you alive."

"You mean the guys can at least drink legally?" The man sighed. "I'm wasting my time here, aren't I?"

Dan shook his head. "Stay the evening and have fun. Take the pressure off yourself. Maybe listen to what the others have to say."

Mr. Four made a rueful grin. "My wife always did say I talk too much."

"Now is the time to prove her wrong."

A huge smile spread across Mr. Four's face and took five years off his age. "You are a very wise man, Mr. One. Thank you for not eating me alive. I appreciate it."

"Keep that smile," Dan suggested.

The smile grew even wider, and Mr. Four said, "I will," as the whistle sounded again.

Mr. Six was the polar opposite of Mr. Four. Dan wasn't even sure the man was old enough to drink in the bar, and his uncertainty must have shown on his face, because Mr. Six produced his driving license. "I know I look about fourteen. There's nothing I can do about that. But I am twenty-five, perfectly legal and able to hold my beer."

"That sounds like a rehearsed speech," Dan said, unable to hide the smirk on his face.

"It's probably one that I've given out at least five times a night since I was twenty-one. I can say it in Spanish and Korean too."

"I'll take your word for it. So, aside from defending your baby-faced charm, what do you do?"

"I'm studying to be a vet," Mr. Six said. "I want to open up a small animal practice back in my hometown."

Dan thought he'd detected a southern accent. "Where is home?"

"I'm a southern boy. Georgia."

"You're here to study?"

"I'm doing my postgrad training at NYU."

"Do you like it here in New York?"

"It's okay, but I'm a small-town boy," Mr. Six confessed. "New York can be overwhelming. What about you?"

"I'm a New Yorker and a barman. I work here to be honest."

Mr. Six snapped his fingers. "You're the one they're hosting this for?"

Dan nodded. "Guilty as charged."

"I hope you find your date."

Strike three off the list, Dan thought. He didn't think he was ever going to find someone who liked him. Although at least he wasn't wasting his time with men who didn't find him attractive. Mr. Six stayed until the five minutes were up, but he was out of the chair as soon as the whistle blew, as though the end couldn't have come soon enough.

Dan took a minute to look for Gideon, but he couldn't see any sign of him. Strange, Dan thought Gideon would be there to give moral support, but he guessed a room full of gay men wasn't his idea of a good time. Dan was disappointed, but he told himself that Gideon had spent the whole day getting Dan scrubbed up for the evening. He'd done his babysitting duties.

Dan caught Ariel's eye and pretended he was drinking from a bottle. She nodded, and a minute later, a bottle of his favorite beer was in front of him.

Next on the list was Mr. Eight, who was taking his time to appear. Dan felt a bit awkward sitting at the table by himself, but after he had drunk about half the bottle, a man slid into the seat opposite him. Dan stared. It looked like a lion had escaped from Central Park Zoo and walked into Cowboys and Angels.

CHAPTER 12

THE MAN had a mane of red hair that framed his face at crazy angles. His eyebrows and stubble matched. If Dan had been into redheaded men, he would have pulled the guy out of his seat and rushed out the door before someone else could claim him.

"Hi," the man said shyly. I'm Cris…. Mr. Eight."

"Hey, Cris…. Mr. Eight. You are…." What did one say to a lion god?

"Ginger?" The man grimaced as though he'd heard it a lot.

"I was going to say something like a lion god, but ginger will do."

Cris blushed almost the color of his hair. "It's the first time anyone has called me a god."

Dan blushed too. "I guess that was a bit over-the-top."

"God or ginger? You are, without doubt, the best one I have seen tonight." Cris pulled a face. "In order—boring, closeted, and tight. You, my friend, are a breath of fresh air."

That was the first time Dan had been called a breath of fresh air. Still, Cris's remarks didn't hold out much hope for Dan's dating prospects. He got the feeling Cris wasn't going to be on his list either. Cris's expectations were probably too high for the Cowboys and Angels crowd.

"Tell me what you do, Cris?"

"I'm a stripper."

Dan choked on a mouthful of beer and had to work hard not to spray beer all over Cris as he tried to get himself under control. When he finally wiped his eyes and looked up, Cris gave him a resigned look.

"Yeah, that's the reaction I usually get."

"I don't have a problem with you being a stripper. Hell, I work in a bar. I'm the last person to judge what a man does."

"And yet you just did."

Dan shook his head fiercely. "No. I don't care what you or anyone else in this room does to pay your bills. You seem like a good man, Cris. That's all I care about."

Cris still looked wary, but he nodded. "Are you the guy who works here?"

"Does everybody know?"

"It was all anyone could talk about before the evening started. Your girl there, the one in the red dress, wasn't exactly subtle."

"I'm going to kill her," Dan muttered.

"Don't do that. She's fiercely protective of you. We all but got told to treat you with kid gloves."

Dan groaned and banged his forehead on the table. "No one's going to date me with her hanging over me."

Cris laughed. "You're probably right there, but it's been good talking to you." He pulled a card out of his pocket. "If you can cope with screaming women, come and see the show when you get a night off."

Dan looked at the card and furrowed his brow. Forbidden Nightz sounded vaguely familiar. "I'm sure I know this place."

"It used to be Bones."

Dan snapped his fingers. "That's where I remember it from. I worked there when I left school."

"As a stripper?"

"No." Dan had been going to say "Hell no," but he remembered who he was talking to. "I worked the bar. That's all I've ever done. It wasn't a strip club then. It closed down because there were fewer customers than bar staff."

Cris grinned. "It's certainly changed now. Give me a call and let me know when you're free to come over. My number's on the back."

Dan turned the card over. A cell number was scrawled messily from one corner to the other. "You're not looking for a date, are you?"

"I don't think I'm your type, Mr. One. It's a shame, because you're definitely mine. But I'll take what I can get. Friendship is good enough… for now."

Dan was almost sad when the whistle went. He liked Cris, and he would have been happy to talk to him for the rest of the evening.

The evening went on and on. Dan pasted on a smile, listened to the small talk, and tried not to look at his watch too much. Finally he was down to the last five. He didn't understand Ariel's numbering system, but he had Fifteen to Twenty left.

Mr. Fifteen was about half Dan's height, twice as loud, and strangely entertaining. Dan let him talk for the entire time, because Mr. Fifteen wasn't short on things to say, and Dan didn't feel like interrupting him. Physically he did nothing for Dan, but then, he'd never been one to base relationships on looks alone. When Mr. Fifteen got up at the whistle, he winked at Dan. "You are a good listener. Next time, try talking a little about yourself."

"I didn't get a chance," Dan pointed out. "You talked enough for both of us."

"Maybe we can go out for a beer, and I can get to know something about you."

Dan nodded. He wasn't someone Dan would want to take to the wedding, but for another date, Dan was willing.

Mr. Sixteen disappeared somewhere. Dan had no idea where he'd gone, so he took the opportunity to use the bathroom and get another drink. Ariel sidled up to him as Bradley handed him a bottle.

"So? Have you met anyone interesting?"

"I'm not sure about a date, but I've seen a couple of people who looked like they could be friends."

"We're looking for a date for the wedding," Ariel said.

"I think that ship has sailed." Dan tugged Ariel into a hug at her crestfallen face. "This was fun, and I might have made some friends from it. Thank you, Ariel."

She hugged him tightly around the waist and then pushed him off in the direction of his chair. "You're a lousy liar, but I love you. Hurry up, the whistle is about to go again."

Dan was going to ask her where Gideon was, but she blew the whistle and the moment was lost. So was Dan's hearing. He really hated that whistle.

Mr. Seventeen—tall, dark, and handsome—slipped into the chair and gave Dan a sheepish smile. Dan smiled automatically, and then he blinked.

"Mikey?"

"I guess you're surprised to see me," Mikey said.

He was a customer of Cowboys and Angels, one of the guys always in the middle of any altercation. Dan had never realized he was gay.

"I had no idea," Dan said honestly.

"Nor me, about you. I thought I was the only one. I can't tell anyone I work with." There was a warning note at the end, and Dan nodded. Message received.

"You were brave to come here."

Mikey sighed and rubbed his temples. "I'm so damn tired of hiding."

It occurred to Dan as he listened to Mikey talk that no one had asked about Dan. It was like they knew he was a barman and that he was looking for a date, but anything else was irrelevant. They didn't view him as a date. He was a commodity. All of a sudden Dan was tired, and he really wanted the evening to be over and done with.

As though Mr. Eighteen had read his thoughts, he sat down, smiled at Dan, and asked him how his day had been. Dan stared at him for a moment as though it were a trick question, and then he threw caution to the wind and told him about his day. Mr. Eighteen laughed as Dan talked about Aunty Vera and admitted he was scared to death of her. He also studied Dan quite carefully as he talked about his shave and Baz's skill with the razor.

"You're right. It's a very close shave. I imagine your chin would be quite smooth."

The implication was that he would like to feel Dan's chin on his skin, and they both knew it. Dan thought about it for a moment, and then he nodded. "It's very smooth."

"I'll remember that," Mr. Eighteen said, and he was gone.

Dan took a deep breath and looked at the piece of paper Ariel had given him for the first time. He ticked Mr. Eighteen.

Chapter 13

"Hello, Dan."

Dan stared in horror as Mr. Nineteen slid into the seat opposite him. Oh fuck no. What the hell was he doing there? Dan hadn't spent the last three weeks avoiding Disastrous Date for him to turn up now. "What the hell are you doing here?" he demanded.

"I heard about this on the grapevine. I knew you'd be here."

Dan wanted to punch the smug expression off the man's face. "I'm not interested."

Disastrous Date looked genuinely confused. "Who wouldn't want Parker Smith?"

"You talk about yourself in the third person?"

Parker shrugged. "Why're you playing hard to get? I'm gay. You're gay and not bad-looking." Dan ground his teeth at the backhanded compliment. "Why don't we just skip number twenty and go fuck?"

"I don't like you," Dan said through gritted teeth. "And even if I did like you, there is no way in hell I would be another lunchtime conversation piece about my dick."

"Is that what your problem is?"

"I don't have a problem. You have the problem. You're the one who thinks good first-date conversation is about all the other men you've fucked."

Parker looked at him as though he were mad. "Is that why you've been ignoring me?"

"I've been ignoring you because I don't want to go out with you, I don't want to go to bed with you, and I'd be very happy never to see your face again."

"I do like my men feisty," Parker said as though Dan hadn't spoken. He certainly wasn't listening to what Dan was telling him. "It makes it so much more fun in bed when I tie them down."

Dan tensed. He was ready to crawl over the table and smack the dude in the face. Wouldn't that be ironic? The newly appointed manager starting a fight. But then someone laid a hand on Dan's shoulder, preventing him from rearranging the dude's face.

"You lay one finger on my man," Gideon said, "and I'll tear you limb from limb."

His words were slow and deadly, and Dan had no doubt he meant every word, but Parker's lip curled as he took in Gideon's full frame dressed in jeans and a figure-hugging black sweater. "Who're you?"

Neither of them noticed Dan's quiet meltdown as he stared at Gideon. What was he doing?

"I'm Mr. Twenty, and you're in my seat. Move."

"My time isn't up yet," Parker protested.

"Your time was up weeks ago," Dan spat. "You just won't take the hint."

Gideon put his hand on Parker's chair and made it very obvious by the way he loomed over Parker that if he didn't move voluntarily, Gideon would make him move. For one moment Dan thought Parker was going to create a scene, but then he seemed to think better of it and got to his feet. Dan was almost disappointed. After weeks of hassle, the thought of Parker's face being rearranged was very satisfying. Then he scolded himself for turning into a savage. Gideon took Parker's place and grinned across at Dan.

"Well, hello there, my name is Gideon, and I'm your Mr. Twenty."

Dan shook his head. "There's going to be a very disappointed Mr. Twenty in a minute if you're sitting in his seat."

Gideon gave him an enigmatic smile. "No, not really. I *am* Mr. Twenty."

"You are?" Dan blinked at him. "But… you're not…. Why are—?"

"Are you going to manage to get a whole sentence out at some point?"

Dan leaned forward over the table. "The whole point of this evening is to find me a date."

"And have you found one yet?"

Dan looked over the list of people to find one he could say would be the date. "Well, I suppose numbers fifteen or eighteen. Fourteen was okay."

Gideon gave a low rolling chuckle. "Do you even remember who they are?" When Dan just stared at him, the chuckle turned smug. "I thought not."

"You're not gay," Dan hissed.

"No, I'm not," Gideon agreed, and Dan's heart sank. "I'm bisexual, and before you ask, this isn't a midlife crisis. I had boyfriends and girlfriends before I met my wife. I don't think bi is on the way to gay, or men are to play with and women are for relationships, or anything else you might think of."

Dan's brain hadn't gotten that far. He stuttered and faltered on the idea that Gideon was sitting opposite him. Until Gideon had ended their telephone conversation with a casual comment about not being straight, he'd never had a clue Gideon was anything except heterosexual. For five years he'd been completely oblivious. "You never told me."

"You never asked." Gideon shrugged. "I loved Sarah, and I wasn't ready to go out with anyone else for a very long time—man or woman. Now I think I'm ready, and I thought this was one way to take the plunge."

"By speed dating," Dan said flatly.

"I knew who I wanted to go out with before the whole thing started, but this was fun. I would do it again."

Dan frowned and looked down the list. "You've met one of these men before? Which one?"

Gideon rolled his eyes. "I swear flirting never used to be this hard." He leaned forward and fixed Dan with his intense gaze. "There's only one man I've been interested in for a long time, Mr. One."

It took Dan a minute—a very long minute. But then his jaw dropped open. Finally he managed to splutter "Me?"

"Yes, Dan. You're the one I am interested in. You're the reason I'm here, dressed up like a Christmas turkey and talking to all these men."

"You couldn't have just told me this beforehand?"

Gideon looked shocked, as though the idea hadn't occurred to him. "It wouldn't have been as much fun," he finally managed.

"You and I have a very different idea of fun. I would rather pull my eyelashes out than go through this again." A thought occurred to Dan. "Oh my God. Ariel set this all up. Did you tell her about me? Did she know you're bi?"

Gideon grinned wickedly. "Where do you think she got the idea from? Yes, she knows I'm bisexual. No, she doesn't care. And you were always going to be my Mr. Twenty."

"I'm going to kill her," Dan muttered. "And I should have been your Mr. One, not your Mr. Twenty."

"I said that to her, but she said that being the end person would be better. You'd end up with the man you wanted."

"What makes you think I want you? What if I found someone else?"

Dammit, Gideon's confidence was absolute. He didn't bat an eyelash. "Do you want me?"

"That's not the point," Dan muttered.

"You can get up and walk away now if you want. I won't stop you, and it won't affect your job. Whatever happens tonight won't affect your job."

Dan looked at him uncertainly. "You still want me as your manager, even if I turn you down."

Gideon nodded. "I'm big enough and ugly enough and secure enough not to force a man. But if you like me as much as I like you, then why not take the plunge? It's for one day, that's all."

One day? Dan wasn't sure what he meant for a minute, and then he suddenly realized. Marty's wedding. That's what Gideon was talking about. He wasn't looking for a relationship. He was looking for one day of fun. The disappointment rested bitterly in the back of Dan's throat.

"Sure. Why not. One day of fun at the wedding. You can be my date. You have to deal with two sets of religious parents. But what the hell?"

Gideon narrowed his eyes at Dan's staccato tone. "What just happened there?"

"Nothing. I've got myself a date for the wedding. I'm going home now. Bradley can close up."

Dan got to his feet and smiled bleakly down at Gideon. "Thanks for hosting the evening. Hope it gave you a good laugh. You won the bet. Here's $100. I'll have to work off the rest."

"Dan, what's wrong?"

"Nothing. It all worked out. I'm going home now. I've got the early shift tomorrow." Dan walked away, holding his head up high, because no way was he going to let Gideon see how upset he was. Mr. Eighteen grinned hopefully at him, but Dan shook his head and headed for the door.

Ariel rushed toward him, a concerned look on her face. "Dan, where're you going? It's not over yet."

"It is for me. I got my date for the wedding, you had a laugh at my expense. G'night."

Dan grabbed his jacket, shrugged it on, and pulled out his gloves and hat. The cool, clear air was a relief after the stuffiness of the bar.

He walked away quickly, half-afraid someone—Gideon—would try to stop him and half-disappointed no one did. But he made it back to his apartment and closed the door. He rested against it with his eyes shut and tried to process what just happened.

He should have realized it was a setup. Gideon and Ariel played him well. He would get through tomorrow with his head held high and his dignity intact, and then he would find another job and get as far away from Gideon as he could. It was one thing to have an unrequited crush on his boss, it was another to find out the boss knew and was laughing at him.

Wearily Dan shucked his clothes, set his alarm for an early start, and collapsed into bed. SmokeyJo settled against his chest and purred as he stroked her.

"I'm a fool, SmokeyJo."

She purred in agreement.

Dan huffed. "You weren't supposed to agree with me. I should push you off the bed, you worthless hunk of fur."

But the cat stayed where she was, a slightly vibrating comfort to Dan's troubled soul.

CHAPTER 14

SMOKEYJO WAS still there when Dan woke up, feeling like a complete tool. He'd thrown Ariel and Gideon's hard work in their faces, and for what? Just because they'd arranged a pity date for him didn't mean he couldn't take Gideon to the wedding and maybe meet some of the other guys outside of Cowboys and Angels. At least two of the guys had shown an interest in him, and he really needed to expand his social circle outside the bar. He might even call the stripper, Cris.

Dan sat up and stroked SmokeyJo's head. "I've gotta eat humble pie and apologize to Ariel and the boss." She purred in agreement. "That's if they're still talking to me after I walked out last night."

He rolled out of bed and skinned into his usual hoodie and sweats. Coffee, hot shower, and pastries from the bakery a block away would be next. He fed the cat because, of course, she demanded it. Then he wrapped up against the cold and left his apartment.

Dan had real hatred of the early morning shifts, which was why Gideon generally gave him the late shift and Juan the early start. But he was grateful for the ass-bitingly cold air to clear his head as he thought about what to say to Gideon and Ariel. Neither of them was around when he arrived. He didn't expect any different. Gideon employed people to open up the bar because he hated early mornings too.

All the furniture from the previous night had been cleared away, and the usual tables and chairs were in their place. Dan went through his normal procedure to get the bar ready for the day. Eddie arrived soon after to help him with the deliveries.

"How did it go last night?" Eddie asked when he'd divested himself of his coat.

Dan eyed him cautiously. Eddie was a nice enough guy, and they'd never had an issue, but he was a Catholic and very traditional in his views. "It was good. I think they made money on the bar."

"And less damage." Eddie chuckled at his own joke.

"Yeah," Dan agreed.

"Maybe they'll have to do it again."

"Are you okay with that?"

Eddie shrugged. "I am. Times have changed, and some of us have changed with them."

Dan stopped what he was doing to look at him. "Thanks, Eddie."

The man flushed and muttered something about deliveries. Dan let him go. They both needed a moment to process their exchange.

They had a new draft beer on tap, and Eddie chatted away with the delivery man about the new arrival. Eddie could work hard when he wanted to talk beer, and the deliveries were finished soon enough. The bar opened just after eleven, and not long after that, the usual suspects arrived. They ordered their drinks and vanished into various corners of the bar to read the newspapers and do the crossword.

Just after opening, Ariel came downstairs and spotted Dan. He braced himself as she walked over. Before she could even speak, he said, "I'm sorry. I was an ass yesterday, Ariel."

She nodded with her lips pressed tightly together. "What did I do wrong?"

Dan mopped the same section of the bar several times before he answered. "I didn't need a pity date."

"It wasn't meant to be a pity date," she protested.

"Wasn't it? Because it sure felt like that." He cut himself off because it was meant to be an apology, not an attack.

She shook her head vehemently. "I wanted to do something fun to help you. It was my dad who suggested he should end up being your date. You know him, and you know you'll be looked after at the wedding."

"Looked after?"

"What Ariel means is you don't have to worry about me," Gideon said from the bottom of the stairs. "You have enough to take care of at the wedding. I'm just the pretty boy on the side. If you took a date you didn't know, you'd be worrying about them. This way you don't even have to think about it."

"I wouldn't have to worry at all if I went stag."

"Just let us help," Gideon said, wearily. "I'm sorry if you felt we were laughing at you last night, but it really wasn't like that. It was just meant to be fun."

Dan gritted his teeth. He was angry but mainly at himself. This wasn't the way his apology was meant to go. "I know, and I'm being an ass. Again. Thanks for thinking of me."

“I loved it,” Ariel said. “I can’t wait to do it again.”

Dan’s eyes widened, and he held his hands up as though to ward off the oncoming threat. “Oh no. No, no, no. I am not putting myself through that again.”

She waved a hand dismissively. “What makes you think you’ll be invited? We’ve done your one, now we need to do boys-and-girls speed-dating night. You never know. I might find a date.”

“So, we get your dad to run interference on this one too?” Dan asked sweetly.

“Once is enough. I’m not dating my father. That’s ewww.”

He raised an eyebrow at her horrified look. “It’s all right for me to be set up, but not you, missy?”

“That’s right.” She smirked at him.

Dan rolled his eyes, and then he caught a matching smirk on Gideon’s face. “Now what?”

“Nothing,” Gideon said. “Nothing at all.”

He vanished back upstairs, and Dan wondered why he’d come down in the first place. Ariel leaned over the bar to give him a kiss, and then she, too, disappeared back upstairs, leaving Dan feeling better than he had before. He’d apologized, kind of, and they didn’t seem to hate him, so all was right with the world.

THE WEEK passed by at a breakneck pace. Dan was either at work, head down in his studies, feeding his cat, or running interference between Marty and Lena. For some unfathomable reason, considering it was Marty’s third wedding, he was working himself into a panic about all the arrangements. Dan spent hours on the phone trying to calm him down as he worried about this detail and that detail. After the fourth time Marty rang him up in a panic about party favors, Dan called Lena and they concocted a plan to “calm Marty the fuck down.” That involved Dan taking Marty for a squash game—which nearly killed both of them—and a meal with Lena at his favorite restaurant followed by a movie and late-night drinks at a jazz club.

Marty called Dan very apologetically the next day. “I guess I was over-the-top.”

"Ya think?" Dan injected all the sarcasm he could manage into the two words. He was polishing the bar at the time, and he took pleasure in the mindless task.

"Lena told me if I don't calm down, the wedding is off."

"You're gonna get an ulcer if you don't calm down."

"I know." Marty sighed. "I'm leaving all the arrangements to the wedding planner."

"You had a wedding planner and you were worrying about wedding favors? Isn't that like having a dog and barking yourself?"

"I just wanted to it be perfect."

"It will be perfect. You're marrying Lena," Dan assured him.

"That's probably the sappiest thing you've ever said. Anyone would think you're a romantic."

Dan choked. "Don't say that out loud. Someone could hear you. I haven't got a romantic bone in my body."

He left Marty scoffing at him and disconnected the call.

"You know that's a lie, don't you?" Gideon said. As far as Dan knew, Gideon had been in his office. Now he was sitting on a stool by the bar, and he had an amused smirk on his face.

"What's the lie?"

"The fact that you're not romantic."

"I'm not," Dan protested. "I leave romance to straight guys."

"Romance is for everyone."

Dan threw the cloth under the bar and leaned over on his elbows. "I suppose I've never thought of myself as someone… you know. Love and romance and the two point four kids and white picket fence have always been something for heterosexual families, not people like me."

Gideon shook his head. "That's not true. Many guys have long-term relationships. Why don't you think you're worthy of it?"

Dan gave a bitter laugh. "I don't have good experience with marriage. Or rather my mother doesn't."

"How many times has she been married?"

"Just once."

"Not a happy marriage?"

"Not the best." Dan was a master of understatement when he wanted to be. "It put me off marriage."

"But not romance. You're still a romantic soul at heart."

Dan gave a wry look. "You keep telling yourself that."

"I don't need to. You forget, I've known you for five years. I probably know you better than most people."

Dan narrowed his eyes. He wasn't about to be psychoanalyzed by his boss. "You spend most of your time upstairs. What makes you think you know me?"

Gideon didn't seem fazed by the snap in Dan's tone. "I've worked with you enough to know what sort of man you are. You know your customers, don't you?"

"Yeah, quite a few of them. What's that got to do with me being romantic?"

"You talk to them about their lives—the families and the kids. You know when they're in love and when they've broken up with someone."

Dan couldn't see where Gideon was going with his reasoning. "I'm a barman. I talk to people. I'm not like a hairstylist, but people want to tell me what's happening in their day."

"And you listen to them. The others, they nod and say yes, but you actually listen to them. You pay attention."

"I still don't see—"

"You think I'm upstairs, but I'm down here more than you realize. I watch you when people tell you about their families, and I see the look on your face. And I see the longing when somebody tells you about their loved one. I know you're a romantic, and I know that what you really want is a husband and a house—"

Dan had had enough. "If you mention the white picket fence, I'm walking out that door. I don't care what you think you know about me. I'm the least romantic person you've ever met."

Gideon slowly got to his feet, and Dan couldn't take his eyes away. It was like watching a snake uncoil—all power and strength and ready to strike at any moment. Gideon walked over to him, and Dan knew he must have had that deer-in-the-headlights look again.

"Tell me the real reason you haven't gone out with anyone in a very long time," Gideon whispered. "Not the hours, or the lack of dating opportunity. Tell me the reason." He cupped Dan's jaw in his hands.

Dan panicked and tried to look around, but it wasn't easy with Gideon gripping his chin. No one seemed to be in the bar at that moment. He had no idea where Bradley and Eddie were.

"Focus on me," Gideon said. His voice was a rumble in Dan's ears.

Dan licked his lips. "I don't know what you want me to say."

"Just tell me the reason you haven't dated."

"Because I'm in love with somebody."

No way in hell was Dan ever going to admit he was in love with the man standing in front of him. The devil himself would have to be there before Dan would admit that. But his answer seemed to satisfy Gideon, who smiled and dropped his hands. But he didn't step away, and he remained well inside Dan's personal space.

"You've been in love with this person for a long time." That wasn't a question. Gideon spoke with an assurance he shouldn't have had.

"Yes," Dan admitted reluctantly.

"Why have you never told him?"

"Because I'm not his type."

Gideon raised an eyebrow. "Are you sure about that?"

"I'm sure. You don't think I've had crushes on straight guys before?" Gideon opened his mouth to speak, but Dan didn't let him. "It doesn't matter if he's straight or not. Sometimes being in love with someone isn't enough. I want to be that person's everything. I want him to look at me the way Marty looks at Lena. I don't want to be second best, and I think, in this instance, I'd definitely be the runner-up."

Gideon sighed and shook his head. "You seem so sure."

"I'm not sure about anything," Dan admitted. "These last few weeks have turned my world upside down. But I do know I don't want to be anybody's consolation prize." Dan squared his shoulders and looked up into Gideon's dark eyes. "I don't want to be a date, or a plus-one, or a notch on the bedpost. I don't know that I'm romantic, but I do know I deserve better. I'm not going to jump into dating someone without knowing their feelings about me. At least Parker was honest. He wanted to fuck and that was all. He's an asshole but an honest asshole. I want the person who gets me to know what they're getting. I want them to take care of me the way I want to take care of them. I'm not looking for a sugar daddy. I'm looking for a partner." Dan took a deep breath and smiled as brightly as he could at Gideon. "I guess what I'm saying is I want the person who goes out with me to know what he wants too."

Gideon had remained silent through Dan's speech. Now he nodded and said, "I understand."

Dan was a bit bewildered by the two-word answer. "You do?" Dan wasn't sure he understood the workings of his own mind.

"Yeah, I think I do. And I'm glad you told me all this. You're right. Anyone who wants you needs to know they're worthy of you."

"That makes me sound high-maintenance," Dan protested. "I don't need a white knight."

"No, you don't. You need a partner. That's what you said." Gideon stroked Dan's cheek, and his touch was a gentle brush over the nick from the broken glass incident. "I'm going to go away and think about what you said."

Then he was gone, leaving Dan confused but strangely reassured by their conversation.

CHAPTER 15

DAN HADN'T stopped since the moment he entered Cowboys and Angels. Happy hour had only just finished, and the crowd was ten-deep at the bar. When Bradley waved the phone at him to say someone wanted to speak to him, Dan shook his head.

"Take a message and tell them I'll call back later."

Bradley repeated what he'd said to the person at the other end of the line, and then he looked apologetically at Dan. "He says it's kind of an emergency."

Dan apologized to the man he'd been serving and took the phone. "You take over from me. It's the guy in the blue shirt." He didn't know who the heck would be calling him with an emergency on the bar phone. If it were his family they'd call his cell, the same with his friends. "Hi, this better be important."

"Is that Dan Collins?" The male voice seemed vaguely familiar, but Dan couldn't place it.

"Yes, who is this?"

"This is Cris."

"Cris?"

"The stripper. I'm the redhead from the speed-dating night."

"Oh!" He was the last person Dan expected to hear from. "Hey, it's nice to hear from you, but it's really busy at the moment. I haven't got time to talk."

"Thanks, but this is not a booty call. I'm at the club, and I've got a bachelorette party here. I've got a bride who's feeling unwell. She tried to get hold of her fiancé, but he's out of town."

"Okay," Dan said slowly. "But what's that got to do with me?"

"Her name is Lena. She says she is a friend of yours. I figured she might be part of the wedding you're going to."

"Lena? What's the matter with her?" The noise in the bar suddenly increased, and Dan clapped a hand over his ear to hear better.

"She says she's feeling sick and dizzy. I could put her in a cab, but I'd rather she was with somebody she knew. You were the first person I thought of, but if you're working I could—"

"No, it's okay. I'll be there in thirty minutes. She's pregnant, which is probably why she's feeling sick."

"Come to the door and tell them your name. I'll make sure you're let in immediately."

Dan disconnected the call and dialed Gideon's phone.

"Have they started fighting already?" Gideon rumbled. "It's a little early, isn't it?"

"I'm really sorry, boss. But Lena's been taken ill at a club, and Marty is out of town. Is it okay if I take her home? I'll be gone an hour, two tops. I'll make up the time."

"Where's the club?"

"It's what used to be Bones. It's a strip club now. Forbidden Nightz. I'll get a cab and take her home."

"I know it. I'll drive you," Gideon said. "Ariel can take your place for an hour. Give me five minutes, and we'll be down."

"You don't have to do that," Dan protested.

"Lena is my friend. I'm not going to leave her feeling ill and alone without friends."

Gideon disconnected the call before Dan could protest again. He stared at the phone and then shrugged. Even if Gideon just dropped him at the club, it would save him a lot of time. He told Bradley Ariel was coming down to help, and under no circumstances was she allowed to flirt with any of the customers.

Bradley stared at him as though he were stupid. "She's Ariel, the boss's daughter. I don't have any control over what she does."

"I know, but it was worth a try. Just try not to get the place completely destroyed before I get back."

"Maybe you should be telling her that," Bradley suggested.

Dan collected his jacket and wallet, and when he got back to the bar, Gideon was there waiting with a plastic bag. Ariel was behind the bar, already serving customers.

"Thanks for doing this, Gideon," Dan said.

"Not a problem. Ariel will take over for as long as necessary. She's under orders to keep the place intact."

"You mean not to start a fight."

Gideon winked. "That's exactly what I mean."

Dan thought there was more chance of snow in August, but Gideon had faith in his daughter, and if Dan thought it was misplaced, it was still none of his business.

They reached Forbidden Nightz in good time, although Gideon grumbled about leaving his car to the mercies of the neighborhood. Dan refrained from saying he could have gotten a cab. He was curious to know what was in the plastic bag that Gideon brought with him, but they got to the club before he could ask, and they walked straight to the door, ignoring the annoyed rumbling from the waiting line.

One of the doormen stepped forward and held up his hand. "You have to wait along with everyone else."

"My name is Dan Collins. One of your… dancers called me about a friend of mine who is feeling sick." Dan said.

"Dancers?" The guy looked amused. "You do know what type of club this is, don't you?"

A huge, burly man wearing a thick black coat and hat overheard the conversation. "It's okay, Sam. Lionman told me to look out for him."

Lionman? Dan smirked a little. He wasn't the only one who spotted Cris's resemblance to a big cat.

The first doorman stood back and let them through into the club. Sam led the way through the club, which appeared to be filled with women hooting and hollering at the show on the stage. Dan caught a glimpse of two men with tanned and oiled skin. They were dressed in red jockstraps and gyrating around a pole.

They continued into a small office where Lena and Cris sat. The look of relief on Lena's face when she saw Dan made him feel guilty for his initial annoyance about the interruption to his evening.

He rushed over, knelt at her feet, and took her hands in his. "Hey, how're you feeling?"

"Nauseous and feeling like an idiot for being ill at my bachelorette party. I'm really sorry for dragging you away from work. I told Cris not to bother you." She seemed to notice Gideon for the first time. "I'm so sorry, Gideon."

Gideon joined them and gently patted her shoulder. "Don't be silly, Lena. You can't help feeling sick. Let's get you home now."

"I think I might be sick in the car," she said in a little voice.

"Not a problem," Gideon said. "I've brought a bowl, a towel, and some saltines. Have a couple of these crackers before we leave. It will help to settle your stomach."

Now Dan knew what was in the bag. "You were a Boy Scout, weren't you?"

"No, but I did have a wife with very bad morning sickness. I always had a bag packed in case she threw up."

Gideon opened the packet of saltines and handed her a couple of the crackers. As she ate, Dan looked at Cris, who wore sweats but was bare chested and rather shiny. "Thanks for looking after her."

"No worries. I'm just glad I put two and two together." Cris looked at Lena. "Is it all right if I leave you with your friends now? I have another set in fifteen minutes."

She smiled at him, even if it was a shadow of her usual smile. "You've been wonderful. I'm so glad we met at last. Dan mentioned you after the speed-dating event."

"He did?" Cris's smile was sudden and bright in its intensity and lit up the small room. But he must have caught the sudden scowl on Gideon's face, because the smile faded. He murmured something noncommittal, said goodbye to them all, and left the office.

"Where are your bachelorettes?" Dan asked. "Why aren't they looking after you?"

Lena pulled a face. "Is it sad that I don't even know most of the people in my party? Some women from work found out I was getting married and insisted I have a bachelorette party. I only said yes because Marty was out of town. They don't know I'm pregnant. I told them to carry on without me, and they did."

Dan was unimpressed by a group of women who would leave the bride when she was feeling sick. From the scowl on Gideon's face, he was of similar mind. "How did you meet Cris?"

"He caught me coming out of the bathroom and asked me if I was all right. He was lovely. When he realized I was the bride, he asked if I knew you. I didn't know who else to call. I couldn't call my parents, and my matron of honor is on vacation. Mama wouldn't understand me coming to a place like this."

Dan nodded. "Come on, then. Let's get you home."

He helped her on with her coat, and he and Gideon flanked her as they left the club. On the stage, Cris was dancing. He waved to Dan and wiggled his butt at him, and Dan could have sworn he heard a growl from Gideon. He thanked the doormen who had initially helped them and then guided Lena to Gideon's car. She collapsed on the back seat with a sigh of relief. Gideon produced a pillow and a blanket and the bowl, together with more saltines.

"Tell me the address and then just relax, darlin'."

"I want to go back to my apartment." She rattled off the address.

"Are you sure you don't want to go back to your parents' place?" Dan asked. "You should have someone to look after you."

"They don't know I'm pregnant. It would be too hard to explain. I just want to go home, crawl into bed, and forget about tonight."

She closed her eyes, and Dan looked at Gideon, who nodded.

"We'll take you home," Gideon said. "You need to be tucked up in your own bed."

It was probably the best place she could be if she had all-day morning sickness. They drove to her condo in a quiet part of Sunset Park. Dan had never been there before. The area was well out of his price range.

Gideon and Dan escorted her to her apartment door, and she thanked them for helping her.

"You need us and we'll be here," Dan assured her.

She smiled wearily. "I'm really glad Marty knows you. He's very lucky to have friends who drop everything to help."

"I didn't do this for Marty," Dan said. "You're my friend too."

Tears filled her eyes, and she blinked rapidly. "I'm going to go inside before I either throw up or make a complete idiot of myself. Good night, both of you."

Lena disappeared inside and shut the door, and Dan and Gideon walked in silence back to the car. As Gideon pulled away, he said, "I don't like the idea that someone would leave a friend in need."

Dan looked over. It had started to rain, and Gideon's face was illuminated by the light caught in the raindrops on the windshield. "You mean the bachelorettes?"

"Yes. If Ariel were out and in trouble, I'd expect one of her friends to help her."

"Those aren't her friends. Those are her office coworkers. From what I know, Lena's a very efficient and organized individual. They probably didn't see her as somebody sick and vulnerable and thought she would just get a cab home."

"I still don't like it," Gideon insisted.

"That's because you have a big heart, and you would never leave anyone in trouble."

"You don't know that."

"Yes, I do," Dan argued. "I've worked for you for a long time. You took me home the night I covered for the boys. You didn't have to do that. You also made sure I was in bed and covered up. You even fed the damn cat. That's someone who cares for others."

"My momma drummed it into me you always look after your own."

"You were very lucky to have a momma with good instincts."

Gideon glanced over and then back at the road. "Your mom wasn't like that?"

"She… looks after herself. Mom isn't a bad woman, but she comes first." Dan had a lot of things he could say about his mother, but that wasn't the time. He loved her, but they had a complicated relationship, and he didn't think Gideon would understand. Gideon loved unconditionally, and Dan's mother loved with restrictions. Dan understood that, although it had been hard when he was growing up. The benefit of space and years had enhanced their relationship.

"Where's your father?"

"He died, not long before I started at the bar."

"Oh yeah. I forgot that. I'm sorry."

"That's okay. You had your own family to mourn then."

"That I did. If it hadn't been for you keeping the bar running and little Ariel to look after, I might have sunk into my own grief."

"I never told you how much I admired how you kept going after the loss of your son and your wife." It wasn't the sort of thing he and Gideon had ever talked about, but maybe it was time.

"Thanks, Dan." Gideon drove for a few minutes, and then he spoke again. "I've got to ask. You and Cris?"

"What about me and Cris?"

"I… arrogantly assumed you would want to go to the wedding with me. I never considered you might have met another man who you'd rather go with. I know you like him, and he certainly likes you. If you would rather take Cris as your plus-one to the wedding, I'll step back."

Dan swallowed hard. "Would you rather not be my date?"

"Darlin', nothing would give me greater pleasure than to be your plus-one at Marty and Lena's wedding, but I'm an old man compared to Cris, and I don't want to stand in your way."

An old man? Dan nearly burst out laughing. Gideon was thirty-seven—anything but old. Dan sought for the right words to convey how he felt. "Don't get me wrong. I like Cris, and if things hadn't turned out as they did, I might have called him and asked him to come with me to the wedding. But I want you to come with me, to be my plus-one. And as for saying you're an old man, get over yourself."

Gideon burst out laughing. "You're never going to let me wallow in self-pity, are you?"

"Not when you're talking bullshit, no."

"It's not easy going back into the dating market at my age."

"Some of us have never left the dating market, and let me tell you, that's even harder. Especially for a gay man. You go from desirable to invisible very quickly."

"Women say the same thing."

"Have you been reading Ariel's *Cosmopolitan* magazine again?" Dan snarked.

"And there you slap me down again."

"I only slap you down when you deserve it."

Gideon turned into the street. "You and Ariel are the only ones I let do that."

Dan thought about it for a while. "Am I crossing the boundary?"

"Anybody else I'd say yes. You, definitely not." He parked in front of Cowboys and Angels and turned to look at Dan. "Don't change, Daniel Collins. I like you just as you are."

Gideon was out the door before Dan could reply, and maybe that was a good thing because Dan didn't know what the hell to say to that.

THE NEXT morning, before Dan went to work, he called Lena to see how she was.

"It was a very long night," she groaned.

"You kept being sick?"

"Dude, I was the Vomit Comet. If I didn't know better, I'd have thought I was drunk."

Dan frowned. "You don't think anyone spiked your drink, do you?"

"I asked the bar to ensure they only gave me soft drinks no matter what the girls ordered for me. Once I told them I was pregnant, they were happy to assist. The girls may have thought I was drinking double vodkas, but I was only drinking club soda."

Dan was pleased to hear it, but he decided he would check with Cris all the same. If Lena had been drinking alcohol, perhaps she should get checked out by her doctor. "How do you feel this morning?"

"Like the living dead."

"Are you at home?" Dan asked.

Lena chuckled in his ear. "I'm at work, and none of the bachelorettes are here. They all called in sick. The partners think I'm the golden girl for coming in the day after my party. Little do they know the truth."

"It's a Sunday. Why are you at work?"

"The law doesn't stop on a Friday, Dan."

"I know it's none of my business, but will the baby affect your promotion prospects?"

"Probably. Almost certainly," Lena said with a remarkable honesty. "The baby wasn't planned, and if I'm being honest, this is lousy timing. But Marty is the right person, and if we can't make it work now, then when can we make it work?"

Dan stupidly felt his eyes fill. He blinked rapidly and coughed a little to clear the lump in his throat. "Marty's a very lucky man."

"I'm a very lucky woman," she countered. "Not only for marrying the most wonderful man in the world, but for getting his wonderful friends too. I won't forget what you did last night, you and Gideon. I called Marty this morning, and I'm sure you'll be hearing from him soon."

"Oh no. He didn't get all emotional, did he?" he teased to cover his own sudden emotional moment.

"He might have been a little tearful."

"You know I'm going to tease him about that, don't you?"

"I'd expect nothing less. That's why I told you." Dan heard talking in the background, and Lena said, "I've got to go. I've got a meeting in fifteen minutes."

"I'll wait breathlessly for Marty's call."

"You're an ass." She was gone, and her snicker rang in his ear.

To give Marty credit, he managed to last till nearly midday before he called. And, just as Dan and Lena predicted, he was very emotional as he thanked Dan.

"It wasn't only me, dude. My boss was the one who thought of the saltines and the bowl and the blanket and pillows. If it had been me, Lena would have gone home with a taxi and a plastic bag."

"You mean I'm wasting all my thanks on the wrong person?" Marty said.

"Oh no, you can carry on. Just remember now, you owe my boss, and he is definitely going to collect."

"Consider me warned. I've got to know—how did he react to meeting Cris?"

"He was… growly. And I think jealous. He gave me the speech about standing back and letting Cris take his place at the wedding."

"What did you say?" Marty asked breathlessly.

"I told him thanks very much and I'd be happy to go out with the Lionman."

"You didn't?" Marty sounded disgusted.

"Of course I didn't. You're so gullible. I did say that under different circumstances I might—*might*—have gone out with Cris and asked him to the wedding. But I wouldn't want Cris to take Gideon's place. He then said he knew he was an old man, so I told him he'd been reading *Cosmopolitan* too much, and it ended there."

Marty sighed. "This is a conversation I would never have with a straight guy."

"I can belch and fart if you want me to make it more authentic," Dan suggested helpfully.

"That's more like it. I can feel the straight points returning."

"Weren't you the one crying down the phone to me a few minutes ago? You lost all your straight points then."

Marty swore cheerfully and hung up. Dan grinned. He was going to be milking that one for a very long time.

Chapter 16

DAN SHOULD have been paying attention, but he was lost in thought. He was going through the daily routine and failed to spot the signs until Bradley tapped him on the shoulder.

"There's gonna be trouble soon," Bradley muttered.

Dan snapped to attention and surveyed the bar. Bradley was right. There was an edge to the chatter that hadn't been there before. The place was a powder keg. Customers were waiting for the moment when they could all kick off, and it wouldn't take much to light the touch paper. In the center sat the cause of the trouble, two men either side of her, vying for her attention. Her knowing eyes signaled that she was enjoying every moment.

"Dammit. Thanks for the heads-up."

"She's been stringing them along for weeks. They both think they've got a chance with her."

Dan studied the two men. He'd noticed Ariel with them before, but his focus had been elsewhere.

"Should I call the boss?" Bradley asked.

Dan hesitated. Gideon had been unwell for a couple of days. A sniffle had turned to a streaming head cold, and Gideon had retired to rest. Dan knew Gideon had to be feeling lousy because he never stayed in bed. "Let's see if we can head this off. You know any reason why she wants to cause trouble this evening?"

Bradley shook his head. "I haven't seen her since the start of the week. I thought she was away. Why would she want to start trouble when her dad is feeling so poorly?"

"Who knows? Ariel is a law unto herself. You mind the bar. I'll go and talk to her."

Dan walked over to Ariel and heard her trilling laugh as one of the men leaned in to whisper in her ear. To Dan's mind, he was just getting in closer to look down her cleavage, but maybe he was damning the guy. Then the man licked his lips, and Dan knew his instinct was correct. The man was a pig. There was another guy on the other side of

Ariel, as broad as the other one was tall and just as anxious for Ariel's attention. He touched her arm, Ariel turned to look at him, and the first guy snarled. Immediately the people around them paused to see what would happen next.

Dan glared at them, and they subsided at least for a moment. He looked at Ariel. "You all right?"

Ariel tossed her hair. "Why wouldn't I be all right?"

Dan didn't know much about women, but he did know about Ariel, and under the sweet exterior, she was seething. "Do you want to come and talk to me?"

"No. Why would I want to talk to the hired hand? I've got my friends here to keep me company." She indicated the two men on either side of her. They nodded and scowled at Dan.

Broad leaned forward, saying, "That's right, man. So piss off."

Dan ignored them and focused on Ariel. "Don't cause trouble tonight, Ariel. I don't want to have to get Gideon down here. He's not well. You know that."

She tossed her hair again. Dan always thought she could make a fortune in hair commercials. "There'll be no trouble. Will there?" She looked at Broad and Tall, who glared at each other but gave her a nod.

"See that there isn't," Dan warned. "This really isn't the night to be stupid." He stabbed a finger at Tall. "You keep your eyes above her neck. *Capisce?*" Then he looked at Broad. "You know her daddy owns this bar. You cause any trouble, and you're out for good. Don't think it's an idle threat."

Ariel trilled an irritating laugh. "Run along, barman. Haven't you got a job to do?"

Dan gave her a steady look, and she had the grace to blush. As he walked away, Dan heard the three of them snicker behind him.

Back at the bar, Bradley raised an eyebrow. "Are you going to let her get away with speaking to you like that?"

Dan shrugged. "I do tend bar. It's water off a duck's back." He'd had years of people disparaging him because he poured drinks. "She's unhappy. I don't know what's wrong, but she'll tell me sooner or later."

"She's a brat." Bradley stumbled over the last word, and Dan was pretty sure he'd been about to use a completely different *B* word but stopped himself just in time. Dan made it clear in the bar that everyone should be respectful to Ariel, even when she was being a complete bitch.

"Hopefully, they'll mind their manners now, and I can leave Gideon in bed." Dan's mind went to a whole different image of Gideon in bed, rather than the snot-dripping individual who was shivering his way through a nasty cold.

"Are you sure you don't want to go and see if he's all right?" Bradley teased.

Dan ignored him. Bradley had cottoned on to Dan's unrequited crush a long time back and, to his credit, never said a word to anyone else. But it didn't mean that, out of earshot, Dan wasn't fair game for relentless teasing.

The evening settled down for a while. Ariel's suitors continued to woo her, and every time Broad or Tall came over to purchase a drink, they smirked at Dan as though they had gotten one over on him. Dan ignored that too, but closing time couldn't come soon enough.

"We might get through the entire night without anything being broken," Dan said.

Bradley made a hushing noise. "You can't say that. You'll jinx it."

"What are you? Twelve?"

"Everyone knows when you say something's not going to happen, it always does."

Dan snorted. "Definitely twelve."

Bradley flipped him off and served the next customer, who was leaning at an odd angle against the bar. "Are you all right, man?"

The guy's slurred answer was enough for Dan to say, "It's time you went home."

"You're not my father. Give me a drink. I got money." He waved a note in Dan's face and almost punched him.

"Save your money and go home." Dan had had many years of dealing with drunks. He really hoped the guy would take his advice.

"I wanna drink!" The drunk's voice rose, and the level of chatter in the bar diminished. Again the tension became palpable.

Dan looked around the room. "If anyone here wants to cause trouble, I'm calling the cops. I don't care who you are. I don't care if you're drunk or who you are related to." He said that with long look at Ariel, who gave him another toss of the head. "No one gets away with it tonight. Do you understand?"

The customers looked at him and then away, and the conversation started again. Dan breathed a sigh of relief, and then he focused his attention on the drunk dude. "Go home now, and I won't ban you for good."

"You can't do that. You're not the owner."

"No, but I am the manager, and this is your last chance."

Finally, it seemed to penetrate the alcoholic haze in the guy's head that Dan was serious, and with a lot of grumbling, he headed for the door. He tripped on the way and landed on his knees, but two burly guys hauled him up and escorted him out.

"You did good," Gideon said.

Dan jumped. He wasn't even aware Gideon was behind him. "What are you doing down here?"

"I needed a drink. I forgot to restock the soda in my fridge." Gideon held up a couple of bottles of Coca-Cola. He looked exhausted, his face fever-flushed, and his hair was flattened as though he'd just gotten out of bed. He was dressed in a faded Giants long-sleeve T-shirt and sweats, rather than his usual Wranglers and button-down shirt. Dan could have eaten him up, but instead he said, "You look a lot less like hammered shit than you did yesterday."

Gideon grimaced. "It's totally fake. The makeup I'm wearing is really good."

"You still feel bad?"

"Maybe less head monster and more Kathleen Turner."

Dan considered that. Gideon always had a deep drawl, but it was more husky than usual. "What's up with Ariel?"

"I don't know." Gideon looked over at his daughter with a frown between his eyes. She was laughing at something one of the men had said and hadn't acknowledged her father at all. Dan was pretty sure she knew Gideon was in the bar. "Do you want me to find out?"

"No. She can hold court tonight if she wants. You go back to bed."

"I think I'm going to have to if I'm going to be well enough for the weekend."

"It's a quiet night. We'll be fine closing up."

Gideon smirked at him. "I'm sure you will, manager."

"You heard that, huh?"

"I did. It looks good on you. Do it again."

Dan looked at him with a puzzled expression. "Do you want me to stand on the bar and shout out that I'm the manager?"

"No need. You said you're taking the job now. There's no backsies."

"No backsies? I swear I'm surrounded by kids."

"I certainly hope not in my bar."

"Our bar," Dan corrected.

Gideon inclined his head. "Our bar indeed."

A shout alerted Dan that something was wrong. He looked over and groaned. Broad and Tall were facing up to each other while Ariel sat back calmly and watched.

"I'm gonna kill her," Dan muttered under his breath, but obviously not quietly enough, because Gideon nodded.

"I'm going to let you. What the hell does she think she's playing at?"

Dan stormed over to the two men, who were glaring into each other's eyes. Tall had about six inches on Broad, but Broad could make three of him. "What the hell is going on?"

"Stay out of it, faggot," Broad snarled.

For a moment Dan was taken aback. His sexuality had never been an issue at Cowboys and Angels. He never talked about the fact that he was gay, and the customers never cared, as long as he was serving the drinks. This was the first time somebody had publicly demeaned him in his workplace, and it took his breath away. It was stupid. He'd been called faggot many times. But now, for some reason, it really hurt. He caught the shamefaced look on Ariel's face and understood what the whole evening had been about. Ariel finally understood that her father was interested in someone else for the first time since her mother died. She might have known before and understood it in the abstract, but with the wedding coming up, she had the reality in her face. He wondered what the whole speed-dating evening had been about? She seemed so supportive. What had changed in the meantime?

But he didn't have time for speculation. "It's time you two went home."

"We don't take orders from queers." That time it was Tall who was the asshole.

"Right. You're both banned. Get out of here now."

Tall laughed in his face. "Or what? You can call the cops or have your big boyfriend over there save your skinny hide."

Dan faced him down. "I know who you are, and I know where you work. Your boss is a friend of mine. It wouldn't take much to put in a call to him right now. So get out of here before you get arrested, and don't bother coming back."

"Just go, please?" Ariel begged the two men, seeming to understand that Dan's patience had run out.

The two men snarled in Dan's face again, but they stormed out without causing any more trouble. Dan watched them stalk out the door, and then he looked at Ariel. "I don't know what your problem is, but you just crossed a line there, and I won't forget it."

Her bottom lip wobbled, and tears filled her eyes. "I'm really sorry, Dan. I never meant for them to hurt you."

"They weren't the ones who hurt me, Ariel. It was my friend, or the person I thought was my friend, who hurt me."

He walked away without waiting to see Ariel's reaction. Gideon looked at him when he got to the bar.

"Are you all right?"

"I'm okay." Dan took a deep breath and exhaled slowly. "What about you? You realize if she's been talking, people are gonna know about us. The date?"

Gideon shrugged. "I don't care. This is my bar. They don't have to come here."

"I told you this would happen."

"You did, and my answer is still the same. I don't care. They can call me what they like. At the end of the day, it was my decision—not yours, not theirs."

"You know it was Ariel who talked?"

"I do now. I'll talk to her, but right now I'm more concerned about you."

It was Dan's turn to shrug. "Those are all words I've heard before. I'm not going to fall apart because somebody calls me a faggot and a queer." He smiled viciously. "'Course, if they keep calling me that, they might just end up with their teeth down their throat."

Gideon smiled just as viciously in return. "That's my boy."

"Your boy?" Dan raised an eyebrow.

"Gonna argue?"

No. Dan would save that argument for another day.

"Dan?" Ariel stood on the other side of the bar. "Could we talk?"

"Not now," Gideon said. "Dan's got a job to do."

"I want to apologize."

"You should have thought of that sooner," Gideon said flatly.

It was the first time Dan had heard Gideon take that tone with his daughter. "It's okay, Gideon."

Gideon shook his head. "It's not okay. It's very far from okay. I can't believe you would put Dan in danger like that."

Ariel's face crumpled. "I didn't think."

"No, you didn't. Go home, Ariel. I don't want you here right now."

Clearly aghast, she looked at her father. But Gideon just stared back, and Ariel fled. The second she was out of sight, Gideon's legs wobbled, and Dan guided him to a chair as he started to cough. Bradley brought over a glass of water, and Gideon sipped it until the wracking cough died. Dan stayed by his side, not willing to leave him in such a vulnerable state.

Finally Gideon put the glass down and took a cautious breath. "Damn, that hurts."

"Is there anything I can get you?"

Gideon shook his head. "I'm gonna go back to bed. Are you okay to close up?"

"Sure." Dan wanted to rest his hand on Gideon's shoulder, but he was conscious of the curious glances being sent their way. He collected the forgotten soda bottles and handed them to Gideon.

Gideon didn't move, and eventually he said, "I'm sorry, Dan. About Ariel. I never thought she'd react this way."

"I don't think she meant any harm. She's just acting out."

"But she was the one who planned your speed-dating event."

"It's not about me, Gideon. Don't you see? This is all about you. The speed-dating event was fun. She loved that. But now the reality's hit home. You're showing interest in someone else other than her. She'd be the same if you were going out with a woman."

"She's worried she's lost my attention?" Gideon sounded bewildered. "She's twenty-one, not five. She needs to grow up."

There were so many things Dan could say to that, but it wasn't the time.

Gideon was struggling as it was. "Give her time. She's been daddy's girl for a long time."

Gideon sighed and scrubbed his hand through his hair, which left it sticking up all over the place. Dan itched to smooth it down. "I don't have the energy for this."

"Go back upstairs. It's a quiet night. We're fine here."

"Thanks." Gideon smiled wearily and vanished up the stairs.

Dan joined Bradley behind the bar. "Sorry for leaving you to hold down the fort. Everything okay?"

"We're fine. Is the boss okay?"

"He will be."

Bradley nodded. "He's facing some home truths, huh?"

"Something like that."

"No one likes to think their kid is a bigot."

"I don't think Ariel is a bigot." Dan found it ironic that he was the one to defend Ariel to Gideon and Bradley. "Not really. She's just struggling with the idea that she might not be the sole focus of her daddy's attention."

Bradley gave a derisive snort, but he left it there, and Dan was thankful. He was worn out and just wanted the night to be finished.

Cashing up and closing the bar added another hour to Dan's shift. He knew Gideon would pay him for the time, but he was shattered by the time he left and thankful he didn't have the early shift. Otherwise he might well sleep at Cowboys and Angels.

Dan left by the back entrance, locked the door, and started down the street toward his apartment. He'd just reached the intersection when there were running footsteps behind him. On instinct Dan turned, and someone punched his cheek. He was unconscious before he hit the ground.

CHAPTER 17

"HEY, YOU'RE awake."

Dan blinked and tried to focus on Gideon's worried face. "Wha' happened?" He struggled to get the words out, his mouth was so dry.

Gideon handed him some ice chips, which helped to moisten his mouth a little. "You were found unconscious near the bar. Do you remember what happened?"

Dan shook his head and wished he hadn't. "My head hurts."

"Two guys attacked you."

Dan gingerly moved his jaw and winced. "They did a good job."

"You're lucky. They didn't get a chance to do any real damage. A man saw it happen and scared them off. He called the cops and paramedics."

"Do they know who hit me?"

Gideon gave him a tight smile. "The witness described one man as very tall and the other as stocky. Sound familiar?"

Too familiar. He really didn't think they'd go that far. "They waited until the end of my shift to beat me up?"

"Sounds like it. I've given the cops the video footage from the club."

Dan tried to sit up, and Gideon was there to help him rest against the pillows. "Why are you here?"

"Someone must have recognized you. The cops knocked on my door about twenty minutes after it happened.

"I'm sorry, Gideon."

Gideon took his hand and threaded their fingers together. "Don't be ridiculous. I know Marty's your emergency contact, but he's still out of town. He's spoken to the hospital, and they allowed me in here because I'm your employer."

"When can I go home? I don't want to be racking up hospital bills."

"You've got insurance," Gideon pointed out. "You're going nowhere until the doctor's checked you for concussion. They were waiting for you to wake up."

"What time is it?"

Gideon checked the clock. "Nearly six."

A nurse poked her head around the door. "Oh good. You're awake."

"Awake and ready to go home."

She frowned at him as she entered the room. "You're not going to give me any trouble, are you?"

Dan ignored Gideon's snicker and shook his head, but he winced as pain shot through his head.

"I bet you wish you hadn't done that, don't you?" She smiled brightly, and Gideon's snicker turned into a chuckle. "Hang tight, and I'll get the doctor to look at you. We'll have you out of here as soon as possible."

"As soon as possible" turned into several hours, and Dan spent most of it asleep, knocked out by the pain medication and the long night. He was vaguely aware of nurses checking on him a few times and Gideon as a silent presence by his side. Eventually he stayed awake long enough to discover Gideon asleep in the chair, although he woke as soon as Dan tried to get out of bed.

Gideon yawned, and got to his feet, rolling his shoulders. "Are you running away?"

"I need a leak."

"I'll help you." Thankfully Gideon didn't offer a bottle.

Dan wobbled to his feet. "I can manage."

"Sure you can, darlin'," Gideon said far too cheerfully, "but I'm still gonna help you."

He was by Dan's shoulder as Dan shuffled to the bathroom, not holding him, but not more than a few inches away. He waited outside the door as Dan did his business and then escorted him back to bed. Dan sat down and sighed. Just that short walk had knocked the energy out of him. But he still wanted to go home, and he said so to Gideon.

"Let's find out when you can escape."

Gideon went off to speak to whoever would spring him from this joint. Finally, after they agreed he wasn't suffering from a concussion and his cheek was bruised, not cracked, they agreed to let him go. The paperwork took longer, but eventually he was a free man and settled in Gideon's car.

Gideon slid in behind the steering wheel. "Home?"

"Yeah." Dan yawned, winced, and yawned again.

He woke up outside his apartment block. "You must have knockout drops in here. I'm always sleeping in your car."

"I work you too hard."

"I'm not gonna deny that, but you weren't the one who assaulted me." At Gideon's silence, he said, "This is not your fault, Gideon."

"I can't help feeling responsible."

Dan patted Gideon's thigh. "I don't hold you responsible. Okay. I'm gonna go home and sleep before the shift."

Gideon shook his head. "I've got Juan to cover your shift today."

Juan was another senior barman. Dan rarely saw him because they covered different shifts.

"I can't take time off, Gideon. I need the money."

"You'll get full pay, and if you need to take tomorrow off, that's covered too. I mean it, Dan. Don't argue with me."

Dan recognized the implacable expression on Gideon's face, and he conceded, but he couldn't resist saying, "I'll see you tomorrow."

Gideon huffed at him as he got out of car.

"You don't need to come with me. I'm awake this time." Just. He would be asleep as soon as he fed the cat.

"Dan, just for once, shut up. I'm feeding your cat and seeing you into bed." Gideon sounded exhausted, and that, more than anything, kept Dan quiet.

SmokeyJo protested her starvation as soon as Dan walked in the door. She took one look at him and weaved around his legs to greet Gideon.

"Traitor," Dan said to her.

She presented her tail to him and purred at Gideon, who scratched her under the chin. "She knows who's going to feed her. Get into bed, and I'll sort her out."

Dan staggered into the bathroom and got a look at his face for the first time. "Lena's going to kill me."

"What's that?" Gideon called.

"My face. It's going to ruin the wedding photos." He poked at the puffiness. Of course it hurt.

Gideon appeared in the doorway. "You've got over a week. The swelling will be down, and any bruising we can cover with concealer."

"You know about makeup?"

Gideon got a rueful look. "I got a black eye two nights before my wedding. You can't see it in the photos, but I'm wearing heavy stage makeup. My wife was furious when she found out and insisted I cover it up."

Dan laughed even harder, but that hurt his jaw. He cupped the injured side of his face and sighed. "I really need to go to bed."

Gideon nodded. "You get changed. I'll see myself out when you're in bed."

"I thought you'd insist on staying with me and sleeping in the chair or some such shit." Then he saw the guilty look on Gideon's face. "You were going to wait until I was asleep, weren't you? I'm gonna wake up and find you asleep on the sofa, and you'll tell me you sat down and fell asleep."

"Busted," Gideon admitted.

"Who's opening up at Cowboys and Angels?"

"Juan is working all day. I didn't know when we'd be out of the hospital. He's not expecting me back until later."

Dan sat down on the bed. He looked over at his sofa, which, he had to admit, was very uncomfortable and not the place for Gideon to be sleeping when he didn't feel 100 percent. His bed, on the other hand, was incredibly comfortable. Dan gave himself a mental slap over the head and then looked up at Gideon. "Come on," he said. "You lie down here with me. I mean, not with me, but on the bed. We're both exhausted, and we need to sleep."

"You want to share the bed?" Gideon asked cautiously.

"Unless you can see another bed, this is the only one available." Dan yawned and started to strip off his clothes. He got down to his boxers, climbed into bed, and snuggled down under the comforter. He cracked open one eye when he didn't hear anything from Gideon and found him with a conflicted expression on his face. "Dude, either get in here or go home, one or the other. I'm not letting you stare at me while I'm asleep. That's just stalkery and weird."

"You trust me?" Gideon asked.

"You look worse than I feel." It was true. Gideon looked almost gray from exhaustion. "Come on, man, just get into bed." He closed his eyes as though he wouldn't be bothered by Gideon's decision one way or the other. Then he heard rustling and realized Gideon was getting undressed. Dan concealed his smile and waited.

Gideon slid under the covers on the other side of the bed and settled down, careful not to touch Dan. "Let me know if you need anything, if you need any more pain medication."

"At the moment I'm stoned. All I need is ten hours sleep."

He felt a soft caress of fingers on his bare shoulder.

"You go to sleep, then," Gideon murmured. "I'll be here when you wake up."

Dan did as he was told and fell into a deep sleep.

HE WAS disorientated for a moment when he woke up. The light in his bedroom was wrong, and he could hear voices. He sat up and looked around. Gideon was gone. No, not gone, just not in bed. He could hear him talking in the living area.

"Not now, Ariel. I know you're sorry, and I know you're upset about what happened to Dan, but he doesn't need your drama at the moment. Yes, I know I don't normally speak to you like this, and maybe I should have done it sooner. Then this wouldn't have happened. I'll call you tomorrow, and if Dan wants to speak to you, he can."

Dan wondered if he should pretend to still be asleep, but he decided against it, got out of bed, and went into the living area. Gideon was staring at his phone with a distraught look on his face. Treating Ariel so coldly went against everything he believed in. His daughter had been the center of his life so long. Dan didn't want to be the reason for an estrangement between them. He sat down next to Gideon.

"I heard you talking to Ariel."

"I'm sorry. I didn't mean to wake you up." Gideon sounded defeated, and Dan's heart ached for him.

"I think you should invite Ariel over here. We can talk."

Gideon shook his head. "It's not just about you, Dan. She's walked all over me for too long now. I love my daughter, and I know in her heart she's a really good girl, but I don't want to see her ruining her life by thinking she can get away with everything. She's twenty-one, not twelve. It's time she understands I have a life too."

"She does know that," Dan assured him.

"I think she does, but a little reinforcement won't harm the situation."

"Does she know you're here?"

"Yes. I wouldn't lie to her. I told her I was looking after you. She wanted to come over and help. But she would be too much, both to you and me. She's a lousy nurse."

Dan knew that from previous experience. Ariel was too lively and erratic to make a good bedside companion. The one thing he never wanted was a headache around her. Her father, on the other hand, was exactly the teddy bear Dan needed when he wasn't feeling well.

"How're you feeling?" Dan asked. "How did you sleep?"

Gideon took a deep breath and smiled. "Like a log. Your bed is better than mine. It's nearly five o'clock. Are you hungry?"

"Starving," Dan confessed.

Gideon grinned. "Pizza?"

"You read my mind. Sicilian?"

"Sounds good to me."

They bickered for a couple of minutes about who would pay, but Dan insisted because Gideon had gotten out of his sick bed to help him and was still paying him while he was lazing about at home.

"You're the only man I know who would consider recovery after being beaten up as lazing around." Gideon shook his head. "You can pay for the pizza, but only because my phone is running out of charge."

Dan ordered the pizza and then went in search of soda. He couldn't face coffee, which he found vaguely alarming. He always wanted coffee. No one had ever told him being smacked in the face decreased the desire for coffee.

He got dressed in his standard home uniform of sweats and hoodie and then looked at Gideon. He was still wearing the Giants long-sleeve shirt and sweats from the night before. "I don't think I have anything to offer you. My clothes are way too small to fit you."

"It's okay. I'll go home later and have a shower. Do you need any pain meds?"

"I'll take some Tylenol. The pain's not too bad. It's more of a dull roar than screaming in agony."

Gideon's lips twitched. "I'm glad to hear it."

"Do you need anything? You sound more like yourself than you did yesterday."

"I think what happened to you shocked the cold out of me. I actually feel fine. I'll be all ready for the date next week."

"It's a wedding, not a date."

Gideon waved his hand as though that were unimportant. “Wedding, date—it’s all the same.”

“I hope you never suggest that a woman get married instead of go on a first date.”

“Why would I do that?” Gideon sounded genuinely puzzled. “I’m going out with you, not a woman.”

Dan bit down on his lip. Gideon seemed so damn sure of what was going on, and yet he was only acting as Dan’s plus-one for the day. He decided the safest thing to do was change the subject.

“I’m gonna take a shower. The pizza should be here soon.”

Gideon gave him a mischievous smirk. “Do you want me to wash your back?”

“You just look out for the pizza. You can practice your lines on the delivery boy.”

“Why? Is he cute?”

“No, but you need someone to practice on. Your lines are way out of date.” Dan smirked at Gideon and then headed into the bathroom. Sometimes he needed to get the upper hand. Didn’t happen very often, so he would enjoy it while it lasted.

After a quick shower, Dan wandered back into the living room with a towel wrapped around his waist.

Gideon was at the front door. He had his back to Dan, but the pizza delivery guy spotted him, and his eyes opened wide. It must have alerted Gideon, because he turned and looked at Dan. Gideon turned back to the delivery man and muttered something to him. Whatever it was, he immediately stopped staring at Dan.

When Gideon shut the door, Dan raised an eyebrow at him. “What did you say to scare the delivery man?”

“I told him if he didn’t stop ogling you, I’d gouge his eyes out.”

“He probably saw my face and thought you smacked me around.”

At Gideon’s flinch Dan said, “Sorry, that was a bad joke. Anyway, you’d better not have scared him off. That’s my favorite pizza place.”

Gideon shrugged. “They can find someone else to deliver. Preferably someone who is blind.”

“You must have been a nightmare when Ariel started dating.”

Gideon smirked, but he didn’t say anything.

The aroma of the pizza reached Dan, and his stomach rumbled. Gideon laughed and said, “I guess that means it’s time to eat. You grab the beer and… I guess you shouldn't really drink if you're taking pain meds."

"I keep the beer for Marty. I don't drink much. I'll have a soda. You can have a beer, but not too many if you're driving back to the bar tonight."

He pulled out a bottle of beer and a can of soda for himself and brought them over to the coffee table. "I'm just gonna get dressed."

"I like you dressed as you are." Gideon rolled his eyes suggestively over Dan's body.

"Down boy," Dan said dryly. "I'm not sitting in a damp towel to eat good pizza."

"You could just drop the towel."

"No."

"It's a real shame," Gideon assured him.

Aware of Gideon's eyes on him, Dan put just a suggestion of a wiggle in his walk as he went back into the bedroom. Then he got changed as quickly as he could. Because pizza.

Gideon had already opened one of the boxes and was stuffing a large slice into his mouth.

"Dude, chew."

With a full mouth, Gideon wasn't in a position to answer, and it took a few moments for him to say, "I am chewing."

"You're a pig," Dan said cheerfully, and then he filled his mouth with pizza and shut up.

They managed to demolish a large pizza, and Dan contemplated sending out for another. They decided to leave it a while and watch a movie on Dan's tiny TV set.

"You know they make TVs bigger than the size of a microwave these days, don't you?" Gideon grumbled.

"Sure they do," Dan agreed, "for people who are around to watch them. I'm barely here, and I watch TV even less. I'm either working, at school, or in the library. My cat's starting to forget what I look like."

Gideon grumbled all the same, although he couldn't argue with Dan's reasoning. Dan picked an action movie, and they sat back to watch. He wasn't even aware he was falling asleep, but he woke up with his head resting on Gideon shoulder, the end credits rolling, and the uncomfortable realization that he'd drooled over Gideon's shirt.

"I'm so sorry," he blurted out as he eyed the wet patch.

"It's not a problem," Gideon assured him. "I was asleep too. I only woke up when you moved."

"I didn't realize I was so tired."

"How's your face?"

"It's sore," Dan admitted. "I'll take a couple of Tylenol now."

"It's almost nine o'clock. I think I ought to get back to the bar. Juan could probably do with a break."

Dan quashed the ridiculous feeling of disappointment in his gut and nodded. "I'll see you tomorrow."

Gideon shook his head. "Take another day off. Come back on Friday."

"I'm fine. I don't need—"

"I know," Gideon said. "But humor me. I'm your boss. You still get paid for your shift, but I want you to recover."

With regret Dan watched Gideon go. He cleared away the pizza boxes and the drinks, brushed his teeth, and collapsed into bed again. Gideon was all over the side where he'd slept, and Dan buried his nose and inhaled the musky scent. He'd had Gideon Tyler in his bed, and nothing had happened. Wasn't that the story of his life?

Dear Reader,

I really want to suck your cock and want to taste your CUM

So please, don't waste your CUM and save for me?

How does your CUM Taste?

Sweet, Sour, bitter,

Mine to tastes bitter,

CHAPTER 18

DAN RETURNED to work on Friday for the early shift as planned. He would never admit it to Gideon, but he appreciated the extra day off. When he woke up, he discovered aches and pains all over his body, and he was too tired to fight through it. He spent most of Thursday asleep with SmokeyJo curled up in the crook of his leg. She appreciated the extra time Dan was at home too.

He was sorting out a delivery of beer when he became aware of Ariel watching him. He looked up, and she gave him a cautious smile. She looked tired, her usual radiance dimmed. Dan guessed she hadn't been sleeping too well since Dan was attacked.

"Let me just finish this," he said, holding up a couple of bottles.

She nodded and went to wait in the bar. Finally he couldn't put off talking to her any longer, and he sat down opposite her at the table—the same table where she had held court with Tall and Broad. He wondered if she knew that and then decided it was a deliberate move.

Ariel rushed to speak, as though she had to get it out before she lost her confidence. "I'm sorry. I am so sorry for what happened to you."

Dan studied her unflinchingly. She reddened but she didn't look away.

"Do you understand what you did?"

"I think so," she whispered.

"I need you to realize what you did was a complete betrayal of my trust. I know my friends know I'm gay, but they never take advantage of that fact. That's what you did. It may have been a joke to you, but the consequences were real to me."

Her bottom lip wobbled. "I never intended you to get hurt. You know that."

"From where I sit that's exactly what you wanted." Dan didn't relent. It was too important to ignore.

"I was jealous," she said, her voice so low he could barely hear her. A couple of tears spilled over onto her cheeks.

Dan gently brushed the tears away. "There's no reason to be jealous of me. You know me, Ariel."

"But he *likes* you." Her voice cracked at the end. She sounded distraught.

Dan's stomach did a whirl, but he told it to settle down.

"He's just providing me with a date for the wedding."

She shook her head. "It's more than that. He talks about you all the time."

Baz had said that too, but Dan worked for Gideon. It wasn't surprising he talked about Dan.

"It's one date to a wedding, which you arranged," he said. "Your father isn't going to suddenly put a ring on my finger. You're seeing zebras where there are only horses, Ariel. Even if he does like me—someone—you need to understand that just because your father is showing an interest in someone else, it doesn't mean he doesn't love you. You know that you're the center of his universe."

Ariel bit her lip. "It's hard, you know? Since Mom and Simon died, it's just been me and Dad. He loved Mom so much. I never thought he'd look for anyone else."

"Is it worse because I'm a man, not a woman?" Dan asked.

She shook her head vehemently, and Dan felt a little of the tension seep away. "I'm not homophobic. I didn't care that he liked a man. I just cared…."

"He liked someone else." Dan finished the sentence for her.

"I was just being a bitch. I never thought they'd attack you."

"I believe you." Dan did believe Ariel had just been jealous. He didn't blame her for the attack by Tall and Broad, even though she had provoked it.

Ariel gave him a tentative smile. "I wish there were some way I could make it up to you."

Dan leaned back in his chair and crossed his arms. "You mean that? Are you just saying that because you think that's what I want to hear?"

"I really mean it."

He decided to take the earnest declaration at face value. "There is something you can do."

"Anything," she assured him.

He gave her a thin smile. "I suggest you hear me out before you agree."

She gave him a brief nod. "Go on."

"I want the fights to stop. I know you're not the one doing the fighting, but you're certainly the one provoking it. It's time to grow up,

Ariel. Someone's gonna go home with more than cuts and bruises." He touched his cheek, and her gaze followed his action. She flinched, and he nodded. "You did real good putting on that event so quickly. Everything was organized, and people had fun. Even me," he admitted, "although you're never putting me through that again. But you're endangering Cowboys and Angels with the way you act. Think of everybody who works here. Bradley, Juan, and Luis, even Liam. Eddie's got little kids. And me. We rely on Cowboys and Angels for our income. While you're off at NYU, we're working for a living."

It was the longest speech he had given in a long time, and by the end of it, he was tired. He didn't have anything left to say.

Ariel stared down at her hands for a long time. Finally she said, "I'll never do that to you again. I promise."

"See that you don't or our friendship is over."

"I've always thought of you as my big brother. It was hard when I suddenly had to think of you as my stepfather." Tears spilled onto her cheeks, and she wiped them away impatiently and left a black smudge from her mascara. "Daddy won't talk to me. I really fucked up, Dan."

"Yeah, you did," Dan said honestly. "But it's retrievable. Not talking to you is killing him, but he wanted to make a point. You've said sorry to me, and that's a good start. Now you owe your dad an apology."

"Where is he?"

"He's gone to find a tuxedo for the wedding. For some reason he's grown out of the one he wore for his own wedding, and he's really annoyed." Dan rolled his eyes, and Ariel giggled. He pulled out his phone and hit Gideon's number.

"Dan? Is everything okay?"

"The bar is still standing."

"What about you?"

"I'm still standing." Only just, but he didn't want to worry Gideon. "I have Ariel here. She wants to talk to you."

Dan didn't wait for his response. He just held the phone out to Ariel, and she took it with a shaky hand.

"Daddy, I'm really sorry. I've apologized to Dan too."

She wandered upstairs with Dan's phone, and he slumped back in the chair, feeling as though he'd been put through a ringer.

"You did good there," Bradley said as he handed Dan a soda.

"And my mom wonders why I never had kids?"

"You would have been a good mom," Bradley teased.

"Don't push it," Dan growled, but he smiled, relieved that the conversation with Ariel was over. "Has the soft drinks delivery arrived?"

"Not yet, but it's due any minute."

The day returned to normal. Ariel returned the phone to Dan and then vanished. Dan handled more deliveries, although he was aching fiercely by the time the last one arrived, and he didn't see Gideon again until early evening when he was stacking glasses in the dishwashers.

Dan jumped out of his skin when he turned to find someone standing behind him. "What the hell?"

Gideon steadied him with his hands on Dan's upper arms. "Didn't mean to scare you. I just wanted to see how you're feeling."

Heart still pounding, Dan took a few deep breaths. "I'm okay, no thanks to you. Just don't do that again."

"Do what?"

"Stand behind me." At Gideon's look of confusion, Dan reluctantly admitted, "I'm nervous about people behind me."

Gideon's eyes widened. "Since the attack?"

Dan nodded. "I'll get over it." He wouldn't have confessed that to anyone but Gideon, but he didn't examine the reasons. He nodded at the suit bag over Gideon's arm. "You got your tux?"

"Yes, I did. What about you?"

"Marty's organizing that for me. I'm renting one." At Gideon's vaguely horrified expression, Dan said defensively, "I don't have much use for a penguin suit."

Gideon gave a wry smile. "I guess not. Sorry."

"Goodness, two apologies from the Tylers in one day. Is it snowing out there?"

Gideon pretended to cuff him over the head, and Dan backed out of his reach and left him alone with a mocking laugh. It was good to have things return to normal.

DAN WENT to the local precinct to give a statement about what he remembered of the assault. The detective dealing with his case was remarkably cheerful, considering Dan remembered very little, but with the video evidence from the bar and from a store nearby, they had clear images of Tall and Broad as they rushed him and of Broad's punch to his face. They were interested in Ariel's involvement in the lead-up to the assault, but he assured them Ariel had insisted the two men leave before there was trouble, and he hoped they wouldn't take it further.

On his return to the bar, Gideon took him up to his apartment and handed him a coffee. He studied Dan's face. "Are you okay?"

Dan sighed. "I'm just frustrated. I honestly can't remember much."

"It's not like you need to," Gideon pointed out. "We know who did it."

"They've been arrested and bailed. With the video footage, my statement is just a formality."

Since the attack Dan's biggest fear was that Tall and Broad would come back to finish the job. They knew where he worked, and it wasn't difficult to find out where he lived. He hadn't told anyone of his fears, but he spent a lot of time looking over his shoulder.

"What's worrying you?" Gideon asked perceptively as he sat down beside Dan.

"Nothing. I'm okay."

Gideon made a disbelieving noise. "They're banned from the bar, Dan."

"I know that."

"But you're still concerned they might come back?"

Dan looked away from Gideon, embarrassed to admit his fears. "Yeah. I know it's stupid."

"They're not gonna get near you."

Dan wrapped his hands around his mug to hide the fact that they were shaking. "Promise?"

"I promise."

Dan drank the coffee and appreciated the warmth as it flowed through his body. He knew some nerves were normal after an assault, but he couldn't afford to let it get the better of him.

"I've made an appointment for you to see a shrink," Gideon said.

Dan's jaw dropped. Of all the typically high-handed and overbearing things Gideon could do. "You did what?"

"A shrink. It's tomorrow, before your shift. Don't argue." Dan opened his mouth to do just that, but Gideon placed a finger over his lips. "I know him. Ariel and I saw him after Sarah and Simon died. It's not a weakness to admit you need extra support."

Just then there was a beep from Dan's phone. Gideon removed his fingers, and Dan pulled it out. He growled as he looked at the screen. Disastrous Date—Parker—again. It was the last thing he needed to deal with.

"What's wrong?" Gideon asked. Dan showed him the screen, and Gideon scowled. "You're gonna have to confront this head-on."

Dan rubbed his temple. "I thought I did at the dating evening. I'll sort it after the wedding. I'm too tired now."

"If you don't, I will."

To his relief, Gideon let it drop then, and Dan escaped down to the bar. He didn't see any more of Gideon until Dan finished his shift, only to find him dressed in coat and hat and holding his car keys.

"Are you going somewhere?" Dan asked curiously.

"I'm taking you home."

"I know you did it last week, but I don't need a ride. I can get an Uber."

Gideon jangled the keys.

Dan rolled his eyes. "You're gonna insist, aren't you?"

"Yep. And I'll be there to pick you up at one for your appointment with the shrink."

Dan shrugged on his coat. "You may as well stay the night," he grumbled.

"If I didn't have morning meetings, I'd take you up on that kind offer."

"It's nearly four in the morning. Why are you awake if you have an early meeting?"

"Just making sure the best man is in one piece for Saturday."

If Dan hadn't looked at Gideon's face, he would have taken that statement at face value. Instead he had a feeling that what Gideon said and what Gideon meant were two different things.

He wasn't surprised when Gideon escorted him all the way to his front door. "Do you want to come in?"

"I'd better not. Otherwise I won't want to leave you alone in that big bed."

"SmokeyJo and I are willing to share."

Gideon groaned under his throat. "Don't say that, darlin'. I'm having a hard time holding back as it is."

It was on the tip of Dan's tongue to tell him not to hold back, to take him inside and pound him into the mattress, because God knew Dan had wanted that for long enough.

Before he could articulate the words, Gideon gave him the briefest of kisses, murmured, "Good night," and disappeared toward the stairs, leaving Dan frustrated and relieved at the same time.

CHAPTER 19

GIDEON TURNED into Dan's shadow for the rest of the week. No matter how much Dan assured him he didn't need a chaperone, Gideon was always by his side, keys in hand, ready to drive him to and from the bar. It did highlight to Dan that working was pretty much all he did, but it's not like he didn't know that already.

His visit to the therapist was… useful. That was all Dan was going to admit. The therapist was a quiet thirtysomething man with a ready smile, who worked from his home in a comfortable brownstone. Privately Dan thought the therapy business must be paying well to own a house like that, but he liked the man and his surroundings. And he would go back. Dan discovered he had a lot of things to get off his chest.

After the appointment Gideon drove him back to the bar with an air of smug satisfaction. Dan let him have his moment. One day he'd get the better of his boss, but today was not that day.

Gideon acted as chauffeur during the day, and Dan told him he didn't have to drive him home. But he wasn't surprised to find Gideon sitting at the bar with his car keys in hand at the end of his shift. It didn't keep Dan from complaining to his friends.

"I'm a grown-ass man," Dan grumbled to Marty and Lena when they met two days before the wedding for a last-minute conference of war.

Lena rolled her eyes. "If it were me or Marty or Gideon or—"

"I get the point," Dan said.

"Do you? If it were anybody else you'd be doing the same thing. Leave him alone if it makes him feel happy. Your safety matters to him."

"Isn't that some kind of public-safety information?" Marty said. "Your safety matters, dot-dot-dot."

Lena notched his elbow. "Idiot."

"Your idiot," Marty agreed.

Now it was Dan's turn to roll his eyes. "You two are really sickening."

"I know," Marty agreed.

Lena opened her mouth, but Dan held up his hand. "If you're about to say 'Wait until it's your turn,' I really suggest you don't."

She smiled sweetly at him. "I won't say it, then."

Marty laughed. "I'd give up now, dude. You'll never win."

Dan gave a grunt of disgust, and they laughed at him again.

Operation Wedding was in hand. Despite pressure from both families, they refused to have a rehearsal dinner, citing the cost as an issue, although Lena admitted privately that the real reason was morning sickness, or rather all-day sickness. Between that, fatigue, and finding food she couldn't eat, it was dragging her down. The thought of two long-winded public events was more than she could handle.

They nearly canceled the wedding, but Lena had decided she could manage if she paced herself. Although Marty's parents had offered to pay for the dinner, Marty and Lena stuck to their guns. Dan was impressed by how well Marty stood up to his parents. Without being demeaning to his friend, Dan felt Marty had really grown a spine, and he put it down to Lena's influence.

"What are you doing Friday night?" Dan said. He was going to the wedding rehearsal and working Friday night so he could get the weekend off for the wedding.

"Todd is coming over for movies and a couple of beers. It's a quiet night in," Marty said.

"Does *he* know that?" Dan asked cautiously. "It's your brother we're talking about."

"He's under instructions from Lena. Besides, I'm working late after the rehearsal on Friday, so he won't have time to do any damage."

Dan wasn't convinced. He knew Todd of old. "If you want, I can try and get the time off." He'd have to beg Juan to cover. Then he'd probably end up doing five early shifts.

Marty shook his head. "It's fine. I may just cancel him and go to bed anyway. I can't believe how long this project is taking."

He launched into a diatribe about his latest clients, and Dan listened with half an ear. He would find Todd's number and warn him to behave. Todd was a fun guy to be around, but he was the eternal prankster and never considered the consequences of his actions until it was too late. Dan liked him well enough, but the man was in his early thirties and still single. No woman ever hung around long enough to calm him down.

GOOD INTENTIONS and all that, but Dan still hadn't called Todd by Friday afternoon. When he suddenly remembered, he tried him on his break, but Todd didn't pick up. He left a text asking Todd to call him ASAP, but he wasn't surprised not to hear from him. The guy was a flake.

Cowboys and Angels was packed on Friday night, and Dan didn't have time to try again. He was busy behind the bar all evening. It was payday, and all the patrons were determined to get as liquored up as possible.

In fairness to Ariel, the fight that broke out was not her fault. She'd left an hour before, saying she was off to meet friends. It was just a normal Friday night, and Dan ducked as a stool came flying over the bar. Instead of calling Gideon on the bar phone, Dan waded into the melee. If he was going to be manager, he needed to handle these things himself, instead of always calling the boss. Dan yelled at everyone to sit down and shut up and then worked his way to the nexus of the fight. Most took him at his word, picked up their chairs, and continued on with the evening, but two men hadn't seemed to notice that everyone around them had gone quiet. They continued to beat the living daylights out of each other until Dan and Bradley hauled them apart.

"Enough," Dan shouted.

One of the men launched himself at the other one, but Bradley grabbed him again.

Dan glared at two men. He knew them, knew they were both regulars. The younger guy had been at the speed-dating evening. Dan stabbed a finger at him. "I don't care what your problem is, Mikey, but fighting days in this bar are over. Do you understand?"

Mikey glared at him, his fists clenching, and Dan tensed, ready to defend himself from a punch.

"But—" Mikey burst out.

"No buts. Do this again and you're banned."

The other man tried to intervene. "Gideon don't care if we fight."

Dan whirled on him, and the man took a step back. "Gideon made me manager, which means you two don't get to be assholes in *my* bar. Now you can either sit down and shut up, or you can take your business and your fight somewhere else. Which is it to be?"

Both men grumbled, but the aggression seemed to have been knocked out of them, at least for the moment. Dan went back to the bar with a fierce look on his face, and nobody got in his way.

"You're very good at this," Gideon said. Dan had noticed him in the stairway, but Gideon didn't try to interfere, and Dan was thankful.

Dan gave a curt nod. "Tonight, they behave. I'm not going to the wedding with another goddam bruise on my face."

"It might be the start of a new era at Cowboys and Angels." Gideon sounded almost shocked.

"The next thing you know, we'll be serving tea and biscuits to the ladies."

It was a joke, but he grinned as Gideon shuddered. "We'd better not."

"I'm in charge now, boss." Dan couldn't resist teasing him. "You're lucky we're not serving pink cocktails and froufrou canapés."

Gideon looked at him skeptically. "Do you even know what a canapé is?"

"I have spent the last month looking at wedding plans and wedding menus. I not only know what a canapé is, I know all the variations, and I would be happy to ram them up the next man who decides to pick a fight here."

Gideon held his hands up in surrender. "No argument from me, darlin'."

"Makes a change. I'd better get back to work, but I'm going to Marty's first thing in the morning. And yes, I'll get an Uber. I'll meet you at the church. The service is at four."

"I remember. You're getting an Uber tonight?" Gideon had apologetically said he couldn't take Dan home at the end of his shift because he had a late video chat with a friend halfway across the world.

"It's all booked," Dan assured him.

"Are you sure there's nothing I can do for you before then?"

Dan shook his head. "Unless you're going to bring me breakfast in bed at five thirty in the morning, I'm good. See you tomorrow."

Chapter 20

Bang! Bang! Bang!

"What the hell?"

Dan shot up out of bed, his heart pounding and his pulse racing. What the hell was that noise? He looked at his clock and growled. It was five twenty-five, five minutes before his alarm was due to go off. He'd gotten home at one, an hour later than he planned. Those extra five minutes counted.

The banging started again, and he rushed to the door and flung it open. His boss grinned at him, his arms full of take-out coffee cups and a bag of something that smelled suspiciously like breakfast sandwiches.

"Morning, darlin'." Gideon looked him up and down. "Well, this is a good way to be greeted."

Dan stared at him. "What are you doing here?"

"You wanted breakfast in bed," Gideon said, as though it were obvious.

"I'm meeting you at the church. This afternoon. What the hell are you doing here now?"

"Who gives a fuck," his portly neighbor across the hall growled, standing in a terry-cloth robe that didn't quite meet where it should. "It's five thirty in the goddamn morning. Shut up before I call the cops."

"Oh my God," Dan moaned. He pulled Gideon into his hallway and apologized profusely to his half-naked neighbor. "I'm so sorry, Mr. Lewis. It won't happen again."

Mr. Lewis huffed, slammed his door, and caught his robe in it. He had to open the door again, and Dan pretended not to notice as he shut his own. He glared at Gideon, who grinned back.

"What the—" Then Dan's alarm sounded raucously through his apartment. "Please let this be a nightmare," Dan muttered as he fled to his bedroom to turn off the racket.

"I've got lattes and breakfast sandwiches," Gideon said cheerfully, as though it were normal to turn up at dark thirty on Dan's doorstep.

"There's no real time to go back to bed, unfortunately. You've got time to eat and then have a shower before we need to go."

Dan went into the bathroom to take a leak and then stalked back into his living room. Gideon was busy stroking SmokeyJo as she wove and purred around his ankles. Of course Dan's cat would fall for Gideon. He'd unpacked the food, and it sat invitingly on the breakfast bar. Dan ignored it, even though his stomach growled. "There is no *we*. I don't know what you're doing here, but I don't need you."

"I know you don't need me for the wedding. You got everything organized. But I'm here to look after you. I know you, Dan. You're going to forget to eat, and we don't want you passing out at the altar."

"It's not me getting married," Dan muttered.

"Not this time," Gideon said cryptically. He handed Dan a hash brown and a sandwich. "Sit and eat. We haven't got much time."

"I need to feed my cat."

"I've already done it, darlin'," Gideon said, pointing to the empty can on the counter.

Of course he had.

"Sit down and eat," Gideon repeated.

Dan sat and stared at him. "How did you know what time I'd be getting up?"

Gideon had just taken a large mouthful of food, so it took him a minute to answer the question. "You told me last night, darlin'. Now eat."

Dan huffed, gave up the fight, and tucked into his food. It was too early in the morning to argue with Gideon. He ate his way through the hash browns and bacon-and-egg sandwich, and then he drank the latte.

"You need to get into the shower," Gideon said.

"There's more coffee if you want it. I set up the coffee machine before bed."

Gideon grabbed a mug and filled it from the coffeepot. "Take that with you. It'll help you to wake up."

Dan took a large slurp of coffee. "What time did you get up?"

"About an hour ago." Gideon spoke as though waking up at four thirty was the usual thing for him.

"You're mad," Dan said and disappeared into the bathroom.

Ten minutes later he reappeared dressed in jeans and a button-down shirt. He had left his tux at Marty's place, together with the rings. Half-asleep as he was, he couldn't fail to notice Gideon's admiring slow perusal, and his body perked up. He told it firmly to shut up and go back to sleep as he refilled his mug.

"What's the time?" he asked.

"You got five minutes."

Gideon had finished his food and coffee, cleared everything away, and was reading one of the books Dan left lying around.

"You like thrillers?" Dan asked.

"I prefer horror, but I don't mind this writer."

Dan ran through the list of things he had to bring with him—key, wallet, breath mints. "Where is your suit?"

"I've got everything in the car. You can come with me. I'll drive you back. That way you can have a drink."

"I don't think I ought to be getting drunk. I'm the best man."

Gideon smirked at him. "I thought it was the best man's job to get trashed, make a really bad speech, and embarrass everyone."

Dan pulled a face. "Don't remind me. I've been dreading making the speech since Marty mentioned the wedding. Marty's brother is *that* best man. At his last wedding, Todd threw up all over the matron of honor. It should have been a warning sign for Marty."

Gideon laughed. "I promise I'll keep you under control, darlin'."

"Why do you keep calling me that?"

"What?"

"Darling. You keep calling me *darling*."

Gideon pulled Dan to his feet. "I've only called three people in my life *darlin'*. My wife, my daughter, and now you. I hope that tells you something."

Dan stared into Gideon's eyes, for the first time recognizing Gideon's expression for what it was. Pure affection, and maybe something else, something more. He wanted to ask, to know Gideon wanted him, boring old Dan Collins, but as he tried to think what to say, Gideon looked over his shoulder.

"It's six twenty. We need to move. Will your cat be all right by herself?"

"I've asked one of my neighbors to come in and feed her later on. She loves SmokeyJo. She'll probably take the cat back to her place for a cuddle. I swear she's trying to find a way to steal her."

Gideon bent down for a scritch behind the cat's ears and smiled expectantly at Dan. "Let's get going, then."

Dan picked up his keys and wallet, and they headed out. Dan halted as Gideon opened the door, and Gideon raised an eyebrow in question.

"Wait a minute." Dan rushed into the bedroom and returned a minute later. "I forgot the speech." He held up a couple of sheets of paper.

"Good call." Gideon ushered Dan out of the apartment as though it were his place rather than Dan's and held out his hand for Dan's keys. Dan huffed and locked the door himself. He didn't need Gideon to do the job for him.

Gideon's chuckle echoed in his ear as he headed for the stairs, and Dan gritted his teeth and took the steps two at a time.

He was happy to climb into Gideon's Nissan, though, rather than taking the subway to Marty's house. The car was still warm, and he relaxed against the comfortable seat and yawned as Gideon merged into the early morning traffic.

"You look tired."

"Thanks." Dan's sarcastic tone was spoiled by another yawn. "I haven't slept much recently."

"Worrying about your speech?" Gideon sounded genuinely concerned.

"Yeah." And dealing with his changing relationship with Gideon after hopelessly crushing on him for so long, the speed-dating evening, and Disastrous Date, who'd texted him twice the day before.

"Well, at least that's over and done with after today. You won't have to worry about the speech again."

One out of four was good. He supposed the speed-dating evening was over, so maybe two out of four. Dan was sure his crush on Gideon wasn't going to go away anytime soon, and Parker had the hide of a rhino. Dan wasn't convinced even using Gideon as his boyfriend would persuade Parker to leave him alone.

"I've done public speaking before," Gideon said. "If you like, we could run through your speech before the reception and I could give you pointers."

"You could deliver the speech if you want," Dan said, only half joking. The thought of having to stand up in front of all the guests was making his stomach churn.

Gideon patted Dan's knee, and Dan tried not to squirm because he wanted Gideon's hand a little farther up. Gideon didn't seem to appreciate Dan's feelings, because he said, "You'll be fine. I have faith in you. I've seen you face down a bar full of drunk men. You can give a speech to a room full of drunk wedding guests. There's no difference, except the guests might heckle you more."

Dan couldn't help but laugh. Gideon was right. Dan had dealt with more than one drunken crowd. He could deal with a room full of wedding guests, religious or not. The only thing he had to worry about was getting Marty to the church on time and remembering the rings. The speech was just gravy. Dan relaxed into the seat and closed his eyes. He would look after Marty, and Gideon would look after him. It was fine.

Dear Reader,
I like to Collect men's dirty underwears, with CUM stains in them.
I have about 1 dozen underwears.
I like to sniff them.
Would you like to give me, your underwear to ME?

Chapter 21

"He's supposed to be here." Dan banged on Marty's door for the third time, but as he hadn't answered the first or second time, Dan didn't hold out much hope.

Gideon peered into the window of Marty's living room. "There are no lights on in the house. I don't think anyone is at home, darlin'."

Dan rubbed a hand over his head. If he had hair, he'd be clutching it by then. "Oh hell n[illegible] You're not telling me I've lost the groom. We haven't gotten [illegible]urch, and the groom is already missing."

"He [illegible]sleep."

Dan [illegible] "Marty sleeps worse than anyone I know. He wouldn't [illegible]gh me banging on the door. Is his Jeep outside?" Dan poi[illegible] of the house, and Gideon went to investigate.

He [illegible]or a moment and then reappeared. "It's still here, and the hood is cold. There isn't any sign he used the car this morning."

Worry gnawing at his gut, Dan pulled out his phone and scrolled down to Marty's number. It rang and rang and eventually went to voicemail. After Marty's brief message, Dan left one of his own.

"I'm not sure how many words that didn't start with the letter *F* were in that sentence," Gideon commented. From the smirk on his face, he was obviously a lot less worried about Marty than Dan was.

Dan scowled. "Perhaps he should be here when he's meant to be here if he wants polite language."

He was at a loss. Marty was impulsive but very predictable. If he said he was going to be somewhere, he would be there. Dan was worried. Marty could be lying in the house injured… or worse. What if he'd fallen down the stairs? Dan raced through a list of possible scenarios, all of them dire.

"Do you have a key?" Gideon asked.

"Would I be standing out here if I did?"

Gideon frowned at Dan's snappy tone, but he felt along the porch roof and looked under the mat and in the flowerpots. "I can't find a spare."

"I don't want to worry Lena just yet," Dan said. "I'll call his brother. He might know where the spare key is." He had Todd's phone number in his contact list from years past, and he was scrolling through his contacts when Gideon spoke.

"Is Todd a taller, thinner version of Marty?"

"Yes, why?"

"Because he's dragging Marty up the street."

Dan looked up to see the two men shuffling toward them, both with sloppy grins on their faces.

"Hey look, Todd, they're already here. I told you we needed to get up earlier." Marty tripped over his feet, and it was only Todd's loose grip that kept him from taking a tumble on the asphalt.

Dan rushed forward to prevent any more accidents. Lena was going to kill him if her groom turned up with a black eye and a broken nose. "Where the hell have you been?" Then he inhaled and nearly gagged. "You reek. Are you drunk?"

"Not drunk. Definitely not drunk." Marty would have sounded more convincing if he hadn't slurred every word.

"He's not drunk. Drinking last night. More hangover." Todd sounded very pleased with himself.

Dan took Marty before he could do himself more damage. Gideon was by his side and took Marty's weight.

A short round man stomped up the path, scowling at Marty and stabbing a thick finger at him. "You owe me for the ride."

"Oh yeah." Marty hung on to Dan's jacket. "We ran out of money. Could you pay the cab driver?"

"How much?"

Dan blanched as the driver named a fare which was his grocery bill for the next month, but Gideon stepped forward. "I'll handle it. You get him inside."

Dan smiled at him gratefully. Then the smile slipped off his face as he turned to Marty. "Where are your keys?"

Marty pulled out a bunch of keys. He squinted at the keys, taking a long time to focus before he picked one and nearly inserted it up Dan's nose as he thrust it in Dan's direction. Dan got the door open and dragged Marty to the sofa. He left Todd behind, not caring what happened to him.

"Thought you were going to have an early night last night?" Dan said. He looked up at Gideon, who'd come in pushing Todd ahead of him and shut the front door. "Can you make coffee? Strong. Really strong."

Gideon nodded and headed into the kitchen. Todd slumped on the opposite sofa in a sprawl of loose limbs.

"Todd said I didn't have a bachelor party, so he would take me on a boys' night out." Marty rolled his head to look at his brother for confirmation. "I would have invited you, but you were working."

"But why on earth did you get drunk? You know Lena's parents hate alcohol. You said you were going to stay sober. She's gonna kill you after she's done killing me."

"I didn't," Marty protested indignantly. "I drank club soda all evening."

Dan made a disbelieving snort and turned to Todd. "What did he really drink?"

Todd opened one eye. "He drank soda… and vodka." He grinned as though he'd done something good.

Dan rested back on his haunches. "Christ, Todd, you know he can't handle liquor. What the hell did you think you were doing?"

"He needed a bachelor party, man," Todd protested. "You weren't going to do it, so it was up to me. That's why I'm the best best man."

"Didn't want a bachelor party because I didn't want to be drunk for Lena." Marty grinned at them both, and then the color drained out of his face and he clutched on to Dan.

"Shit. Grab that trashcan." Dan barked at Todd. He knew what was coming next.

Todd, for once, did as he was told. Dan dumped out the contents and shoved it in front of Marty just as Marty gave up the contents of his stomach.

"Gross, dude." Todd also turned green, and Dan pointed at the downstairs bathroom.

"If you're gonna hurl, do it in there. I'm not cleaning up after you."

Todd rushed away, and Dan heard retching that seemed to go on forever. It was turning out to be a fine morning.

"Just peachy," he muttered and looked at his first patient who groaned and clutched the trashcan as though it were a lifesaver.

"Lena is going to kill me," Marty slurred.

"You'll be lucky if she still marries you," Dan snarled. "Gideon, could we have water as well as the coffee."

Gideon walked in bearing two large glasses of water as though he'd anticipated Dan's request. "Coffee is almost finished."

Dan helped Marty sip the water, but he was unsurprised when it made a reappearance a couple of minutes later.

"I'm dying," Marty moaned. He rested back against the sofa and closed his eyes.

"You're not dying, dude. You must have realized you were drinking alcohol after the first couple of drinks. Why didn't you stop?"

"Todd insisted it was club soda with a kick."

"What the hell did you think the kick was?"

"Lime?" Marty squinted at Dan as though he wanted validation that that was the right answer.

"You're an idiot." Dan got to his feet and stretched. It was too early in the morning for this.

"Here." Gideon laid his hands on Dan's shoulders and massaged them, digging his thumbs into the muscle to roll out the sore knots. Dan groaned in pleasure, and dropped his head to give Gideon more access.

But then Todd stumbled out of the bathroom, and the moment was lost. Gideon stepped away and handed Todd the water. He muttered his thanks, took a sip, and headed straight back into the bathroom.

"It's going to be a long morning," Gideon observed.

Dan nodded in agreement. "Thank God we've got plenty of time to sober up these idiots."

"What time is the photographer arriving?"

Dan nudged Marty, who groaned loudly. "What time is the photographer getting here?"

"She'll be here around one."

"We've got four hours to get you sober and into your tux."

Gideon looked down at Marty. "How much sleep have you had?"

"Sleep?" Marty stared at him as though it were a trick question.

Dan sighed and tugged on Marty's arm. "Go to bed until eleven. We'll make sure you're ready for the photos."

Marty stayed where he was.

Gideon snorted and hoisted Marty to his feet. "Come on, man. Where's your bedroom?"

"Don't need sleep," Marty said petulantly.

"Sure you don't." Gideon half carried him to the stairs.

Dan stayed where he was and wished he were the one in Gideon's arms being taken into the bedroom. A loud, raucous snore broke into his thoughts. Todd had passed out in the bathroom, and Dan left him where he was. He was obviously breathing.

In Marty's small, neat kitchen, Dan cleaned out the trashcan and tried not to breathe as he kept hold of his own stomach with difficulty. He heard Gideon coming down the stairs and poured coffee into two mugs that were already waiting on the countertop. No point letting good coffee go to waste. "I guess he's asleep?"

"Like a baby." Gideon wrinkled his nose. "A very smelly baby. I left another trashcan by his head. God knows if he'll aim straight."

"This is not how I planned my morning. I should never have left him alone last night."

Gideon squeezed Dan's shoulder and then let go to lean against the kitchen counter. "It's my fault. I should have given you the night off."

Dan resisted the temptation to lean against him. "You couldn't know Marty was gonna go out and get trashed."

"I don't think he planned to get hammered. He had help."

"This is all his own fault. Marty knows what Todd is like. He should never have trusted him."

"Maybe Marty wanted to get drunk. A last rebellious fling?"

"It's not like he's gonna be teetotal forever. It was one damn day."

Gideon's lips curved into a wry smile. "Marty was just being an idiot?"

"That's more like it."

Dan was caught by an unexpected yawn, and Gideon put an arm around his shoulders and pulled him in close. "Do you need a nap?"

"You like mothering people, don't you?" Dan yawned again and rested his head against Gideon's shoulder.

Gideon chuckled and held him closer. He was a snuggler. Who knew? "I prefer to call it parenting, but yes, Ariel says I'm always fussing."

"She'd hate it if you stopped."

Ariel complained about her father's strong-arm parenting, but the minute Gideon stopped, she wanted his attention. Last week proved that point.

"And what about you?"

"What about me?" Dan tilted his head to look up at Gideon and noticed how his gold-tipped lashes caught the light.

“Do you want me to stop fussing?” Gideon’s voice dropped to a low rumble.

“No.” Dan held his breath and only relaxed when Gideon smiled.

It would be so easy to reach up and kiss him on that wide, curved mouth. Dan would only have to turn a couple of inches. The temptation was there, and from the way Gideon was staring at Dan’s mouth, he was having the same thought.

Then Dan’s phone rang.

Saved by the bell or the worst timing ever? Dan wasn’t sure. It was a number he didn’t know.

“Hey?”

“Dan? It’s Lena. Is Marty all right?”

The worried tone of Marty’s fiancée penetrated Dan’s cuddle haze. He stepped back and mouthed “Lena” to Gideon.

“Hi, Lena. Marty’s fine.”

“Yes, but how is he really? My friend saw him out last night and said he was wasted.”

So much for keeping quiet.

“Todd took him on a boys’ night out. In all fairness Marty thought he was drinking club soda. Todd spiked his drinks.”

“I’m gonna kill him,” Lena growled, and Dan held the phone away from his ear as she cursed loudly and with a vocabulary he was more used to hearing at Cowboys and Angels. Eventually she settled down, and he listened cautiously. “Where is Marty now?”

“He’s in bed and asleep.” Dan was glad Lena had calmed down because he didn’t want to be responsible for a bride losing her shit on her wedding day. “I’m gonna wake him up in time for the photographer.”

“Just make sure he’s sober by the time you reach the church. And plenty of breath mints. I’m not joking when I say my parents don’t like alcohol.”

“I’m sorry I let you down,” Dan said. “I should never have let him out with Todd. I know what the man’s like.”

“You didn’t let me down,” Lena assured him. “You had to work. Marty’s a grown man and should have realized he was getting drunk.”

“I’ll look after him,” Dan promised.

“Is Gideon there?”

“Yeah. How did you know?” Dan asked suspiciously.

Lena ignored the question. "Good. At least you don't have to handle two drunk asses. Was Gideon already at your place?"

"He picked me up, and shouldn't you be getting ready?" Dan didn't need Lena to run off with wild fantasies about him and Gideon.

Lena crowed loudly in his ear. "I *am* ready. Hair done, makeup done, and ready to hassle you."

"Thanks. Remember I have your groom."

"I knew he was into you from the first time I met you. I told Marty, but he wouldn't believe me. That man couldn't keep his eyes off you at the café."

Dan glanced over and caught Gideon watching him. "It's just a date for the wedding." To his surprise, he saw Gideon narrow his eyes as he turned away from Dan. "Anyway, I've got to go. I'll see you later, and don't be late."

"I'm not the one dealing with the hungover groom," she pointed out. "Any problems, call me. If I have to, I'll come over and get him myself."

"You focus on making yourself even more beautiful than you already are. I'll do the hard work."

He disconnected the call and looked at Gideon, who was staring into space. "I think Todd's ass is toast after today."

"How did she know about Marty?" Gideon asked.

"A friend saw them drinking last night. She's not very happy with her husband-to-be right now. My orders are to deliver him to the church—on time, sober, and with plenty of breath mints."

"We'll do our best."

Gideon sounded strange, almost disinterested, and Dan wasn't sure what had gotten into him. He'd been fine through most of the call until Dan mentioned their date.

Dan laid a hand on Gideon's forearm and felt the strength of his muscles play beneath his fingers. "Did I say something wrong?"

Gideon sighed, turned away, and took his cup to the sink to rinse it out. He turned back to look at Dan. "Everything's fine."

Everything clearly wasn't fine, but Dan didn't have a clue how to fix it. He looked at the clock above the fridge. It was just after eight thirty, so they still had a few hours before the photographer arrived. Dan had planned to take Marty out to breakfast and then go for a walk around their old haunts. Clearly that plan was void, and Dan didn't know what to do with Gideon, who was scowling at his feet.

Dan took a chance. "Would you like to come for a walk?"

Gideon looked startled. "Now?"

Dan shrugged. "We've got nothing else to do for a couple of hours. Marty and Todd aren't going anywhere. I was planning on showing Marty the old haunts, but I could show you instead. Unless you're not interested."

Gideon shook his head. "I'd like that. I didn't realize you were a local."

"I grew up around here. Marty and I met at the local grade school. He was new, and I was pretty much ignored by everyone else. We became friends and stayed friends ever since."

Gideon picked up his jacket and shrugged it on. "You're lucky to still be friends with someone from school. I've lost contact with all my old school friends."

"Marty was special. He didn't care that I was different from all the others."

"By different you mean gay?"

Dan nodded. "I knew from an early age I was into men and not women. Marty didn't care, and he ignored all the teasing from the other kids."

Bullying would have been more accurate, but Gideon didn't need to know the details of his miserable school years. Gideon cast him a shrewd look as though he were well aware what Dan was leaving out. He was a parent and probably knew kids a lot better than Dan did.

Dan checked on Marty, who was sound asleep and snoring loudly, while Gideon did the same for Todd. Dan felt slightly guilty that Todd was still in the downstairs bathroom, but Gideon had covered him with a throw and placed a cushion under his head, and that was more than Dan would have done. He grabbed Marty's keys, and they left the house. It was still cold, and Dan was glad for his thick jacket as they walked down the street.

"I know I should know this, but I can't remember. Did you start college?" Gideon asked.

Dan shook his head. "No. No money, and Mom needed me working. I wasn't college material anyway."

"Not then. But you are now."

"I barely graduated school. Marty was the clever one, not me. I mean look at us now. Marty's got his own business, and I'm still a barman."

"You're the manager of the bar," Gideon pointed out.

"It's more than I ever thought I'd be." Dan pushed his hands into his pockets. "I'm not bitter about my lack of smarts. Some men are destined for greatness, and others like me pull beer. My time will come."

Gideon made a disapproving noise in the back of his throat. "You've got more intelligence then you give yourself credit for, darlin'. You put yourself through college because you have plans."

"Yeah, I did." Dan remembered the early days as he struggled with his assignments. Then he'd wondered what the hell he was doing it for. It had been a long, hard slog and many times he'd nearly given up. He grinned at Gideon. "Keep reminding me of that."

Gideon gave a brief nod. "I will. You're a smart man, Dan Collins."

His intense gaze warmed Dan, who smiled as they walked on.

CHAPTER 22

THEY ENDED up walking past the local playground, gloved hands wrapped around take-out cups of hot chocolate as they watched kids play on the same swings Dan had played on as a child. Dan took Gideon on exactly the same tour he'd planned to take with Marty, and to give him credit, Gideon showed a great deal of interest. He asked questions about Dan's childhood, and maybe Dan gave away a little more about himself than he intended.

"I used to bring Ariel to a playground just like this," Gideon said. "She used to drive her mom mad because she was always into everything. I'd get home, and Sarah would hand me a very wiggly daughter and tell me to run some energy off her."

Dan grinned. Ariel hadn't changed in the slightest, and the fights in the bar were probably the equivalent of swings as a child. "Did you always want to be a dad?"

"Not really. My wife got pregnant in the last year of high school, and I didn't really have a choice. But once Ariel arrived, I couldn't imagine life without her. She's been the best thing that ever happened to me."

"You didn't think of…." Dan tried to find a way to ask the question tactfully. "Adoption or…."

"Abortion?" At Dan's nod, Gideon said, "We thought about it, but Sarah was a Catholic, and there was no way she would have an abortion. We considered adoption, but in the end, she wanted to keep the baby, and I wanted to support her."

"Did you ever regret getting married so young and having children?"

"Not at all. Not for one second."

Dan looked at where Gideon's hand rested on a railing, and he covered it with his own. It was the only form of comfort he could offer. Gideon gazed at him sadly, but he didn't move his hand, and Dan let it lie there for a moment.

Eventually Gideon huffed out a breath captured in the cold air and said, "It's about time we went back to the house. As best man, it's your job to hose Marty down for the wedding."

"Thanks," Dan said dryly. "I really appreciate you reminding me about that. Does that mean you're going to do the same for Todd?"

Gideon barked out a laugh. "Hell no. Todd can go stinky, for all I care."

"That was my thought too. One scrubbing down is more than enough."

They walked back in companionable silence, Dan's thoughts revolving around the man at his side. As Dan put the key in the lock, Gideon said, "Thank you for showing me your life."

"You're probably the only person I would have done that with, except Marty. I don't open up to many people."

"Thank you for trusting me."

"You're welcome." Dan pushed the door open and listened, but the house was as quiet as when they left it. "I think it's time the buckets of water were brought into action, don't you?"

"You're not really going to throw water over them, are you?"

"If they don't get up, water is the least of their worries." Dan would not let Lena down.

Gideon snickered and headed into the kitchen. "I'll put another pot of coffee on."

Dan ran up the stairs and went into the bedroom. Marty, thankfully, appeared to be awake and sitting up in bed, although awake was probably optimistic. Asleep sitting up was nearer the mark. "Marty, you awake?"

Marty groaned. That was good enough.

"You need a shower, dude. I promised your bride a clean and tidy groom, and that's what I'm going to deliver. Shift your ass and get in the shower."

"Stop shouting," Marty begged. "Your voice is too loud."

"That's tough, because you're going to hear a lot more of it, and louder, if you don't get out of bed. And Lena will come over and drag you out of bed herself if you're uncooperative."

Marty cranked one eye open to glare at Dan. "I hate you. I don't know why I ever thought you'd be a good best man."

Dan tapped his wrist where his watch would be if he wore one. "Tick tock, Marty. Get out of bed or I call your bride."

The threat worked. Marty threw back the covers, stood, and swayed as he tried to get his balance. Dan stood by in case he was needed, but Marty managed to stay vertical, which Dan counted as a win.

"I need coffee," Marty demanded.

"You get in the shower, and I'll bring you coffee."

Marty headed into the bathroom. Dan waited until he heard the sound of running water before he left the bedroom and went in search of coffee.

Downstairs, the smell of coffee heralded success, and Dan went into the kitchen to discover Gideon pouring four mugs and a cranky-looking Todd sitting at the breakfast bar. Gideon looked up as Dan came in.

"Is he awake?"

"Awake and in the shower. Also demanding coffee, which I promised to take back up to him." Dan looked at Todd. "How are you feeling?"

"Like death," Todd mumbled.

Dan waited, but that seemed to be all Todd could manage. Dan went to the fridge, took out the cream, and filled one of the coffee mugs to the brim. Then he returned to the upstairs bathroom and held it gingerly around the shower curtain. The mug was taken immediately with mumbled thanks.

"See you downstairs. What do you want to eat?"

"I don't think I can manage food," Marty said.

"You'd better eat something or you're never going to survive the day. What about toast?" Dan didn't wait for Marty to say no. He left him to his coffee and his shower.

Back in the kitchen, Gideon was alone at the breakfast bar.

"Where's Todd?" Dan asked.

"He's going to have a shower when Marty is finished. His clothes are in the guest bedroom. He wasn't going to cooperate, and then I said Lena would drag him in by his short and curlies if he didn't turn up looking presentable."

Dan grinned. The threat of Lena was obviously the key to opening many doors. "I don't know if Todd's tux is here."

Gideon got to his feet. "You drink your coffee. I'll go find out."

To Dan's surprise, Gideon leaned down and gave Dan a kiss on the cheek as he walked by. It was quick and over before Dan had a chance to react, but Dan touched the spot with his fingers as Gideon walked out of the room. Gideon was a more tender and affectionate man than he ever realized. He wondered why he hadn't seen it before.

He was halfway through his own coffee when he heard shouting upstairs. Dan took the stairs two at a time to find Marty rushing into the guest bedroom. Dan followed him in and discovered a naked Todd glaring at Gideon.

"What the hell?" Todd shouted.

Dan looked at Gideon. "What's happened?"

Gideon shrugged. "He went back to sleep. I woke him up." He held up a jug.

"You threw water over me, you bastard," Todd snarled, wiping the water from his face.

"I warned you if you didn't cooperate there would be consequences." Gideon spoke as though Todd's anger was of no consequence.

"I'm tired. I need more sleep."

"You stink," Marty said bluntly. "Even I can smell you. Go take a shower, and use a lot of soap."

"I'll stay here with him and make sure he's clean." Gideon leaned against the bedroom wall, folded his arms, and stared pointedly at Todd.

"You're not my mother," Todd spat.

Dan tried really hard, but he only had to catch the twitch of Gideon's lips, and that was it. He burst out laughing, and Gideon started to laugh too. Even Marty joined in, although he held his head as he did. Todd appeared to be on the point of stamping his foot, but even he must have realized how childish that would be, because he huffed and stomped into the bathroom. The shower started again.

Gideon grinned at Dan and said, "You take care of Marty. I'll make sure Mr. Stinky really does wash this time."

"Make sure he washes behind his ears," Dan teased.

Gideon saluted him and then followed Todd into the bathroom. Dan heard Todd's outraged squawk and knew the job was in hand. He looked at Marty, who was sagging on the bed. "Do I need to supervise your shower?"

"I've already had my shower, and yes, Mom, I did wash behind my ears. And I cleaned my nails." He held hands out like a child for his mom to check. "Lena said she'd have my balls if my hands looked grubby for the photos."

Dan automatically glanced at Marty's hands. "You manicure your nails, dude."

Marty frowned. "Yeah. Doesn't everyone?"

Dan kept quiet about his first manicure. “Let’s get coffee into you. The photographer will be here in about an hour. Do you need to get into your suit before he arrives?”

Marty shook his head and then groaned, holding his head in his hands. “I really shouldn’t have done that. She wants me dressed in pants and a shirt. Then she’s going to do some fancy shit with the tie and cummerbund. I’m not really sure. I just agreed and nodded to whatever she said.”

“Then let’s get downstairs and fill you up with coffee.”

“Not too much,” Marty said. “I don’t want to need a piss during the service.”

“It’s five hours to the service, I think you can cope.”

They went downstairs, and Marty sat at the breakfast bar while Dan poured him more coffee.

Marty took a satisfied slurp. “I’m sorry for ruining our plans this morning. I really had no idea he was spiking my drinks until it was too late.”

“I’m going to talk to him about that,” Dan said grimly. “It’s one thing to do that to your brother, but I don’t want him to think he can try that on a woman.”

Marty looked taken aback, as though the thought had never occurred to him. “Do you really think he would do that to anyone else?”

“I don’t know. But, Marty, it’s not the first time he’s done this to you. It doesn’t hurt to check.”

Marty drank in silence for a couple of minutes. Then he said, “You’re a good friend.”

“Right back atcha, Marty-moo.”

“Please tell me you haven’t put that in your speech?”

Dan realized he hadn’t thought about the speech in hours. It was amazing how unimportant it was in the scheme of things when you had a drunk groom to deal with. “You’re gonna have to wait for the speech like everyone else.

Marty scowled at him. “I lied. You’re a lousy friend.”

“Drink your coffee and shut up.”

GIDEON AND a sullen Todd made it back to the kitchen fifteen minutes later. If Dan were a betting man—and he *had* been known to place the odd bet—he would have guessed that Gideon had stood over Todd until he cleaned every inch of himself. Todd had that freshly scrubbed-raw-skin vibe. Dan handed Todd the coffee and cream and left him to sulk while he paid attention to Gideon.

"Do you want any toast?"

Gideon shook his head. "I'm fine. Do you think you'll be all right here for a while? Bradley called. There's a problem with one of the deliveries."

Dan frowned. "He didn't ring me." Dan was responsible for the deliveries to the bar and was used to calls at all hours from the staff.

"Because I told him, on pain of death, if he rang you today, he shouldn't bother coming back."

"You didn't."

Gideon raised an eyebrow. "It's my bar, and he knows I mean what I say. Anyway, are you okay if I leave for an hour?"

Dan knew it would be a lot longer than an hour if he was going to deal with a delivery question, but he merely nodded. Gideon had gone above and beyond that morning. He could take the time off to deal with his business. "We'll be at the church about four o'clock."

"I should be back well before then."

Dan made a noncommittal hum and walked him to the door. "I'll see you later."

Gideon wrapped his hands around Dan's biceps, pulled him in for another one of those small, quick kisses on his cheek, and left him standing on the doorstep watching Gideon drive away. Dan touched his cheek. He would really like to know what a proper kiss felt like if a small kiss could make his stomach flutter.

"You've really got it bad for him."

CHAPTER 23

DAN TURNED to see Marty watching him from the kitchen doorway. He thought about denying it, but Marty knew him far too well. "I think I have."

"What are you going to do about it, then?"

"I have no clue. Not a single one."

Marty rolled his eyes, then winced as if it hurt. He managed an acerbic, "You're clueless, Daniel Collins."

"What do you mean?"

"He looks at you like I look at Lena."

Dan had seen the soppy looks Marty gave Lena, and Gideon looked nothing like that. "You need to get your eyes tested."

"I mean it. He can't take his eyes off you."

"He's my boss. He wants to check I'm doing things right."

Marty rolled his eyes again. "You keep telling yourself that. I'm telling you he's besotted with you."

"Yeah, yeah. I'll make you toast, and then you need to get dressed or the photographer will be here while you're still in your underwear."

Marty swallowed hard. "I hoped you'd forgotten about the toast."

"You have to eat something."

Dan herded Marty back into the kitchen, and within a couple of minutes, he had Marty and Todd buttering slices of toast. The job seemed to revive them and improve their humor. Todd only marginally complained about the spread on the bread, and his brother told him to shut the fuck up. Then Marty went upstairs to get dressed while Dan cleaned up. Todd stayed down in the kitchen and watched Dan work. He didn't offer to help, which didn't surprise Dan in the least.

"I'm sorry I screwed up your plans," Todd said.

Dan looked up, surprised at Todd's apology. "It's okay." It wasn't okay, but he could be magnanimous. "At least this time you didn't tie Marty to a streetlight." He looked up at the silence. The guilty look on Todd's face made him groan. "Please tell me you didn't do that."

"It wasn't a streetlight."

"What did you do?" Dan muttered through gritted teeth. He threw the cloth onto the countertop and stalked toward Todd.

Todd obviously knew he'd fucked up badly because he held up his hands as though to ward off Dan's attack. "It was a tree. Okay? A tree."

"A tree where?"

"In the park."

"Are there photos?"

"I took some. It was only ten minutes."

Dan held out his hand. "Give me your phone."

"No."

"Give. Me. Your. Phone. Are these transferred to the cloud?"

From the blank stare Todd gave him, he made the assumption that he didn't have a clue what the cloud was.

Todd unlocked and handed over his iPhone with a snarl. Dan scrolled through the photos and deleted photo after photo of a naked Marty grinning stupidly. He noticed Lena was a lucky woman. Marty had certainly filled out since they were at school. He made sure he deleted them all before he returned the phone to Todd.

"Go get dressed," Dan ordered. "Just your pants and shirt."

Muttering to himself—Dan decided it was better not to know what he was saying—Todd headed for the stairs. Dan finished the last of the cleaning up and looked at the clock. They had an hour before the photographer was due. They could do it. *He* could do it without killing anyone. Marty was off-limits. But Todd was fair game.

THE PHOTOGRAPHER was a cute Japanese woman with short hair. She was dressed in a pantsuit and a pale peach blouse. She introduced herself as Akiko, and she told Dan they had to do exactly what she said and all would go well. Her two assistants hung back, both carrying enough equipment to bring them to their knees.

"You do know he's the client," Todd said, pointing at Marty.

She looked unimpressed. Marty hissed at Todd to be quiet and introduced himself. "I'm Marty. This is my best man, Dan. He's the one to talk to if you need anything. Ignore Todd. We all do."

Akiko flicked her gaze to Dan, who felt judged and found wanting. But he met her gaze, and she nodded.

"We'll start in here," Akiko said. She frowned as she studied the two men. "You need to comb your hair."

Partway through the photographic session, Dan felt like he'd been put through a wringer. Akiko was relentless. At least Dan had the benefit of being sober. Marty and Todd were both ashen, and Dan was seriously worried that Marty was about to pass out.

He insisted they stop for a coffee break, and that restored some of the color to their faces. Todd asked for the hair of the dog, but Dan ignored him. They would stay sober until they reached the church. After that, Todd wasn't Dan's problem.

By the time Akiko and her crack team of assistants left, all the men were dressed in their tuxes with burgundy cummerbunds and ties. There was still time before they had to leave for the church, and Dan was left with two men who didn't know what to do with themselves. It was like herding cats. Todd was still clearly hungover and had the grouchy mood to go with it. Marty was nervous and prone to pacing the floor. It didn't help when Todd pointed out that it was his third wedding and shouldn't he have it down pat by now? As Marty snarled, Dan shoved both men down on the sofa and told them to shut up and watch a movie. He picked one at random from Marty's Blu-ray collection and blinked.

"You watch teen romance?"

Marty flushed. "They're Lena's."

"Sure they are."

Todd scoffed loudly, and Marty seemed about to launch himself at his brother, but he subsided under a stern glare from Dan. The two men started to watch the movie, and Dan retreated into the kitchen. Gideon still hadn't made a reappearance, and Dan could have done with Gideon's calming presence right about then. On impulse, Dan texted him.

How's it going?

The reply was almost instantaneous. *I'm going to kill everyone.*

Dan chuckled. Dealing with delivery people required all of Dan's patience. *Problem?*

Dealt with. I'll meet you at the church.

You don't have to.

Shut up! See you there. Don't forget the rings!

Dan's lips curved into a smile. He shouldn't feel as ridiculously pleased as he did at Gideon's reminder. The man was still looking out for him. He patted his pocket where he'd put the small box of rings for safekeeping.

The doorbell rang. "Please let it be the chauffeur."

It was, and Dan herded his recalcitrant charges into the back of the car. He pointed a finger at them. "No fighting."

They scowled at him, and he glared back. Then he shut the door and slipped into the passenger seat. He didn't want to sit next to either of them.

The chauffeur shot him an amused look. "Bad day?"

Dan expelled a long breath. "It's times like this I'm glad I don't have kids."

"I hear you, brother. I hear you."

"You have kids?"

"Five of them, and every last one is both a joy and a pain."

"These two are just a pain."

The driver chuckled and pulled away. Dan relaxed into the seat and closed his eyes. Next time Marty got married, he could ask someone else to be best man.

At the church, Akiko wanted to take more photos. Before he let her get her claws into Marty, Dan shoved Todd in the direction of the pews. Then he turned back to the groom, who was leaning against the car, looking miserable.

"You need to get it together," Dan said. "From the looks they're giving you, Lena's parents are over there."

He smiled at a very well-dressed group. One of the women looked like an older version of Lena.

"Kill me now," Marty moaned, but he turned around to acknowledge them. They waved, although the frowns didn't leave their faces.

Dan handed him a pack of breath mints. "Chew one of these." He took one too, and the wintergreen was a burst of life in his mouth. "Now fake it, Marty. Fake it like you've never done before."

Marty straightened his spine, pasted a smile on his face, and did his best to pretend he didn't have a raging hangover.

"Are you ready?" Akiko asked. She looked less than sympathetic for Marty's predicament.

"I'm all yours," Marty said.

She gave him a knowing look. "Oh, Marty, it takes a good woman to handle someone like me."

Dan smirked at her, and she smirked back. Marty rolled his eyes and then groaned.

"Let's just do this before my head falls off."

In the church Dan scanned the small crowd at the front. Gideon wasn't there, and Dan swallowed back bitter disappointment. There must have been more problems at the bar. He sighed and went through the motions until they were finally at the altar.

The guests chatted among themselves until the music started. Marty paced until Dan told him to sit down. The last few guests appeared to take their seats, and bringing up the rear was Gideon. He mouthed an apology at Dan and took his seat in the pew behind Dan's. When his large hand landed on Dan's shoulder, the tension in Dan faded away. Gideon was there as he promised. He came through.

It was a blessing rather than a traditional wedding service, and Marty and Lena had picked their favorite songs for the walk up and down the aisle. The opening chords of "Songbird" sounded in the church, and the priest instructed them to stand for the bride.

Dan stood and squeezed Marty's shoulder. "This is it, buddy. Your forever moment. Don't fu—screw it up again."

Marty saw Lena, and his smile lit up the small church. His love for Lena was openly transparent. Dan felt a sudden envy. This was what he'd always wanted. A man who looked at Dan like the sun had come out just because he'd stepped into the room. Not just another notch on the bedpost. He told himself to get over it and focused on the bride.

Lena was stunning. Her hair was swept back with burgundy flowers, and she wore a pale-ivory silk dress with a kind of cape that led into a train. Her matron of honor and best friend, Shona, fussed with the train with the assistance of Rosie, Lena's young niece. Shona and Rosie would walk together behind Lena.

Marty didn't take his eyes off Lena. Even after his past mistakes, he was utterly confident that Lena was the one, and Dan thought that this time he was right. Lena was everything Marty needed and vice versa.

On impulse Dan risked a glance at Gideon, and his heart stuttered. Gideon wasn't looking at the bride. He was gazing at Dan with the same loving, tender smile that was on Marty's face. Just as Marty had said. The certainty in his expression took Dan's breath away.

Gideon caught Dan's gaze, and his smile broadened. Dan smiled tentatively, wondering how many times he'd been oblivious to Gideon's gentle loving.

CHAPTER 24

DAN SHIFTED from side to side. His feet hurt from the hours of standing around waiting for things to happen. That was ironic, considering he spent his working life on his feet. The other guests were taking advantage of the free cocktail bar at the reception in the hotel while more photos were taken, but Dan wouldn't touch a drop until he delivered his speech. After several hours he was starting to regret that decision.

"You look amazing," Gideon purred in Dan's ear, his body pressed up against Dan's back. His hair tickled Dan's neck, and Dan shivered.

"You need your eyes tested."

"My eyes are just fine, Daniel Collins. You're a fine-looking man."

"You need to be careful. We're in public."

"It's a shame, because if we were alone, I'd show you exactly what I think of you."

Dan sucked in a breath. "You—"

"Yes?"

Dan stepped away and turned to look at him. "You can't take risks, Gideon. We can't take risks. These people—" He waved his hand around. "Marty's parents and family are good people, but they don't approve of people like me. Lena's family are even more entrenched in their views. You have a business to run. If it got back to your customers, you could lose your business."

Gideon's face hardened. "I think you're not giving our customers enough credit. They know you, and they like you. They can deal with us, and if they can't, too bad. They aren't important. *You* are."

Dan flushed at the unsubtle emphasis on the you. "You have a good bar, Gideon, but those guys aren't always subtle about what they think of queers, even in front of me."

"Dan, I knew what I was in for when I agreed to the speed-dating evening. Thank you for worrying about me, but you don't have to. I don't care if people see me with my tongue down your throat. The bar could close tomorrow, and I wouldn't care. It's not my life."

"But it *is* my life," Dan reminded him, "and Bradley's and Juan's. We don't have a cushion of money like you."

"Dan, take a deep breath." Gideon stepped into Dan's personal space and forced Dan to look up. "This is New York, not Texas."

"You still get beaten up in New York for being a faggot. Or have you forgotten last week?" Dan said bitterly.

"I know they do, but do you think you're the only blue-collar gay guy at the bar?"

Dan remembered Mr. Seventeen. He'd never consciously been aware of other gay men at the bar. "No, but—"

Gideon chuckled, and it turned into a deep, rumbling laugh. "Oh, Dan, you are oblivious at times."

"I've heard that one before," Dan said ruefully. More than one person had told him his gaydar was shit.

Gideon sighed and ran his hand through his thick hair. "How did we get from me flirting with you to worrying about the bar closing?"

"I'm sorry. I ruined the moment."

"I'm sorry I made you uncomfortable. I'll tone it down, but when the time is right, I am going to flirt, and there will be kissing."

Dan licked his lips. "Kissing?"

"And probably dancing." Gideon held up his hand as Dan opened his mouth to protest. "And maybe some fucking."

Dan fidgeted uncomfortably. "You've gotta stop, dude, or I won't be able to walk."

Gideon rumbled out a laugh. "Just trust me."

"I do trust you." Five years of working for Gideon had imbued a deep and abiding trust. "Thank you." Gideon seemed thrilled by Dan's immediate response.

One of Akiko's assistants jogged over to them. "Best man and partner, Akiko needs you."

"Both of us?" Gideon asked.

The assistant nodded. "Yes, both of you." He waited, obviously not convinced they were going to obey his instructions.

"Okay then, darlin'," Gideon drawled. "Let's go and get our picture taken."

Dan rolled his eyes, but he did as he was told and headed over to the bride and groom with Gideon behind him.

Lena gave him a kiss on the cheek. "You look very cute together."

"I brought my date," Dan said. "You won't make me date the matron of honor?"

Lena giggled. "You're safe. She's brought a date of her own."

Dan looked around and found the matron of honor talking to a tall dark-haired man. Dan's stomach roiled. "Don't tell me that's her date."

Gideon looked over, alerted by Dan's tone. "Are you okay?"

"No, I'm not okay. Look over there." He pointed, and Gideon growled under his breath.

"What's the matter?" Lena asked.

"Who's that man, Lena?"

"Parker?" Lena didn't bother to turn around. "He's an old friend of Shona's."

"Do you know him?"

She shook her head. "Never met him before today. I think he's been working on the West Coast. What's wrong?"

"He's my Disastrous Date."

Her eyes opened comically. "No."

"Yup. And up to last night he was texting me five times a day."

"You didn't tell me that," Gideon growled.

Dan gave him an apologetic smile. "I had other things on my mind."

Gideon looked at Lena. "He was also at the speed-dating evening."

"Your evening?"

Dan nodded. "He was Mr. Nineteen."

"What happened?" Lena asked.

"Mr. Twenty told him to get lost."

"Who was Mr. Twenty?"

Gideon smirked at her. "I was."

She rolled her eyes. "I should have guessed."

"He's an asshole," Dan growled. "He's been hassling me for weeks, and I'm sick of it."

Gideon's arm settled comfortably around Dan's shoulders. "You don't need to worry now, darlin'. He won't bother you again if he knows what's good for him."

Dan didn't know whether to shake him off or settle in closer, but Akiko made the decision for him.

"Groom, bride, best man and partner, matron of honor and partner."

If Parker was coming anywhere near him, Dan would stay by Gideon's side. Shona, the matron of honor who was Lena's best friend, and Parker wandered over to them. Parker didn't look surprised to see Dan, which confirmed Dan's feeling that it was a setup. Or was he being egotistical? Parker smirked at Dan, although he blanched when Gideon scowled at him.

"Marty and Lena in the middle," Akiko ordered. "Dan, you stand next to Marty and Shona next to Lena."

Dan seriously hoped he wasn't expected to stand next to Parker, but Akiko spared him that, and Gideon settled comfortably by his side.

Akiko took a series of photos and then swapped them about. She had a sense of fun, Dan had discovered, and asked them to pretend they were dancing. Dan found himself in Gideon's arms, if only for a second, and Gideon looked highly amused at Dan's discovery that Gideon planned to lead.

"I'll take you dancing, darlin', and you can lead."

Dan gave a curt nod. "You'd better."

"Best man and partner, less talking, more dancing," Akiko snapped, and they both jumped.

"That woman's a nightmare," Gideon muttered into Dan's ear as Akiko told them to pretend they were slow dancing.

"She's one of the best photographers in the business." Dan had listened to an in-depth discussion from Marty until his eyes glazed over. "They were lucky she had a cancellation for today."

"I'll take your word for it."

Dan fit in Gideon's arms as though he were made to be there, but he only just had time to realize it before he was pretending to dance with Shona and then with Lena.

Lena looked up at him as they posed. "You look happy."

"That's supposed to be you and Marty," Dan teased.

She shook her head. "I know I haven't known you for long, but you seemed…." She struggled to find the right words. "Lonely. When you're with Gideon, you don't seem lonely anymore."

"I don't feel lonely when I'm with him," Dan admitted.

Lena patted his cheek. "He's the one? He could be, if you wanted it."

"You and Marty just want everyone to be as happy as you are."

She rolled her eyes. "Duh. Of course we do. You and Gideon are made for each other."

"I hope you're right," Dan said.

"What do you feel in here?" She placed a hand over his heart.

"Alive. He makes me feel alive," he admitted.

"Well, then." Lena smiled at him like it was all settled.

Dan looked at Gideon who smiled at him.

"See?" Lena said. "You're made for each other.

DAN HAD not exactly avoided Lena's family, but he hadn't gone out of his way to get acquainted with them. He'd been aware of a hostile scowl from an elderly woman in a crimson floral dress and a large wide-brimmed hat when the photos were being taken, but he'd been too busy to pay much attention. Once they reached the hotel, however, hostile glances turned into pointed comments. Dan had heard those comments for most of his life, and while he couldn't say they didn't find their mark, he refused to let them ruin his day. The person he worried about was Gideon. More than a few times he saw Gideon's mouth press into a hard line when she made a comment about "that type of individual," or "he'll face Judgment Day soon enough." She was particularly outraged that Gideon was sitting with them on the long table, and she went out of her way to ask Lena—in front of Dan and Gideon—if there had been a mistake with the seating arrangements.

Lena scanned the table. "No, this is correct, Aunty. Why?"

"You have two men sitting together," her aunt said as she shot a scowl at Dan and Gideon.

Gideon looked as though he were about to lay into her, but unseen under the table, Dan laid a hand on his thigh and silently begged him to stay silent.

"That's right. Dan and his partner." Lena gave her a flat stare. "Don't make a fuss, Aunty Celia."

Her aunt had a sour expression. "It's not right."

"You're welcome to leave if it offends you," Lena said flatly.

Aunt Celia gasped, her hand to her mouth. "Lena May Dawson, how could you speak to me like this?"

"I'm Lena May Kennedy now."

Marty came up and hugged Lena. "Yes, you are, my beautiful wife. It's time to sit down now." He smiled at his new aunt-in-law "Come on, Aunty Celia." He offered his arm and led her to her seat, thankfully at a different table.

Lena turned to Dan and Gideon. "Are you all right?"

"We're fine," Dan assured her.

She gave him a skeptical look. "It doesn't matter what my family says. I love you, and I am so happy to have you in my life."

Dan stood, walked around the table, and swept her into his arms. "I love you too. You're the one Marty's been waiting for."

Then Gideon did the same thing, and Lena hugged him close. "Ignore them. Ignore the comments. Nothing matters except you and Dan."

Gideon nodded and let her go. "You go and join your husband."

She smiled at him, and they all took their seats. Marty leaned back to glance at Gideon. "You okay?"

Dan was proud of his friends. It couldn't be easy to go against their families, but they drew their line in the sand and made it clear that Dan and Gideon were on their side of it. Now, if he could just get past the speeches, he'd have a chance to relax.

Chapter 25

LENA HAD made it clear that Dan's speech was not to last longer than five minutes and any mention of ex-wives was off-limits. Other than that, Marty was fair game. His brother's previous speeches had been about getting Marty drunk and letting him get into trouble. Dan's speech focused on the boy Marty had been and the man he'd become—with a few funny stories thrown in. He also gushed about Lena, which definitely eased the hostile glances from her family, and Lena's mother even smiled at him a couple of times. He was nervous, sure, and his hands shook as he stood, but he said his words, and by the time Dan finished, there was more than one person dabbing a tear from their eyes.

Marty stood and pulled Dan in for a hug. "Thanks, buddy. You know your friendship means the world to me."

"Right back atcha, Marty-moo."

They hugged and thumped backs and eventually sat down. Dan took a deep breath of relief, and Gideon handed him a glass of champagne.

"Now you can drink."

Dan caught Lena's aunt scowling at him. "Yes, I can." He raised his glass to her and drank deeply.

"You're supposed to sip champagne," Gideon said.

Dan burped. "After the day I've had, I don't care."

He noticed a bottle of beer had arrived on the table. "Where's that from?"

"From me," Marty said. "You deserve it after today. I know you don't drink, but you're off duty now."

Dan gladly put aside the champagne and took the bottle. "Thanks, bud. I'm real glad my duties are over."

"Uh-huh. There's still the dance with the matron of honor," Marty said.

Dan sighed. "Damn, I'd forgotten."

"You do your duty," Gideon said, "and we'll find somewhere to have a dance together."

Dan shivered at the thought of the two of them wrapped around each other, if only once. "Make sure it's a slow dance."

"You're on."

The meal and speeches over with, Marty and Lena took to the floor for the first dance. Dan leaned back in his seat and watched them sway together.

"They look great together," Gideon said as he draped his arm over the back of Dan's chair.

"They do," Dan agreed.

"I had a wedding like this with Sarah. She wore a huge white dress that was a nightmare to get off."

Dan tilted his head to look at him. "Is this hard for you? Being here? Seeing Marty and Lena together."

Gideon tangled his fingers in Dan's. "A little, but that was a lifetime ago. I don't regret any of my life with Sarah. She was a wonderful woman, and I wish you'd had the chance to meet each other. And Simon. He was so much like her. But now I'm here with you. You're not competing with a memory, Dan. You're not second best."

Dan remembered the conversation in the bar. In his mind, Gideon's love for his wife was a positive trait, not a negative one, but it was good to know he wasn't a runner-up.

"I've never been to a wedding with anyone before," he admitted.

"Not even gay weddings?"

"I spend most of my time at the bar. I don't have many gay friends. A couple of the guys I do know got married last year, but I still didn't go with anyone." Dan looked at their entangled fingers. "It's nice. Just having this. Thank you for being my date."

"You're welcome."

They stayed where they were until Shona claimed Dan for their dance. She pulled him onto the dance floor with an eagerness he found surprising.

Shona heaved a sigh as they started to move. "Next time an old flame calls up the night before a wedding and asks if he can gate-crash, remind me to get my head checked."

"Parker?"

"The one and only. He's so obnoxious, going on and on about the women he's fucked. I only let him come because my boyfriend dumped me a couple of weeks ago. And what's his beef with you?"

Dan blinked as he processed what she'd just said. "Women? He goes on about women?"

"Yeah. Why?"

He smirked at her. "Let me tell the story of my Disastrous Date."

By the end of the dance and the next song—because it took a while—Shona was openmouthed. "What an asshole. He's using me to get to you?"

"Maybe."

"And all those women he's talking about are really men?"

"Who knows? They're the same stories. They might not even exist."

"I was gonna sleep with him just to get some action. Now I'd rather use my vibrator."

Dan grimaced at the thought. "TMI, Shona."

"Sorry, I forgot you're a poor delicate gay dude." She grinned wickedly. "You knew what it was, though."

Then Gideon was by their side. "May I cut in?"

For a second, Dan panicked that Gideon was going to dance with him in public, but then Gideon swept Shona away, and Lena was there, holding out her hand.

"I'd like my dance with the best man."

Marty mock scowled at Dan. "I'm already losing my bride to the cute gay guys."

"Call me cute again, and you and I will have words." Then Dan spun away Lena.

"You're a good dancer," Lena said.

"Weddings are about the only time I get to dance, usually with all the single women." Dan steered her away from another couple.

"You can do it," Lena said.

"Do what?"

"Dance with Gideon. We wouldn't mind."

"Thank you. But I think your family would," Dan said gently.

Lena took on a stubborn look. "It's my wedding."

Dan maneuvered her away from another couple. "There's no point upsetting them. Gideon and I are fine. We don't expect anything more."

"You may not, but I think he does."

Dan was rapidly learning that Lena was very perceptive. "Gideon's used to what it's like for straight folks. It's been a long time since he was out in public with guys—if he ever was. It's gonna be a hard learning curve for him."

"You think he won't be able to handle how gay people are treated?"

"I think he has no idea. No one does unless they have to go through it." Then he realized Lena was wearing a too-stupid-to-live expression. Dan frowned. "What?"

"Look at me."

Dan frowned. "What am I missing?"

"I'm a black woman, Dan, a successful black woman. You don't think I know what you mean?"

Even then it took a minute for him to grasp what she was saying. He groaned, smiling at her apologetically. "I'm a stupid idiot."

Lena grinned at him. "Marty keeps saying you can be oblivious."

"I am. I can't deny it. Thanks for not being offended."

"I'm not offended—much—but I think maybe you need to give Gideon more credit. He's not stupid, and he's a strong man. If he wants you, he'll learn to cope."

Dan wasn't so sure, but he didn't want to argue with the bride on her wedding day. "Can I tell you a secret?"

Her eyes lit up. "Sure."

"I've wanted him since the moment I walked into the bar."

"You did?" Gideon asked behind him.

Lena burst into peals of laughter as Dan hoped the floor would swallow him up. He thunked his head gently on Lena's shoulder. She patted his head. "There, there, baby. I wish I could take a photo of your face right now. Here, Gideon, you take over."

Gideon bowed to Lena. "Save me a dance?"

"It's a date, mister."

She'd only taken two steps before someone else claimed her hand.

Gideon quirked an eyebrow at Dan. "Want a beer?"

"Is that a euphemism?"

"It can be anything you want it to be, darlin'."

What he really wanted was to be alone with Gideon so they could kiss and dance without any interruptions. But in the meantime, a beer would have to do. "Sure." Dan shoved his hands into his pockets to prevent the temptation of taking Gideon's hand.

The evening seemed endless, but Gideon's presence at his side made all the difference. Dan danced with Marty's mom, and she was pleasant enough and willing to talk about old times. Gideon claimed his dance with Lena—an elegant waltz around the floor. Marty made the guests laugh as he took Dan on a careering dance at the same time. It was a joke, but Dan appreciated the point Marty was making to certain other guests.

Toward the end of the evening, Lena threw her bouquet and Shona caught it.

"I really hope she's not expecting Parker to be her intended," Gideon murmured in Dan's ear.

Dan turned his cheek, and he was so close he could almost have leaned forward for a kiss, but out of the corner of his eye, he saw Marty's mother looking at him. "I told her about the disastrous date. It seems Parker is telling the same tales about his amazing love life as he told me, but he's changing the gender."

Gideon gave a bark of laughter. "Why does that not surprise me?"

Finally the crowd gathered around the bride and groom. Marty put his arm around Lena. They looked exhausted but very happy.

"Thank you very much to everyone who came this evening. I will not forget this day for a very long time to come."

"Make this the last one!"

Marty laughed at the heckle from an unknown member of the crowd. "I promise this is the very last time. Lena and I have some news we want to share with you. I know some of you thought we were rushing our wedding, and you were right. But there was a reason. In a little over seven months' time we're going to have a new arrival." He placed a possessive hand on Lena's silk-clad belly. "We're expecting a baby."

The noise from the crowd, the gasps and cheers, was almost overwhelming. Already in the know, Dan stood back and watched people's reactions. Nearly everyone was excited and happy, but he was acutely aware of the angry looks on the faces of Lena's family. After a few minutes Marty and Lena approached them. Dan really hoped the parents weren't going to cause a scene and ruin Lena's day. Of course he probably wouldn't have dropped a bombshell in that way, but that was their decision.

Whatever Marty said to them, it worked, because the next thing Dan saw was Lena and her mother hugging and her father not far behind.

Gideon raised an eyebrow at Dan. "Crisis averted?"

"I think so."

Then Marty's family was there, and everyone seemed really happy. Dan breathed easier, knowing they didn't need an intervention.

After a little while, Marty and Lena came over to them. Marty gave them a tired smile. "We're going to bed now. We've had enough. Thank you so much for what you did for us."

Dan hugged them both close. Gideon did the same and then held out a key card. "I know you tried to book the honeymoon suite, but it was unavailable. I asked again earlier today, and it's now free. I hope you don't mind, but I got everything moved into the honeymoon suite for you. It's yours until Monday."

Marty stared down at the key card in his hand. "But they said the suite had been booked for months."

"I know. I must have just asked at the right time." Gideon paid no attention to Dan's suspicious glance and smiled at the newlyweds. "Go and relax. You deserve it. Breakfast is also booked for tomorrow in your room. You just have to ring down when you're ready."

Lena gave a most un-Lena-like squeal and hugged Gideon again. "I don't know how you managed to do that, and I'm not going to ask, but thank you."

Marty shook Gideon's hand and hugged and thumped Dan again, and then they vanished from sight.

Dan looked at Gideon. "If I ask you what you did, will you tell me?"

Gideon grinned. "Probably not."

Dan decided he didn't care enough to pursue the matter. "I want my dance."

"About time. Let's go." Gideon grabbed Dan's hand. He caught Dan's shocked expression. "I don't care what any of them think. Okay? If I didn't have another plan, I'd take you on the dance floor now and fu—hang all of them."

Dan stared at their hands and then at Gideon. He couldn't think of anything to say except "Yes, Gideon."

CHAPTER 26

GIDEON SEEMED to have a destination in mind as he skirted around the other guests. They were stopped several times by people wanting to talk to them, and Dan discovered many of the guests knew Gideon in one capacity or another. At some point he was going to have to talk to Gideon about just how many fingers he had in what pies. Gideon would let the conversations go on for so long, and then make their excuses. Dan caught their knowing looks, and his face was afire. Gideon, on the other hand, seemed oblivious, or if he knew, he didn't care. Dan suspected it was the latter.

They reached the large open doorway leading to the lobby, and Gideon took a deep breath.

"I don't care if it's the mayor himself, I ain't stopping to talk to anyone else."

"They all seem to know you," Dan pointed out.

"I know a lot of people," Gideon agreed.

Which meant what, exactly? Dan was puzzling on that when Gideon said, "Isn't that Lena's friend, with the guy who won't take no for an answer?" He pointed at Shona and Parker, who seemed to be having some sort of altercation by the elevators. Dan could clearly see the fury on her face. "I'm going over there."

Dan shook his head. "Not yet. Shona's more than capable of taking care of herself. He'll be lucky to leave with his balls intact."

To his amusement, Gideon tugged him behind a large potted plant and pulled Dan against him, his chest plastered to Dan's back and his breath warm against Dan's ear. Dan found it strangely intimate to be hidden away behind the foliage. He leaned back against Gideon and watched the encounter unfold.

"Is she okay?" Gideon asked worriedly.

"I don't think she's the one you need to worry about."

Shona faced Parker, her arms folded, and her head held high. Parker appeared to be pleading with her, although Dan couldn't hear what he was saying. Shona shook her head, and then she stormed off in the direction of the reception room. Parker stood on his own for a moment. Then he shrugged and vanished in the direction of the exit.

"Hopefully that's the last we'll see of him," Dan said.

"He's a weasel." Gideon nudged Dan out from behind the plant. "I think you promised me a dance?"

Dan listened to the music coming from the reception room. "You want to dance to 'The Macarena'?"

Gideon snorted. "I don't think so. We can make our own music."

"You really are an old romantic, aren't you?" Dan said it as a joke, but he was surprised when Gideon looked at him a little sadly.

"Have you only just worked that out?"

Dan thought about it. "I think… you have many great qualities. You're a great father, a good boss. You're kind and generous. But I never got to see this side of you before."

Gideon nodded. "That's fair enough. I've always seen myself as romantic. It's just been a long time since I've wanted to show this side of me."

Dan really wanted to be the one to see Gideon's romantic soul. "Take me for this dance."

"Come this way."

Gideon gestured, and Dan fell into step beside him, not sure where they were going. He didn't know if Gideon really wanted to dance or if it was a euphemism for fuck, but either would work. He had done his duty for the day, and he wanted to be alone with Gideon.

But fate seemed determined to throw one more monkey wrench in the works. They had crossed the lobby and were waiting at the elevator when Parker reappeared with a smarmy smile on his face.

"You guys blowing off this snoozefest? I can't say I blame you. I'm up for a threesome if you are."

Dan stiffened, prepared to turn around and deck Parker if he didn't get lost. But Gideon turned and smiled at Parker, and if Dan had been on the receiving end of that smile, his blood would have run cold. "I don't share, and if I did it wouldn't be with a man like you. If I see your face again, I'm going to file a harassment charge with the police."

Parker scowled at him. "I'm not harassing you."

"But you *are* harassing my boyfriend. He's told you to fuck off, and yet you still come back for more. I don't know if that makes you desperate or stupid, and I don't care. I just want you to walk out of this hotel, and I never want to see you again."

Parker puffed up like an angry cockerel as he leaned into Gideon's space. Dan waited for Gideon to lay him out, but Gideon didn't twitch a finger.

Then Parker stabbed a finger into Gideon's chest. "You don't tell me what to do. If Dan wants to talk to me that's up to him."

"That's the whole point," Dan hissed. "I don't want to talk to you ever again. I've tried ignoring you. I've told you to get lost. My… boyfriend has asked you nicely to go away. Why won't you take the hint? I don't want to see you again. Nor does Shona by the look of it. Go away."

Parker's face was crimson, whether with rage or humiliation, Dan wasn't sure. He didn't care. He just wanted Parker out of his life.

"You think you'll get better than me?" Parker sneered. "I'm an investment banker. What are you? A thirty-year-old barman with no prospects. And him?" Parker stabbed a finger at Gideon. "He owns a run-down bar in Brooklyn. Why would you choose him over me?"

"Because I'm not an asshole, for one," Gideon said.

"Because I love him," Dan said at the same time. He felt the wave of red come up his neck at the same time as Gideon and Parker turned to stare at him.

"You do?" The smile on Gideon's face was worth all the humiliation.

"You're an idiot," Parker spat.

"I love you," Dan said to Gideon, ignoring Parker's splutters. "I've loved you for a long time."

Gideon turned to Parker, his smile obnoxiously smug. "That's the reason you need to fuck off, buddy. He loves me, not you."

"He's an idiot. You'll never have the portfolio I have."

Gideon rolled his eyes. "You really believe a man's worth is determined by his portfolio? That's why you're all alone, and I'm taking home the beau of the ball. He doesn't care how much money I make. He cares about me and my daughter and my bar."

Dan nodded. "You need to look at the big picture, buddy. Another body in your bed is fine for now, but what happens when no one wants to fuck you. Oh right, that's today, isn't it? Both me and Shona have turned you down today. Bad luck."

"You losers deserve each other," Parker spat.

Gideon smiled at Dan, who warmed under his regard. "I really think we do. And one more thing, Parker."

"What?"

"You're going to have to explain to your boss on Monday morning how you've lost your bank one of their biggest clients."

"What are you talking about?"

Gideon's smiled was vicious. "C&A Holdings is your client, I believe?"

The blood drained from Parker's face, and Dan thought he might pass out. He wasn't going to catch him if he did. "How do you know C&A Holdings is my client?"

"*Was* your client," Gideon corrected. "I couldn't work out where I knew you from until you said you were an investment banker, and then it all fell into place. C&A Holdings is my company, and as of Monday, I'll be looking for a new bank to manage my investments. I don't hold out much hope for your promotion prospects when I tell them why I no longer want to do business with them."

As if on cue, the elevator doors opened, and Gideon drew Dan inside. "Have a good weekend, Parker. You're going to need it come Monday."

The doors closed on Parker's horrified face. Gideon stabbed the top button, and the car started to ascend. It was empty apart from them.

"Was any of that true?" Dan asked.

"All of it."

"So, you've got money?"

"Yup."

Dan processed this silently. "A lot of money?"

"Yup. I inherited most of it from my grandparents." Gideon looked down at him. "Is that a problem?"

"I haven't. Got money, I mean."

"I know, darlin'. I don't care."

"I guess that's why you don't care what people think of you."

"Pretty much," Gideon agreed. "Money cushions you from other folks' disapproval."

Dan nodded and stared down at his feet.

"Dan?" Gideon asked gently.

Dan looked at him. "When were you going to tell me?"

"When we discussed our wedding plans."

"Wedding? Gideon, we haven't even kissed yet. Properly, I mean. We haven't even had that damned dance."

"I think we can take care of one of those right now."

Gideon gently tugged Dan into his arms. "Is it all right if I kiss you now?"

"What happens if someone gets into the elevator?"

"They won't. This one goes to the top floor only."

"Of course, it does," Dan said helplessly, "because why wouldn't it?"

Gideon smoothed his hand over Dan's cheek. "You told me you loved me. I never thought I'd hear you say that."

"I wish I'd told you before blurting it out in front of that asshole."

"I don't care if you told the whole world, Daniel Collins. You love me, that's all that matters."

Gideon bent his head and brushed his lips over Dan's. Dan moaned and dragged Gideon down for a proper kiss, his fingers tangling in Gideon's thick curls, and aggressively sought entrance to his mouth. Gideon opened up, and Dan eagerly explored as their tongues slid and dueled in an intimate dance. Gideon grabbed Dan's ass and hauled him close. His hard arousal pushed against Dan's lower belly.

The time for cautious exploration was gone. Dan wanted more than light kisses, more than a gentle dance. He wanted the horizontal tango as his old paw-paw used to call it. His grandfather would have approved of Gideon. They broke apart for air, and Dan caught sight of himself in the mirrored walls of the elevator, his eyes wide and filled with need, his lips ravaged and red.

The elevator doors opened, Gideon leading Dan into the middle of the penthouse. Dan looked around slowly. "You got us a room for the night?"

"I got us a room to dance," Gideon corrected.

"You got a big room for one dance."

Gideon held out his hand to Dan. "I was hoping it would turn into more than one dance."

Dan curled his fingers around Gideon's. "We need music."

Gideon walked over to a unit where there was an iPod docking station. He set up his phone, and Dan heard the strains of Adele flooding the room.

“Dan Collins, would you do me the honor of dancing with me?” Gideon held out his hand again.

Dan took Gideon’s hand and let Gideon twirl him around until he was in Gideon’s arms. Once more he was taking the woman’s role. Oh well, they could argue about that later.

CHAPTER 27

ONE DANCE turned into two and then three. The music got progressively cheesier, and in the end, Dan rested his head in the crook of Gideon's neck as they shuffled around the room, his arms wrapped loosely around Gideon's waist. Gideon didn't seem anxious to push it to the next level. He held Dan, stroked his hair, and occasionally brushed a kiss over his temple.

As the song came to an end, Gideon stopped their gentle swaying. He placed one finger under Dan's chin and tilted it so he could kiss him. Dan shuddered, clutched Gideon's ass and hauled him closer, and opened his mouth for another long kiss that left his toes curling in his fancy dress shoes. From the way Gideon's arms tightened around him and his moan of pleasure as their tongues met and dueled, Gideon was just as affected.

Dan slid one hand up to cup the back of Gideon's neck, and the short hairs prickled his palm. He left the other on Gideon's tight ass and squeezed, relishing the feel of taut muscle beneath his hand.

Gideon snorted as he ran his hand over Dan's head. "You need to grow your hair."

"You just want something to hang on to." Dan had been thinking about growing it out since the barfights had tapered off.

"I want something to hang on to," Gideon agreed. Then he kissed Dan hard again.

And Dan's shaft pressed insistently against Gideon's thigh. He rubbed against him because he wanted to take it to the next stage. He didn't expect Gideon to pick him up. Dan had the choice to struggle or wrap his legs around Gideon's waist. When he chose the latter, Gideon smiled at him as though he'd hung the moon.

But Dan, being Dan, had to growl an "I'm not a girl," even if the thought of Gideon being able to carry him aroused the living fuck out of him.

"I know that, darlin'." Gideon's soothing tone should have stung Dan's pride, and maybe it did a little, but he didn't have time to do more than hang on as Gideon took them into a bedroom which was as large as Dan's entire apartment and deposited Dan on the huge bed. Then he crawled over Dan and pressed him into the mattress.

Dan stared up at him. "We kinda need to get naked. And no shoes."

"I need to ask a question… to know…." Gideon's hesitancy made Dan frown.

He ran a finger along Gideon's cheek. "Ask me anything."

"We haven't talked about if this is okay."

"Is this a consent talk? Because I'm grateful an' all, but I'm not saying no."

While Dan had been joking, he realized from Gideon's serious expression that that *had* been one of the questions. Dan wasn't used to being asked if he consented, but it had been all over the media, and it wasn't the time to laugh at Gideon for taking extra care of him. He smiled, and Gideon gave the briefest of smiles in return, but his gaze was intense.

"Good, because I really wanna fuck you. Is that okay?"

"What if I want to fuck you?" Dan liked changing it up. He loved being filled by a cock, and he was just as happy banging a guy's brains out.

"You can do what you like, darlin'."

Dan knew if he said no, Gideon would accept it without question, but he didn't want to say no. "I want you inside me, filling me up until I can't breathe."

Gideon's smile was huge. "Then let's get naked, because I really need to feel your skin on mine."

Dan was fully onboard with that idea, but then he remembered that getting into the tuxedos had been a two-man job. Stripping out of the tuxedos was easier said than done. "I might need some help here, big guy."

"I can do that."

Dan had never had the experience of being undressed by any man. Gideon took each button slowly, kissed each piece of skin as it was exposed, and nuzzled into the hair on Dan's chest. Dan remembered his shower, when he'd wondered if Gideon could deal with a furry chest. He didn't seem to have an issue.

Then it was Dan's turn to help Gideon. As he pushed off Gideon's shirt, Dan nearly swallowed his tongue. Gideon was all man in clothes, but naked, he was a fucking god.

"Christ," he whispered as he took in the broad shoulders, chest lightly covered in hair, slim waist, and long legs. His cock was thick and long, and Dan wanted to drop to his knees to taste it.

"Gideon, or sir, if you want to," Gideon replied seriously.

"Sir? In your dreams," Dan scoffed, because no way was he calling a lover *sir*.

Gideon smile was wry. "Ah, Daniel, you don't know just how many dreams I've had about you."

"Likewise."

They came together in a clash of hands and teeth, mouths desperate to connect again, dicks leaving sticky trails on bellies and thighs. It was hard and needy and left Daniel in no doubt that Gideon wanted him, Daniel Collins, not some nameless lover.

Gideon tipped them over onto the bed. Dan went down with an *Oof*, the breath knocked out of him. Dan barely had time to inhale before Gideon kissed him again, and Gideon cradled either side of his face with his large hands. He wasn't used to tenderness together with desire. It was as though Gideon wanted to wrap him up as well as fuck him into the mattress.

Dan's eyes slowly drifted shut. He arched his back as Gideon placed wet sucking kisses down his neck and then along a trail to his left nipple. Dan carded his fingers through Gideon's thick hair as Gideon licked and toyed with one nipple and then the other. Each pass of his tongue set Dan's nerve endings on fire, and he rubbed his cock against Gideon, begging for Gideon's attention.

He moaned as Gideon wrapped his hand around Dan's shaft. "More. I want to feel your cock against mine."

"Whatever you want, darlin'," Gideon crooned, and he started a slow jack of their cocks—velvet hardness against velvet hardness.

Dan wasn't sure who moaned or whether they both moaned in unison. The angle was strange, but it didn't matter, because it was Gideon touching him and Gideon pressing him down into the mattress and Gideon's cock sending delicious friction against his. Slow and perfect, it was more than Dan had ever dreamed of. He opened his eyes to see

Gideon staring at him intently, strain around his eyes and mouth, and he realized Gideon was close to the edge already.

He enveloped Gideon's hand in his. "It's okay. You can come now."

Gideon shoved through their joined hands with sharp staccato thrusts until he let out a choking sound and came in warm pulses, spilling through their fingers onto Dan's belly. Dan worked him through his orgasm until Gideon rested his head in the crook of Dan's neck.

It took a few minutes, but finally Gideon drew in a shuddering breath and looked up, his expression sheepish. "I didn't intend it to be that quick."

"It's okay," Dan soothed.

"Can I suck you off?"

"Oh God, yes."

Gideon slithered down the bed and took Dan's cock into his mouth. Dan moaned and arched up as Gideon licked around the glans and ran his tongue up and down the shaft.

"Don't tease. Too close. Need to fuck your mouth."

Gideon pulled off, his mouth glistening. "Do it."

He sucked Dan back into his mouth and waited while he looked up at Dan. If Dan wanted it, then Gideon was ready and willing. It only took a few thrusts, and Dan spilled down Gideon's throat and felt Gideon take it all.

Gideon climbed back onto the bed and handed Dan a packet of wipes that had been on the nightstand. Dan managed to clean them both up, throw the wipes somewhere in the direction of the trashcan, and roll into Gideon's arms. Gideon kissed the top of his head, and Dan closed his eyes.

He was almost asleep when a horrible thought struck him and he sat bolt upright.

"Wassa matter, darlin'?" Gideon murmured all sleepy and warm.

"SmokeyJo. She needs feeding."

"Ariel's gonna feed her tomorrow. We've got your spare keys at the bar, remember?"

"I—but—"

"Stop worrying and go to sleep. Your cat is fine."

Gideon pulled Dan down and enfolded him in his arms again. Dan was asleep in seconds, sated and content in a way he hadn't been for years.

THEY CAME together in the night as urgent desire overtook the need to sleep. Dan woke needing the bathroom and had to wriggle out of Gideon's embrace, because Gideon hadn't let go of him at all during the night. He was like a much larger, although slightly less furry version of his cat.

When he got back into bed, Gideon wanted kisses. He gave them willingly, folding into Gideon's arms and seeking his mouth in the dark. They kissed for a long time, until it was more panting, and their dicks were hard and painting needy trails on their skin.

"Roll over," Gideon said eventually.

Dan did as he was asked, and he heard a quiet *snick*. Gideon's preparation was as tender as he expected, until Dan couldn't take any more and begged him to fuck him. He was starting to realize Gideon liked to hear Dan ask or beg for what he wanted. A crinkle of foil, and then Gideon was pushing his way in. Dan breathed through until Gideon rested behind him, his pubic hair tickling Dan's ass.

Gideon moaned gently and kissed the nape of Dan's neck. "You feel unbelievable."

"So do you." Dan reached behind him with one arm to pull Gideon closer.

Gideon started to move with small thrusts, getting deeper, until the sound of their panting filled the darkened room. Dan tugged on his cock and matched his rhythm to Gideon's. Their rhythm worked and stuttered, and then they climaxed. Dan wasn't sure who was first, but he felt Gideon pump into the condom as he spurted over his hand again. Gideon rested his sweaty forehead against Dan's back until he finally moved and flicked on one of the small lights, and Dan blinked against the brightness. It was Gideon's turn to pad to the bathroom and dispose of the condom. Dan cleaned up as best he could and tried not to lay in the wet patch. The sheets were a mess, and Dan took great satisfaction in that thought.

Dan wrapped himself around Gideon when he returned to bed. He wanted to show the same tenderness that Gideon had shown him.

"Good night," he whispered as they lay in the darkness.

"'Night, darlin'."

CHAPTER 28

DAN WOKE first, disorientated by the strange room, and even more by the fact there was someone in the bed next to him. He rolled over to stare at Gideon, who was still sleeping. It was a rare moment for Dan to study the man he had fallen so hard for. Gideon was on his back, one arm above his head, the other hand resting on his belly. The sheet was draped over his hips, only showing a hint of the springy hair at the base of his abdomen and hiding his morning wood from view. He looked happy and relaxed, and a slight smile curved his generous mouth.

Dan licked his lips. Some men changed when they slept, but Gideon was the same man he was when he was awake—strong, virile, and oozing sex appeal. One of his curls had fallen across his eyes, and Dan itched to push it back but didn't want to disturb him. Gideon snorted and stretched, and Dan held his breath and watched as Gideon turned over onto his belly. He was a study in tanned skin and muscle and broad shoulders. The sheet now draped across his ass, the cleft between the cheeks just visible.

Gideon made Dan's mouth go dry just looking at him. He never thought he would get lucky enough to have Gideon in his bed, let alone in his life. He wondered how much angst could have been saved if he'd known Gideon was bisexual all along. But then, Gideon had admitted that he had mourned his wife for a long time and was only now ready for another relationship. It worried Dan a little. Gideon hadn't really looked elsewhere, and Dan didn't want to be the "getting back in the saddle" relationship.

What if Gideon decided he wanted a woman? Dan would be devastated. But he could walk away now, before he got too involved.

"Who am I kidding?" he murmured, not wanting to disturb Gideon. "I was head over heels the moment I walked into the bar and saw your smile."

Unable to resist the urge, Dan pushed the dark curls away from Gideon's eyes and then gently traced a path down his neck and along the bumps of his spine to the dark valley barely visible under the sheet.

Gideon hadn't moved, and Dan thought he was still asleep until he heard a sleepy "G'morning, darlin'."

"Morning." Dan blushed a little at being caught openly ogling, but Gideon didn't seem to mind. He reached over and pulled Dan in for a long, deep kiss. The kissing was as mind-blowing as the sex had been. And Dan sank into it and wriggled so he straddled Gideon's hips. Gideon wrapped his arms around him. Dan was trapped and happy to be so.

After a long while, Gideon pulled back and buried his face in Dan's neck. "You're going to need a shave soon."

"Mmmm, you too." He rubbed his hand against Gideon's stubble.

"We could go and see Baz," Gideon suggested.

"Or we could just stay here and fuck each other senseless."

Gideon grinned. "That sounds like an excellent idea."

"What time do we have to check out?"

"Tomorrow."

Dan lifted his head and raised his eyebrows in question. "You booked the room for two nights? What about Cowboys and Angels?"

"Juan, Eddie, and Ariel are running the bar. Bradley can take care of deliveries. Liam can be a pain in the ass like he usually is. I'm having a business meeting with my manager."

"A business meeting. A business meeting where you're lying in bed naked with your manager on top of you?"

"Yes," Gideon agreed.

"Do you have many business meetings in bed, Mr. Tyler?" Dan hoped his tone conveyed how much he disapproved of that idea.

"Not recently," Gideon assured him. "And certainly not like this."

"Like what?" Dan asked.

Gideon's arms tightened around Dan and made him cough. "Like I never want to leave this bed. Like I would be happy to drown in your eyes and body. Like I can't believe I've been lucky enough to find you. I never thought I'd be lucky enough to fall in love again, let alone so completely and deeply."

Dan thought he was the one who was going to drown in Gideon's intense gaze. "Don't say that if you don't mean it."

"But I do mean it. I don't say things I don't mean. You know that. I'm in love with you, Daniel Collins, and I want to spend the rest of my life with you."

"I love you too. More than I can say." It felt good to say it out loud. "You're the one with the words. I can only show you how I feel."

"Why don't you just do that, then? Show me how you feel for the rest of our lives together."

Dan sought Gideon's mouth and kissed him with all the longing he possessed. His cock slid against Gideon's and thickened in anticipation of pleasure to come, but right then, meeting Gideon's mouth was more important.

Gideon sighed as though he were coming home, and Dan captured the sound and stored it as his own. Gideon had been more than Dan's plus-one. In such a short time, he'd become a lover and a friend and a partner.

Something occurred to him, and he pulled back, needing an answer before he carried on. Gideon frowned at the interruption. "What's the matter?"

"Parker."

Gideon's frown deepened. "You want to talk about him now? What about him?"

Dan didn't really want to talk about Parker, but this had been bothering him since their encounter in the lobby. "You really going to pull your business from his firm?"

"He deserves it," Gideon said flatly.

"He is an asshole, certainly, but if you do pull your business, he'll lose his job."

Gideon nodded. "I don't want a man like that involved in my affairs."

"I'm not trying to interfere—" Dan started.

"Yes, you are," Gideon teased.

"Maybe a little. But throw him a bone. He's probably spent the weekend wondering what the hell just happened. Find a way of not working with him, but not making him unemployed."

"Why would it bother you if he were unemployed? You said yourself he did nothing but hassle you for weeks. I'm still annoyed at you for not telling me just how much of an ass he was being."

"It wasn't your problem until now," Dan pointed out. "I just know it wouldn't sit right for me to be responsible for a man losing his job."

"He's responsible, not you. You're not the one who was the asshole."

"I know." Dan traced his fingers over Gideon's strong mouth. "Just think about it. Okay? I know you. You're not that sort of man. He lost me. He never can have me. Maybe next time he'll think long and hard before getting another notch on his bedpost."

Gideon pressed his lips together. "I'll think about it. I know you have the best intentions, but the guy is a menace."

Dan nodded. Any decision would have to be Gideon's. Dan leaned forward and kissed the stress out of Gideon's mouth. "I can think of better things to do than talk about him."

"Now we're in agreement." Gideon rolled over, and then it was Dan pressed into the mattress. "I hated the thought of you taking anyone else to the wedding." Gideon's voice was so low Dan could barely hear him.

"You know, you only had to ask."

Gideon's smile was wry. "I didn't think you'd believe me if I asked you out for a date. I thought you'd believe it was a pity date." Dan opened his mouth and shut it again. That's exactly what he *had* thought. Gideon nodded. "I like looking after people. I wanted to take care of you."

"Today?"

"And forever, if you'll have me."

"I'll consider it," Dan teased, but he yelped when Gideon dug two fingers in to tickle his ribs. "Uncle! Uncle!" When Gideon quit tickling him, he asked, "What do you want to talk about now?"

Gideon grunted. "I'm more of an action man, myself. I'd rather show you how I feel than talk about it."

Dan could go along with that plan. He lay out on the bed and surrendered himself to whatever Gideon had planned.

Gideon brushed his lips along the faint traces of the bruise on Dan's cheek. Then he nuzzled into Dan's ear and kissed down his neck. Dan shivered and pressed his skin into Gideon's mouth. The one thing Dan had learned about Gideon last night was that he didn't like to be rushed when he made love. And this was definitely making love. Dan wasn't just another notch on his bedpost. Dan was there in his bed, and Gideon had every intention of keeping him there forever.

He left wet kisses through the hair on Dan's chest until he reached his nipples, which he licked and sucked until they were on the point of being sore. Then he slid a little downward to focus on Dan's belly button. Dan lay there with his eyes closed until he needed to see what Gideon was doing, needed to look at the dark-haired lover intent on driving Dan out of his mind.

"Need more," Dan whispered.

Gideon raised his head. "What you need?"

"I need you inside me."

Gideon slid down farther until his ass was all but off the bed, and he licked the tip of Dan's cock. "What part of me do you want inside you? My tongue, my fingers, or my dick?"

"Yes," Dan moaned. One of them, all of them. He really wasn't fussy, as long as he got it now.

"All of me is yours, darlin'." Gideon reached over for the lube they'd chucked aside overnight and squeezed a little into his fingers.

Dan moaned as the cool lube hit his hole. "Cruel."

Gideon chuckled, but he drove two fingers into Dan, and Dan stopped worrying about the coolness of the lube. Gideon prepared him thoroughly and then replaced two fingers with his thick cock, and Dan sighed in relief. That was what he needed.

They didn't move for a moment as Dan relaxed around Gideon. Then he pulled back and drove in again and drew a moan from Dan that seemed to last forever. Gideon filled him, completed him. He didn't need anything else. Right at that moment, he had everything he wanted. He didn't even really need to come, not yet, anyway. But his body had other ideas, and it wasn't long before he felt his orgasm coiling in his balls. He gasped, and his body spasmed around Gideon as he came. Gideon shouted and joined him in climax.

Finally they stilled, and Gideon collapsed onto his side. He made a desultory attempt to clean up and disposed of the condom, but as soon as he could, Gideon put his knee between Dan's legs and his hand on Dan's chest and tugged lightly at the chest hair.

Dan looked into Gideon's eyes. "I love you, Gideon."

A tear spilled onto Gideon's cheek. "I never thought anyone would say that to me again. Thank you for waiting for me, darlin'."

Dan reached up to kiss away the tear. "You were worth waiting for."

EPILOGUE

COWBOYS AND Angels was closed to the public again. The private function was in full swing, and Bradley, Juan, and Eddie served drinks as fast as they could to people who kept arriving. Most of the regulars were there, including old Buck, who complained it was past his bedtime. But he wasn't about to leave. He sat in his usual seat with his favorite beer and gave a gummy grin to anyone who sat down to talk to him.

Technically it was Dan's night off. But as he now lived above the bar, he didn't spend much time away. He and SmokeyJo had moved in nearly a year earlier, and once the gray cat established her territory and ground rules to Gideon and Ariel, they lived in mostly peaceful harmony.

Once again Dan was the focus of the event, but this time he didn't care. He'd finally received his degree in business and economics. It was his graduation party, and he'd earned every second of his celebration.

Buzzing with happiness and more beer than he usually drank, Dan leaned against Gideon as they talked to Cris, Marty, and Lena. As usual Gideon had one arm wrapped around him, his hand resting over Dan's heart and a bottle of beer in the other. It was a possessive he's-mine attitude that made Dan roll his eyes because Gideon still growled a little if Cris got too close. Dan was where he wanted to be, in the arms of the man he loved. It still made him light-headed just thinking about it.

They'd endured endless ribbing for wearing matching dark-green dress shirts and dark-gray slacks. Dan ran a hand over his newly styled hair. He refused to grow it very long, but now Gideon had his hair to hold on to. They'd both visited Baz for a haircut and a shave. Yes, and a mani-pedi with Aunty Vera too. Dan had finally gotten over his fear of grooming.

He had a chance to unwind after weeks of intense study. He was going to relax with his husband and not think about stats and profit margins at all.

His husband. That was still shiny and new. Like *today* new, which was the reason for the matching clothes. It was also their wedding reception. Gideon had offered him a big affair, but Dan looked at him in horror. City Hall and a party at Cowboys and Angels was all he needed. Dan looked at the platinum ring on his finger and felt the unaccustomed weight. It seemed significant. He was a married man.

"Happy?" Gideon murmured in his ear. His ring was currently over Dan's heart, just where it should be.

Dan tilted his head. "I've never been happier."

"What's next for you two now that Dan's finished his degree and you've tied the knot?" Lena asked.

Marty chuckled. "A house in the burbs and babies?"

Dan choked on his beer, but Gideon just laughed. "We'll leave that to you two."

"As long their uncles, Dan and Gideon and Cris look after them," Lena said.

Daniel Christopher Kennedy had made an early appearance five months after the wedding and had his honorary uncles and grandparents wrapped around his tiny finger. Lena's parents were babysitting tonight. Little Dan was the glue that brought the families together. They were all besotted by their first grandchild. For his part Dan loved his godson and was more than happy to take care of him if Marty and Lena wanted a date. He was also just as happy to give him back to his doting parents. Babies were not on his things-to-do list, and Gideon didn't feel the need to start another family.

"What *are* you going to do now that you've finished your degree?" Cris asked. He'd become a regular at the bar, and Dan—so far without success—was trying to persuade him to come work at Cowboys and Angels.

"I'm not sure," Dan said. "I had plans to start my own bar eventually. I guess my life has changed. We can make new plans together." He smiled at Gideon, who kissed him briefly.

"Talking of plans, now is the time." Gideon squeezed Dan for a moment and waved at Bradley.

Dan shot him a suspicious look. "What are you scheming?"

Gideon grinned at him. "That's my boy. Always suspicious."

"He knows you well," Marty said.

Ignoring them all Gideon stepped away from Dan and rapped his knuckles on the bar to call for silence.

"You promised there would be no speeches tonight." Dan had extracted that promise on pain of no sex for a week.

"This isn't a speech. Kind of." Gideon took a large manila envelope from Bradley. "Quiet!"

They all turned to look at Gideon, and Dan's heart sank. Gideon was up to something. He was sure of it.

"My husband says I'm not allowed to make a speech—"

"Never stopped you before."

There was a ripple of laughter as someone heckled from the back. Gideon flipped them off in their general direction.

"I want to thank you all for being here tonight to celebrate Dan's graduation and our wedding day." Gideon took a deep breath, and Dan saw the sheen of tears in his eyes. "Dan, I know you said no presents, but this is for you. For completing your degree. For joining the Tyler family. For making me a very happy man." He handed Dan the envelope.

Dan stared at it. "What is it?"

"Open it and find out."

Dan slid open the flap and pulled out the official document. A lump formed in his throat, and he swallowed hard. He looked at Gideon and then caught Ariel and Bradley grinning like lunatics from behind the bar, obviously in on the secret.

"You've given me Cowboys and Angels?" Dan could barely speak around the lump in his throat. "Your bar?"

"Your bar," Gideon corrected. "She's all yours now, darlin'."

Dan's hands shook. "I don't know what to say."

"The beer's on us?" Buck suggested from the corner.

"Just for tonight," Gideon said.

"So much for it being my bar?" But Dan laughed at Gideon to let him know he wasn't bothered.

Cheering erupted, and there was a surge for the bar. Dan took the opportunity to haul Gideon into a hug. Then he was mobbed by people wanting to congratulate him on their wedding, his degree, but mainly for becoming owner of Cowboys and Angels. His customers knew their priorities.

When he finally got a breathing space, Ariel handed him a new bottle. "Drink up, Pops."

"Pops?"

"Well, you're my stepfather now."

"No," he said flatly.

She gazed at him, her eyes wide and innocent. "Papa Dan?"

"Not if you want to live."

"Is that a way to talk to your new daughter?"

"Welcome to the family," Gideon drawled as he draped his arm around Dan again.

Dan glowered at both of them. "I'm having second thoughts."

"Too late. You're a Tyler now," Ariel trilled.

Daniel Tyler. Gideon had been willing to double-barrel their names, but Dan was more than happy to leave Collins behind. He'd told his sister about his marriage. She was pleased for him but didn't want to fly back for the wedding. He still hadn't told his mother. The last thing he wanted was her at his celebration. He would take Gideon to meet her in a couple of months… or years.

IT WAS hours later before Dan and Gideon were alone in the bar, nursing coffees and going over the paperwork. Dan was still overwhelmed by the enormity of Gideon's present. He traced his name on the papers with one fingertip.

"Why would you give me the bar?"

Gideon smiled tenderly at him. "I can't think of anyone better to take care of my baby. You walking in the front door was the best thing that ever happened to us."

"But Cowboys and Angels was yours and Sarah's. Why didn't you give it to Ariel?"

"Because she doesn't love Cowboys and Angels like you do. Ariel has her own plans, and I'll support her with those, once she decides what they are. But I know you wanted your own bar, and I never wanted you to give up your dreams just because you married me. You've worked too hard for them, Dan. If you're worried, I talked to Ariel, and she thinks it's a great idea."

Dan laced his fingers with Gideon's. "It's too much. I have nothing to offer you."

"You're so wrong, my darlin'." Gideon tugged Dan off his stool and between Gideon's legs. "I don't need things. I'm wealthy enough not to need anything more. You don't care what I own because you love me for me. You didn't even blink when you found out I had money. Do you know how rare that is?"

That was true. He'd been more concerned about Parker losing his job—he did, but not due to Gideon, and that was another story.

Dan had never cared much for possessions. He loved Gideon, his cat, Ariel, and his friends. He had everything he had ever wanted, his happily ever after. "Life with you is never going to be boring, is it?"

Gideon burst out laughing. "Not if I can help it. Now come and kiss me."

"With pleasure." Dan wrapped his arms around Gideon's neck and kissed him eagerly.

In the background he could hear insistent meowing. Dan smiled against Gideon's mouth. She could wait a while longer while he loved his husband.

Exclusive Excerpt

Secretly Dating the Lionman

Cowboys and Angels: Book Two

By Sue Brown

Can a man burdened with family drama find his way into the arms of a happy-go-lucky stripper called Lionman?

Cris likes a drink at Cowboys and Angels bar after his shift at the strip club—until one night when a trashed young guy named Mikey tries to kiss him. He's not Cris's type, but Cris is good enough to see the kid home safely. There he meets Mikey's handsome older brother, Bennett, and there's an immediate spark between them.

But Bennett might not be in a position to start a relationship, let alone with the carefree Cris. He's trying desperately to hold his family together, with a younger brother who's running off the rails and hostile parents who will never accept not just one, but two gay sons.

When Cris is unexpectedly fired and Bennett's family drama escalates, they turn to each other for support. But can a shoulder to lean on develop into something much closer, something they both deserve?

CRIS PETERS fumbled to make the call, not willing to take off his gloves in the icy-chill of the evening, but the touch screen defeated him, and he had to pull off one glove. The second he pressed Send, Cris tucked the phone under his ear and pulled his glove back on. He waited impatiently for the call to connect.

"Hello?" A deep male voice rumbled in his ear and reminded Cris why he'd been attracted to Paul in the first place.

"Hi, Paul. It's Cris Peters."

"Oh yeah. Hi."

Cris couldn't fail to notice the mixture of wariness and indifference in Paul's voice. He'd already canceled one date with Paul, and he was not going to appreciate Cris doing it again simply because his idiot manager couldn't sort out his schedules. He sighed and launched into an explanation of why he had to rearrange their first date again.

Five minutes later Cris no longer had a date to rearrange. Paul had better things to do with his Saturday night than wait in for a guy who wasn't interested, and no amount of apologies would convince him otherwise.

"You're a stripper, not a surgeon. It's not life or death if you don't turn up for work," Paul sneered as he disconnected.

"It's the difference between a bed and the streets, asshole," Cris snapped, even though Paul had already gone.

Cris sighed as he slipped his phone back into his pocket. He really needed a beer, so he pushed open the door to Cowboys and Angels and was immediately hit by a wave of noise and heat and the seventies rock music that blasted out to deafen anyone within a five-block radius. The bar was packed with men ready to drink away their Friday night. A year ago he'd never have thought he'd be seeking a night out at Cowboys and Angels, a blue-collar bar a few blocks from where he lived. It had an extensive list of great beers, but with a reputation for barroom brawls, it wasn't a place where Cris wanted to spend the night. He preferred more quiet.

But times had changed, and he came in without more than a quick look around to see if any fights were brewing. There were still skirmishes, but Dan, the new owner, stopped them before more than a few fists flew.

And the cause of most of the trouble worked behind the bar now. Ariel, the owner's daughter, no longer had time to stir up the clientele.

He pushed through the crowd toward the bar and greeted some of the customers as he passed.

"Lionman!" One of the men clapped him on the back, and he staggered. Fortunately Cris had excellent reflexes, and he recovered his footing and pasted a smile on his face for the young construction worker who'd accosted him.

"Pat. Good to see you, man."

"My girl saw your show last week." Pat laughed raucously, and his friends joined in. "Now she wants me to dress up in a jockstrap and cowboy hat."

Cris remembered that show, and he remembered Pat's woman, all lush curves and huge dark eyes. "You're a lucky man, Pat." He winked at him. "If you want me to give you lessons on how to strip…."

Pat's friends whistled and jeered, and Pat flushed but grinned good-naturedly. "Maybe I will." He managed a bad hip shimmy.

Cris grinned and left behind a still wildly blushing Pat and a chorus of whistles and cheers. He pushed his way through to the bar and waved at Dan, who came over with a smile and a raised eyebrow.

"Aren't you supposed to be working tonight?" he asked as he pushed a beer across the bar.

Cris took a long swallow. "Mix-up with the schedule. They want me tomorrow night instead."

"Didn't that happen last weekend?"

"And the one before that." Cris rubbed his eyes tiredly. He hadn't been thrilled to discover yet again that the manager of his strip club, Forbidden Nightz, had screwed up his weekend with little more than an apologetic smile and an indifference to how it might affect his life. "Marlon's fuckin' useless, man. And my date didn't appreciate being canceled twice."

"You ought to come and work for me." Dan winked at him.

Cris took another swallow of the honey-based beer. "You don't pay enough."

It was a recurring discussion. Dan had been suggesting almost since they met that Cris come work at Cowboys and Angels, but Cris's answer was always the same. He could make way more money in tips stripping than he could behind the bar, and he needed every cent just to pay his rent at home and at the studio. Cris stripped to live, but his first love was painting. But the manager's disorganization was doing his head in.

Dan just snorted and handed him another beer. Then he went away to serve another customer. If Dan was on duty, Cris never paid for a drink at Cowboys and Angels. He protested, but Dan ignored him. Cris had helped a friend of Dan's at the strip club when she became unwell. As far as Dan was concerned, Cris was golden. Appropriate really. Cris had a flaming mane of unruly red hair, hence Lionman as his stage name. But tonight Cris felt more like a stray alley cat than the king of the jungle.

Cris finished his first drink, picked up the second, and turned around to look at the room. He recognized a lot of the customers now, and a couple of them gave him a sloppy wave. There was a scuffle as the wave smacked into another guy's face, but they settled down after a bellow from Dan. Cris turned away hastily. He didn't want to attract the attention of one of the men. He'd met him before, at a speed-dating evening held at Cowboys and Angels, and he had one foot in the closet. Mr. Seventeen. Why the guy attended the event, Cris had no idea. Mr. Seventeen, whose name was Mikey, panicked every time he saw Cris, as though Cris would out anyone against their will. He knew more secrets than a hair stylist.

The door opened, letting in a blast of cold air. Cris saw Mikey—no, not Mikey, but someone who looked like him—come in and look around. He took off his hat and swept a hand through his thick hair, leaving it rumpled. He was older than Mikey, and he wore a deep frown. For some reason Cris itched to smooth the rumpled hair and the frown. The patrons started to grumble, so the man hastily shut the door and headed over to Mikey, who didn't look pleased to see him. Cris watched curiously as they had what looked like a heated discussion. The older guy pointed to the door, but Mikey shook his head and took a step back, his expression resolute.

"Another beer?" Dan asked.

Cris dragged his gaze away from the tableau. "Thanks. Who's Mikey talking to?"

Dan flicked a glance their way. "Bennett. Mikey's older brother. He's probably trying to get Mikey home before he gets himself into trouble."

"Does it work?"

"Mikey gets into trouble just by breathing."

"They look like each other," Cris observed.

"Yeah, but in personality, they're oil and water. Bennett is steady, works for the family business."

Cris looked at Bennett. His face was set and angry as he tried to persuade Mikey to leave. "And Mikey's the prodigal son?"

"Something like that."

"Lionman!"

Cris rolled his eyes, pasted a smile on his face, and turned to face Gideon, the former owner of Cowboys and Angels, who strode across the room to him. Cris was just over six feet tall and muscled, but Gideon could make three of him. He made Cris feel small, which was a rare feeling, and Cris wasn't sure he liked it. "Hi, Gideon."

He was always wary around Gideon. He'd made the mistake of showing his interest in Dan just as Gideon declared his own. Dan was head-over-heels in love with Gideon, and there had never been any real contest, but Gideon obviously viewed Cris as a rival.

Gideon smiled at him. "Aren't you working tonight?"

"Another mix-up with the schedules," he said flatly.

Gideon frowned. "This not the first time, is it?"

"No." Cris leaned against the bar. "Getting tired of it, you know? Now they want me to work tomorrow night, and I'd planned to go out. But I've gotta work. I can't afford to turn down a shift."

"You should come and work for me."

"Thanks, man." Cris meant it. "I'm grateful for the offer. It's just the money. I can earn a lot more at the club, and I need it to pay my rent. No offense," he added hastily.

"None taken."

Gideon eyed him speculatively, but Gideon just said, "Enjoy your evening. Gotta be visible or Dan gets annoyed."

Cris hid his amusement until Gideon turned away. When Dan became the manager, he'd insisted Gideon show his face in the bar. Gideon complained loudly to anyone who would listen, but he'd do anything for Dan. Now Dan was the owner, it seemed he still had Gideon on a tight leash.

Cris turned and waved his glass at Dan. "'Nother?"

"Is that a question or a request?"

"Just fill it up."

Dan took the glass and refilled it with Cris's favorite beer. "Do I need to get Gideon to pour you home?"

"I'm not wasted on three beers, dude," Cris protested.

"'Kay. He can give you a ride home if you need it."

Cris mumbled his thanks, and Dan went off to serve someone else. Cris sighed. He was used to being the focus of attention on stage, not the sad sack at the bar. Maybe it was time he went home and crashed out in front of the Hallmark Channel to watch sappy romances.

"I really am that sad," he muttered into his glass.

"Lionman!"

Cris cursed under his breath. Thanks to Gideon's incessant use of his stage name, no one called him Cris. He turned to see Mikey lurching toward him and hastily put down his glass. There was no sign of his brother.

"Lionman." Mikey wafted beer fumes in Cris's face as he swayed.

Cris caught him by the biceps, afraid of getting smacked in the head. "Whoa, big man, steady."

Mikey didn't seem to notice. "You look sad, Lionman. Are ya sad?"

He gave Cris a sloppy smile and tried to pat his face, but only succeeded in smacking Cris in the nose. Christ, it was early for the guy to be that trashed. No wonder his brother was trying to get him home.

Cris caught Mikey's wandering hand before he could inflict more damage. "I'm okay, Mikey. Just fed up."

"You don' wanna be tha'. You gotta be happy, like me."

There were a lot of ways Cris could have responded, considering Mikey was the unhappiest man he'd ever met, but he made an effort to smile. "Thanks, Mikey. I'm gonna take a leak and go home now. You take care."

Mikey took a moment to focus on him as his eyes seemed to want to go in different directions. Then he blinked, focused, and nodded. "Okay. 'Night."

Cris squeezed Mikey's arm, ensured he was steady on his feet, and headed off to the bathroom. He pushed the door and was about to walk in when he was shoved from behind, and for the second time that evening, he struggled to stay on his feet.

SUE BROWN is owned by her dog and two children. When she isn't following their orders, she can be found with her laptop in Starbucks, drinking latte and eating chocolate.

Sue discovered M/M romance at the time she woke up to find two men kissing on her favorite television series. The kissing was hot and tender and Sue wanted to write about these men. She may be late to the party, but she's made up for it since, writing fan fiction until she was brave enough to venture out into the world of original fiction.

Sue can be found at:

Website: www.suebrownstories.com
Blog: suebrownsstories.blogspot.co.uk
Twitter: @suebrownstories
Facebook: www.facebook.com/suebrownstories

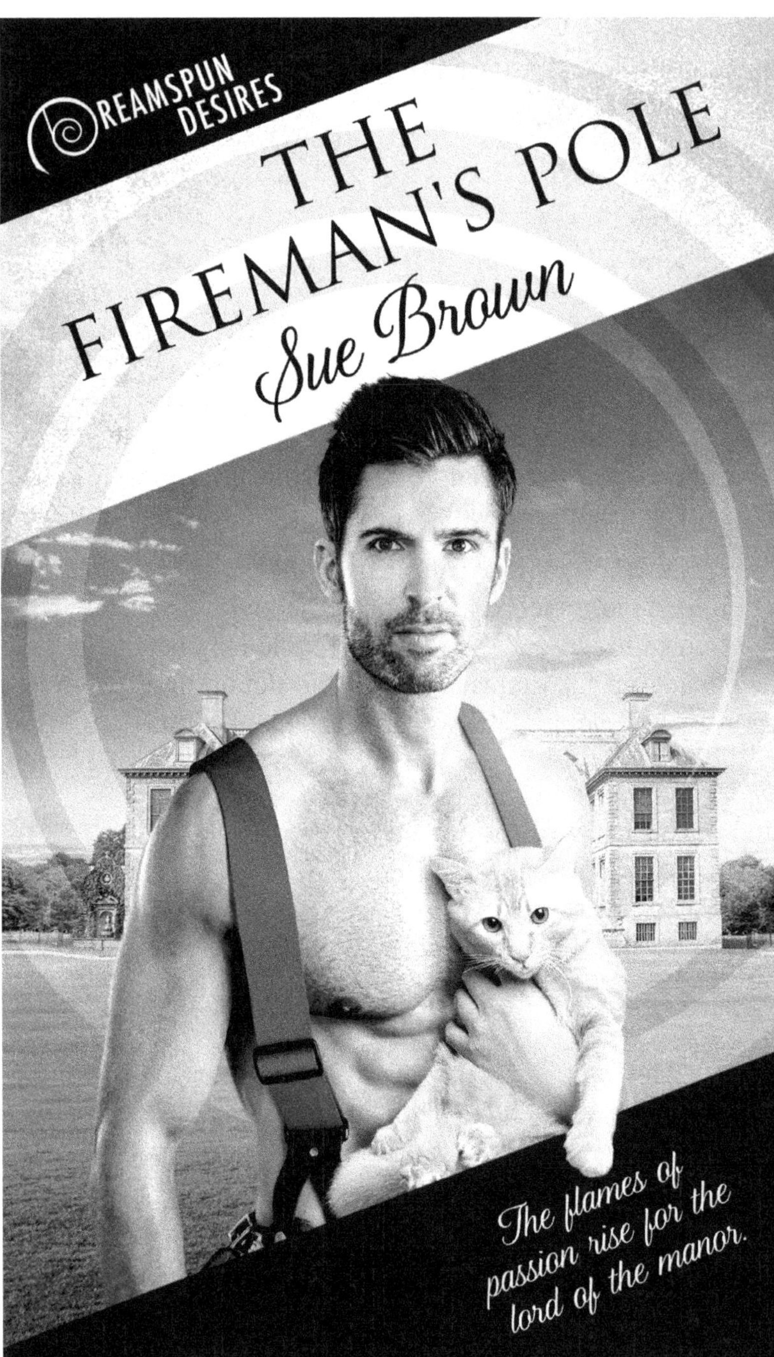
DREAMSPUN DESIRES
THE FIREMAN'S POLE
Sue Brown
The flames of passion rise for the lord of the manor.

The flames of passion rise for the lord of the manor.

It's springtime in Calminster village, but things are already heating up. Sexy firefighter Dale Maloney is new to the local station. When Dale backs the company fire engine into the village maypole, he attracts the ire—and attention—of Benedict Raleigh, the Baron Calminster.

Soon after meeting Dale, Ben breaks off his relationship with his girlfriend, and the sparks between Ben and Dale are quickly fanned into flames.

Unfortunately the passion between the two men isn't the only blaze in the village. An arsonist's crimes are escalating, and it's up to Dale and his crew to stop them. Meanwhile, as they investigate, an unscrupulous business partner attempts to coerce Ben into marrying his daughter. The May Day parade is around the corner, but they have plenty of fires to put out before Ben can finally slide down the fireman's pole.

THE LAYERED MASK

SUE BROWN

Threatened by his father with disinheritance, Lord Edwin Nash arrives in London with a sole purpose: to find a wife. A more than eligible bachelor and titled to boot, the society matrons are determined to shackle him to one of the girls by the end of the season.

During a masquerade ball, Nash hides from the ladies vying for his attention. He is discovered by Lord Thomas Downe, the Duke of Lynwood. Nash is horrified when Downe calmly tells him that he knows the secret Nash has hidden for years and sees through the mask Edwin presents to the rest of the world.

And then he offers him an alternative.

The Next Call

Mark Grayson volunteers for an LGBT helpline, the same one that helpe[illegible] him through his teenage years. One day he takes a call from “Ricky,” [illegible] suicidal man being forced into a marriage he doesn’t want. For w[illegible]ark talks to Ricky and provides support, but he’s frustrated by t[illegible] information Ricky provides and the decisions he’s making. In t[illegible]e, Mark starts a relationship with another volunteer. Then trag[illegible]s and Mark takes time away from the helpline, but when he com[illegible] Ricky is waiting. Mark realizes Ricky is stronger than before and thei[illegible] relationship changes, but Mark isn’t sure what their future holds if their relationship is destined to be at the end of the phone.

www.dreamspinnerpress.com

SUE BROWN
ISLAND
DOCTOR

Island Medics: Book One
An Isle Novel

Dr. Jeff Martin has spent five years as a rural general practitioner on the Isle of Wight, hiding the fact he's gay. He travels in secret to see his partner, Tris, but when he discovers Tris has been cheating on him, he ends their relationship. Then Jeff meets island native Cameron Gillard. Cameron is down-to-earth, lively, and treats Jeff like he's the most important person in his life. Jeff blooms under Cameron's attention, and he decides to come out to his colleagues and friends.

Just when things are going well, Tris reappears out of the blue. Jeff is no longer interested in Tris, but it seems he has two men to convince. Tris, who can't believe Jeff is serious about wanting to end their relationship, and Cameron, who can't hide his jealousy of Tris.

Jeff is certain about one thing—the only man he wants in his life is Cameron. Now he just needs to prove it to him.

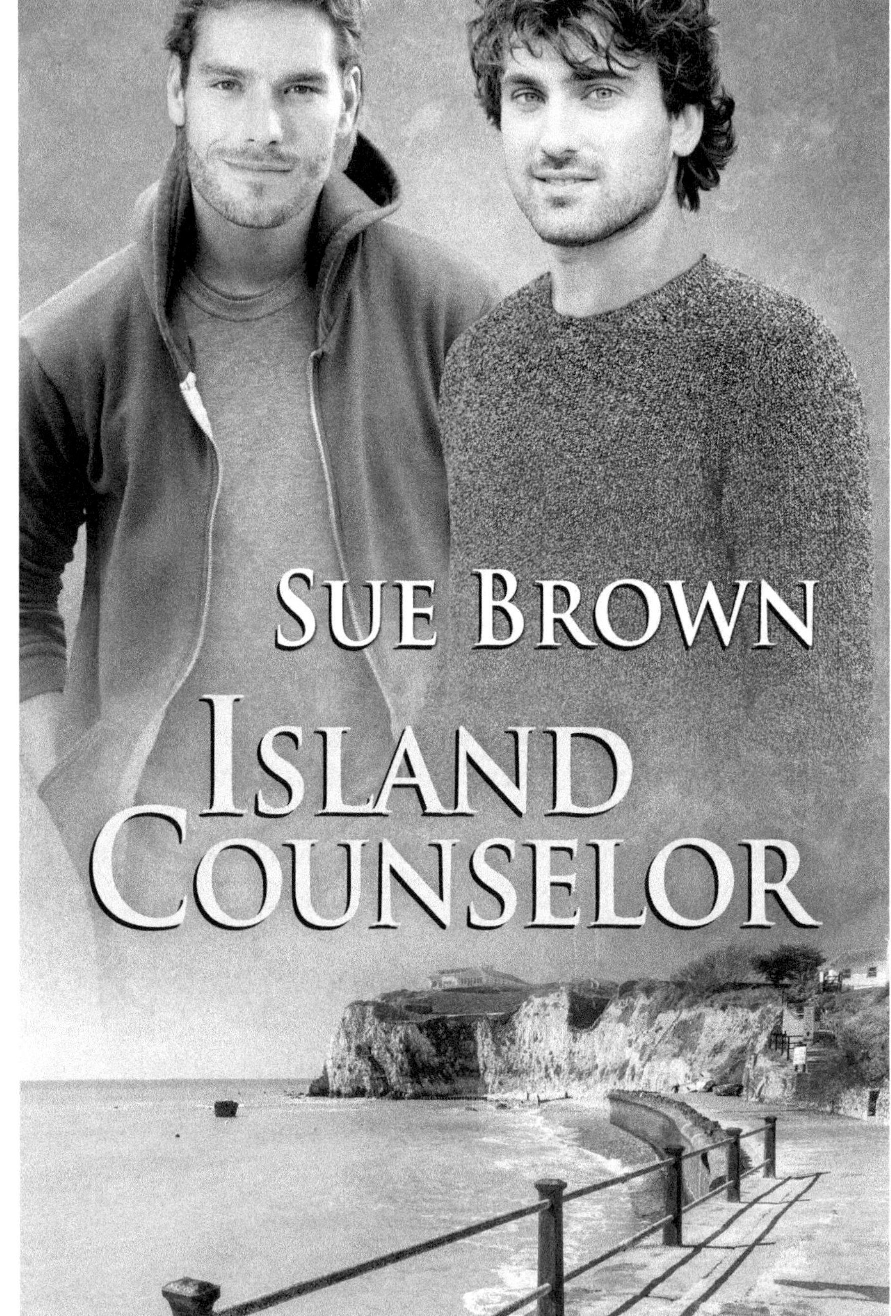
SUE BROWN
ISLAND COUNSELOR

Island Medics: Book Two
An Isle Novel

Counselor Logan Wilde has a successful therapy practice in London, but when a traumatic incident there leaves him suffering from PTSD, he takes refuge in his holiday cottage on the Isle of Wight, unable to face going back to work. Not that he's allowed to relax. Logan's time is taken up with helping Liam Owens, plus there's Nick Brent, whom Logan discovers collapsed on the beach. Nick and Logan spend their time bickering with each other, but that doesn't alter the attraction they feel.

Logan is forced to make some hard decisions about his future, which entails facing up to recent events. Only he's not alone—Nick is with him. Unfortunately someone else makes a decision too, and now trouble is on its way to the Isle of Wight.

www.dreamspinnerpress.com

CPSIA information can be obtained
at www.ICGtesting.com
Printed in the USA
LVHW080511101220
673815LV00025B/411

9 781640 806504